THE RAVEN WHEEL

A F STONE

The Book Guild Ltd

First published in Great Britain in 2019 by
The Book Guild Ltd
9 Priory Business Park
Wistow Road, Kibworth
Leicestershire, LE8 0RX
Freephone: 0800 999 2982
www.bookguild.co.uk
Email: info@bookguild.co.uk
Twitter: @bookguild

Typeset in 11pt Sabon MT

Printed and bound in the UK by TJ International, Padstow, Cornwall

ISBN 978 1912881 741

British Library Cataloguing in Publication Data.
A catalogue record for this book is available from the British Library.

For my family

PART 1

CHAPTER 1
RIA

It felt like the scar she returned to on the back of her knee. That spot where the skin was so thin. A white, fine film that was taut over the threaded network of tissue, veins, blood. It was the fragile perfection that made her want to pierce it. The first time she cut herself, she felt like a butterfly, having its wings torn by a cat's claw. She liked it. She chose a slightly different spot each time, a few millimetres one way or the other, so the skin was new. But it never felt as good. Now, her finger running along the bird's beak, she was acutely aware of the scars on the back of her knee. Raised, bumped yet smooth, hard. It felt the same.

The black shape waited, patient, while she stroked it. Its feet rested on her forearm, hooked into her sleeve.

'You're beautiful,' she said, reaching into her pocket with her other hand. She drew out a glistening, fibrous chunk of raw chicken. The raven thrust its beak forward and snatched the lump, its head like a flint spear, glinting, tilting. One jerk and the gobbet fell down the black trap door. Ria smiled.

'Go on then, Bertie.' She held her arm out and felt the bird's weight push off as it flew out of the gap where a windowpane used to be. The sun was still up, throwing its last rays over the mill. This was Ria's place. From where she stood, at the window of the first floor, she could see all of Talvern Pitts. Even in the sunlight, she could still feel the grey. A grey village in grey hills under a grey sky. Today at least, the sun cast an orange bleed over the horizon, warming it all just enough. Here at the top of the hill, there was even a hint of gold in the long grass, shimmering through the net of leaves cast above the trees, just to the left of the mill. She stood in the stone ruin and decided to walk around the outside of it, to the millpond behind. It would be beautiful now – all bronze ripples and reeds making their lilting sound in the wind.

She scuffed her feet over the floorboards, sending clouds of dust up either side of her trainers. She knelt in the gritty powder and drew with her finger in the dirt: RIA & THE RAVENS.

Suddenly, something scuttled across the floor between two wooden barrels at the far end of the room.

'Shit!' she cried, jumping to her feet.

It's just a mouse, she told herself, *the place is full of them*. She edged over to the barrels and peered over the top. Everything was still there – the multipack of crisps, the box of crackers and the cans of cider. The only casualty was the paper bag of cookies. It had a neat hole in the corner. Her eyes followed the trail of crumbs in the base of the barrel to the edge. She tilted it and discovered a small gap between the base and side.

'Bollocks.'

She lifted out the packet and shook the remaining bits of broken biscuit onto the floor.

'Might as well have it now,' she said, screwing up the bag and tossing it into the empty fireplace.

She heard cawing outside and turned to the window. *Someone's walking up the hillside towards us.* She ducked down and peered over the edge, breathing in the damp cold of the stone wall.

The boy was her age, maybe a bit older. He had dark hair in tight curls, bursting out into the air like a firework. He was frowning, kicking the grass now and then. *Is he crying?* She couldn't tell.

He picked up a stone and hurled it at a tree nearby. He picked up another and looked at the mill. Ria ducked down. A loud smash made her jump up.

'Oi!' she shouted, leaning out of the window.

'Jesus!' the boy cried, quickly stepping backwards.

'That was the only window left with glass in it, you dick!' The boy frowned.

'What do you care? It's not your bloody house,' he said. 'Some fucking dump that's been here a hundred years, should've been knocked down ages ago.'

'It *is* my house, actually. And you've just damaged it. I could call the police.'

'Bullshit. Nobody lives here. And definitely not you.'

'Why am I here then, shouting at you for breaking my bloody window?' she said, smirking. 'And anyway,' she frowned, 'what do you mean *definitely not* me?'

'Okay.' He folded his arms and planted his feet. 'Number one – you don't get tramps and squatters in the countryside. Number two – even if you did, you're too posh to be a squatter.'

'What?! I'm not posh! How do—'

'Oh no, I'm not posh, dahling,' he mimicked.

'Fuck off, I don't sound like that. You don't know anything about me. You don't even know my name.'

'I bet it's something well fancy like one of those *Made in Chelsea* types – Henrietta… Jemima!' he laughed.

'It's Ria. My name is Ria and I'm not posh. I'm just not from round here. Do posh girls drink Frosty Jack's?'

'Definitely not.' He shook his head.

'Want one?'

'All right.'

She went over to the barrel, her feet crunching the cookie crumbs, and lifted out two cans.

Am I going to do this? she asked herself, climbing down the wooden ladder to the ground floor, one hand on the ladder, the other clutching the cans.

A flipbook of her life breezed through her vision. Not her *real* life. Not the black of her past or the grey of her present – but the life she would *make* real. The life she wanted to have lived and to be living now, to live until she died. The life that she would tell this boy all about. He would believe her. And if he believed her, maybe that was the start of living it, for real?

Yes. I'm going to do this.

***

'Come on,' she said, walking round the side of the mill. 'We need to chill it first.'

She heard his footsteps follow. He was taller than she'd expected. She took a deep breath in through her nose and out through her mouth, pressing the pads of her fingers hard against the can rims.

'Here we are.'

She stopped and turned, watching him look around. They were on a small wooden jetty, reaching out over the pond. The wheel was still there, grey and flaking. It was still, but the gentle ripple of the dark water against the slats at the surface made it shimmer, as though it were half a wheel hovering over the water, without the rest submerged in the black depths.

'Pass me that bag,' she said, pointing at a plastic carrier bag tied round a wooden post that marked the join between the jetty and the bank. He untied it and handed it over, looking at her with a half-smile. She laughed, taking it off him.

'Don't worry, I'm not going to suffocate you.'

'That's good to know,' he said, nodding his head.

She put the cider cans in the bag, kicked off her shoes and rolled up her jeans to the knee. The sun was just in her eyes as she sat on the edge of the wooden boards. She squinted as she turned to look at him, tying the handles of the bag round her ankle.

'Come sit,' she said, swinging her legs over the edge and plunging the bag into the water with them. He smiled, bending down, perching next to her. He sat on his haunches, his feet on the floor and his knees bent, leaning his elbows on top of them.

'You're too tall for that, you can't be comfy. Just put your legs over the edge.'

'I'm not getting these wet!' He pointed to his trainers.

'Take them off, obviously...'

'Yeah I know, but then I'll have wet feet going back inside them and they were £200—'

'What?! £200 for trainers? Jesus Christ. You're wearing £200 trainers in Talvern Pitts... you do realise the average age round here is seventy, right? Unless you count the cows, who would bring it down a fair bit. But cows aren't impressed by trainers. Especially if they're leather.'

'You're weird,' he said, taking the trainers off.

'I'm not the one dressed for the MTV Awards afterparty in a field in Talvern Pitts.'

'I think I'd rather look like this than you do right now, with an Aldi bag of Frosty Jack's tied round your ankle in a lake.'

She shrugged.

'At least I'm practical.'

Ria looked down into the water as he slowly lowered his feet in.

'Fuck, that's freezing!' he shouted.

She wasn't listening. Her reflection was staring back at her, between her feet. *You're not Ariadne any more. You're Ria.*

She realised he was talking.

'What?' she asked.

'I said, how do you still have your legs in there? They'll drop off!'

He had shifted right back so his legs were safely lying flat on the boards, with his feet drying over the edge.

'I like being numb,' she said quietly, then leaned forwards and reached into the pond for the bag.

'Cold enough,' she handed him the dripping can.

'Thanks.'

They cracked open the cans and sipped in silence, listening to the wind through the branches above them. *He's right.* She pressed the flesh on her calf and it didn't feel like hers. It felt like she'd lifted a dead body out of the water. She saw herself under the water, tangled in reeds, staring up. She rolled her jeans down and crossed her legs. *Stop thinking like that. Ask him a question.*

'You never said what your name was.'

'Tye.'

'As in tie-a-knot or Thailand?'

'T-Y-E.'

'Oh. Why were you throwing stones at my house, anyway?'

'Come on, it's not your house.'

'I don't own it, but that's where I live… most of the time.'

'Most of the time?'

'My great-aunt lives in the village. She's half lost her marbles but she remembers who I am still. I stay there when the weather's bad, charge my phone there, shower. That kind of thing. She gives me money now and then.'

It just came out – before she even really knew if any of it made sense, it was out there.

'Where does she live?' he asked. 'My nan is on Brindle Lane.'

'Other side to that. Up the hill going out towards Silverton.'

Shit. What am I doing? Why am I saying this?

'Where are your parents?'

8

'They died. In a car crash.' *Fuck.*

'Jesus Christ, I'm sorry – that's awful. When did it happen?'

Think.

'Last year…'

'Shit. How did you… I mean… don't you have any other family?'

'None.'

She thought of her sister and felt a pang of guilt.

'Didn't social services—' he started.

'Well, I do have a sister,' Ria interrupted. 'She's a lot older than me. So they let her adopt me, then they left us alone. But I don't see her. She emigrated.'

'She just left you here alone?! How old are you?'

'Seventeen.'

'Still, that's…' he trailed off, taking a swig.

'It's not her fault, I made her. She had a job offer in America… I told her I'd got a job with boarding… at a stable. I didn't want to hold her back.'

She heard her mother's voice. *You just start talking, Ariadne, and the lies spin themselves into a web that you'll be caught in forever.* Ria suddenly felt a desperate need to cut herself. She wanted him to go so she could do it. But he was still there, asking questions. And it was her fault.

'So she has no idea you're sleeping rough?'

'I'm not *sleeping rough,* I just… spend a lot of time outdoors.'

'And you don't go to school or college, or have a job?'

'Like I said, my great-aunt gives me money now and then. I might go to college next year. Or I might just stay here. I like the moorland. Feels like home.'

'So all your stuff is in there?' he said, pointing back to the mill. She nodded.

This was an opportunity. She knew that if he left now, she'd add a new scar to her collection, but she'd probably never see him again. He was a total stranger, who only knew whatever

9

she told him about herself. She needed to tell him more, to make him believe her, to have someone complicit in her new reality.

'D'you want to see? We need another drink, anyway,' she said, shaking the last drops of her can out onto the grass.

'Okay.'

He smiled. She felt sick. There was no going back now.

'How did you find out about this place?' Tye asked, as they stepped over the threshold. Inside, an empty stone-walled space stared back at them. The only features were a pile of rubble in one corner, a chimney breast surrounding a hearth and a wooden ladder at the far end. The ladder leaned up against a hatch in the ceiling.

'I live up here,' she said, walking over to the ladder.

She beckoned him to follow her up. He hesitated.

'I'm not a serial killer, I promise,' she said, suddenly feeling the weight of the web she had spun. A chain-link web on her shoulders, making it impossible to carry on climbing.

'Never mind,' she said, lowering herself back down.

'No,' he stepped towards the ladder. 'I want to see.'

She took a deep breath and headed up. She could feel him behind her, the ladder bowing under the weight of them both.

'It's not much,' she said, clambering to her feet on the floorboards and turning round to watch his reaction as he did the same.

'Wow…' He looked round. She smiled.

'It's just bits I've collected. Nobody comes here. Not that it's worth stealing. It's all junk, really.'

She followed Tye's gaze. She saw him take in the bookshelf she'd made from loose floorboards, the half-burned candles in old glass bottles, the stack of hay in the corner and her sleeping bag.

'Jesus. You really do live here… where are your clothes and stuff, though? How do you cook or wash or like… do anything except sleep and read?'

'I don't really have much stuff,' she stalled, 'and I don't need to cook. I have food in here.' She opened the barrel and lifted out the multipack of crisps. She put it back and got two more cans out.

'I'm all right, thanks,' he said.

Shit. He's suspicious. He thinks you're weird. He thinks you're lying.

You are *weird and you* are *lying.*

'The rest of my stuff is at Marjory's house. That's my great-aunt's name. I stay there when the weather is shit, if I'm ill, that kind of thing. Get showers, charge my phone. Like I said. I do things for her round the house, keep her company. She doesn't have anyone else.'

Tye didn't say anything. She couldn't read his face. He turned round, looking out of the window.

'I can see my nan's house from here,' he said, pointing at the houses backing onto the farm on the hillside opposite.

'Which one?'

'The one with the red fence at the back. There.'

She made a noise of recognition, but was distracted by something she'd just spotted on the floor. He turned to see before she had chance to cover it over.

'"Ria and the ravens",' he read.

Oh, God.

'Is that like the name of your band or something?' he asked.

She wished it was. *Why not lie about that too? You've made everything else up.* No. She couldn't pull it off. Even though the lies she'd told him so far amounted to a parallel universe, all she had to do to maintain them was pretty much do what she always did anyway. Hang out there. But a band implied friends, rehearsals, gigs, instruments, talent. She thought of how ridiculous the situation was – it was easier for her to pretend to be an orphan than to be in a band. She laughed.

'What?' Tye asked.

'Oh, nothing – just the thought of me in a band. I can't play a thing.'

'Oh. So what is it then?'

She cringed. *Just be honest.*

'The ravens live here too. Well, they don't live here, they just visit…' she trailed off, seeing his expression change.

'Okay…' he said, moving towards the hatch.

'No don't – I promise, I'm not insane. Look—'

She unzipped her pocket and pulled out the bag of raw chicken.

'Fucking hell,' he said, watching the bag. 'I'm sorry, I'm going—' he started to step down the ladder.

'Wait! It's for the ravens! Just wait one minute, I'm not crazy – you'll see!'

He stood still, halfway down the ladder, visible to her only from the shoulders up. She rifled in the bag and drew out a slimy gobbet. She saw Tye wince as she held it out of the window, balanced in the nook her thumb and forefinger made when she rolled her hand into a fist, as though she were about to flip it like a coin. She looked at Tye and whistled. He watched her hand. Nothing happened. They waited. Still nothing. He started down the steps. She held up her other hand in a "stop" sign. He watched again, from one step further down this time.

'Shit!' he shouted, nearly falling backwards, catching himself on either side of the hatch. The raven clattered in, like a half-open black umbrella thrown through the window.

'Don't be scared – he's no harm,' she said.

'Are you sure?' Tye asked, clinging to the floorboards on either side of the hatch.

'I was talking to Bertie…' Ria looked at Tye, stifling a smirk.

'Oh… right.'

She stroked the bird's neck with the back of her finger.

'Now do you believe me?'

12

SIX WEEKS EARLIER

CHAPTER 2
KIAN

'Hey fuckface, why are you walking so fast?' The shout came from behind, on the other side of the road.

Kian kept his eyes down and gripped the straps of his rucksack. He maintained his speed.

'You fucking power-walking or what? Just run, why don't you?' another voice shouted.

They entered the edge of his vision. *Shit.*

'Go on then, you run… see how long you can keep it up for,' the first voice sneered.

Kian carried on, digging his nails into the straps.

'I said run, fuckface,' the boy shouted. 'Fucking run!'

Kian flinched at a sharp hit on his shoulder. A small stone clattered to the curb. *Don't turn round. Keep going.*

'Oi!' the boy shouted, throwing another missile. It hit Kian's cheekbone. He tried to ignore the instinct to put his hand to his face. *Don't cry. Don't cry. Don't cry.*

He heard footsteps running towards him from behind. *Fuck.* He screwed his eyes closed, waiting for the blow.

A hand on his shoulder spun him round. Tye. Kian exhaled.

'He's *my* fucking brother, shitheads!' Tye shouted to the boys, holding Kian's shoulder, pointing at him.

Kian watched the boys' faces change. One turned to walk away, but the other stopped him, shouting back at Tye, 'Oh yeah? How come you're black and he's white then? 'Cos your mum's a fucking slag?'

Tye let go of Kian and ran out into the road. A car screeched to a halt inches from him, horn screaming. Tye darted between the vehicles after the boys, who were already pelting up the road away from him.

'Tye!' shouted Kian. Kian was so far behind Tye, all he could see was the backs of vehicles as they swerved and stopped to avoid him. Tye ran in front of a bus.

'Shit, Tye!' Kian ran towards the bus as it groaned, dragging its bulk to a stop.

Kian felt like he was underwater, like in one of his dreams where his limbs won't move, his shouts cling to the inside of his teeth and his ears seal shut. Everything swam in front of him. The boys had long gone, the bus had stopped, but Tye was nowhere.

'Go fuck yourself!' The words clicked in Kian's ear, resetting everything. Tye was on the driver's side of the bus, shouting, gesturing *wanker* at the window. He made his way back to Kian, holding his middle finger up as the driver leaned out of the window and shouted after him.

They walked together in silence for three roads. Kian kept his eyes on the floor. He knew what Tye was thinking – Kian should stand up for himself. *I'm not you, Tye, I can't.*

'Urgh, look at that!' He stopped suddenly, tugging on Tye's sleeve.

Tye looked down at the road.

'Fucking hell, that's rank!' he laughed.

In front of the wheel of a parked car was a dead pigeon, squashed flat like a raw burger patty. The feathers were mashed into the flesh. The head had separated from the body, except for a stringy pink sinew stretched between the two. This string was being plucked, twanging off the floor and back again, by a large raven. It stopped and stared up at them. They stared back. Kian started filming the bird on his phone. They watched the big black beak as it dived down at the edge of the remains and started scraping them up, peeling the mush off the road and squashing it into a solid clump, gathering as much as it could into one place. The bird cocked its head to one side, sizing up the mound. It squeezed the clod of feathery flesh into its beak, peeled it off the floor and hopped two steps back under the weight.

'No way,' said Tye, as it flew off right over his head, the meat weighing it down.

They looked at each other and laughed.

'Going on YouTube,' Kian said, putting his phone back in his pocket. Tye rolled his eyes.

'Nobody wants to see that.'

'Yeah they do.'

Kian felt lighter for the rest of the walk back. He hated being rescued by Tye, but he hated *not* being rescued more. He remembered last time, when they caught up. *At least that didn't happen this time.* He felt like he should say thank you.

He opened his mouth to speak as he watched Tye put his key in the door. He faltered. Tye spoke first.

'Don't mention the crow thing to Dad,' he said quietly, 'or show him the video, anyway.'

'It was a raven,' Kian corrected him.

'Whatever. He's not good with stuff like that at the moment. Blood and... death and stuff.'

Kian nodded, looking at the doorstep.

'Kian? Look at me,' Tye said, searching his face. 'Don't show him, okay?'

'Jesus, I won't, I said I won't – why would I?'

'Good. I don't know, something to talk about. But don't—'

'For fuck's sake, I won't, now let me in the bloody house.'

'Dad'll be back from work in half an hour. Get off the Xbox. Help me tidy up while I get tea on, yeah?' Tye said.

Kian didn't take his eyes off the screen. He could see Tye in the reflection on the edge of it, stood in the doorway behind him, arms folded. *Fine, I'll die.* He ran out across the dunes in front of enemy fire. He knew it was coming, but still winced at the smack, the red blur and the fade to black.

'Done?' Tye asked.

Kian sighed and stood up.

'Okay, so you do this room,' Tye began. 'I'll do the kitchen. Take all that crap you've dumped on the stairs up too, yeah?'

'This house has no space. We live in a shoebox.'

'Well, it won't take long to tidy then, will it? I need to get on with tea.'

'We're not having that gross cow thing again are we?' Kian asked.

'It's called oxtail stew, and it's Dad's favourite. It's good for you. If it were up to you we'd live off those fucking potato smiley faces.'

'I can't wait till I can move out,' Kian said, gathering up mugs from the coffee table. 'Chicken nuggets all the way—' A noise stopped him. They both looked down at the floor. There was the noise again. Like a shuffling, footsteps maybe. *There's someone in the cellar.*

'What the fuck?' Kian whispered.

Tye mimed "shhh" and listened. A different noise. It sounded like a drill. He frowned.

'I'll call the police,' said Kian, getting his phone out.

'No, wait,' Tye said. 'Stay here.'

'Tye!' Kian hissed, too late. He watched him close the door behind him and lock it. He tried the handle. Locked.

The drill started up again, but this time just for a second before a cry that made Kian's skin prickle. Like an animal in pain – something deep but fragile, then a thud and a clatter. He heard Tye scream.

'Shit – Tye!' Kian kicked the door and pulled the handle, but to no avail. 'I'm calling them Tye, I'm ringing them now!' he shouted. His hands shook so hard he dropped the phone.

'Shit, shit!' He picked it up and managed to dial.

Footsteps. Kian watched the lock click open and the handle turn. *Fuck!*

'Help!' he found himself shouting at the operator. 'Help me, please!'

Tye appeared, his white school shirt shining red with blood.

'It's Dad. Give me the phone,' he said, snatching it from him with slippery-red hands. 'Mine's got no fucking battery.'

'Dad!' Kian cried, making for the door.

'No!' Tye shouted, holding him back, his hand pressed into Kian's chest. He thrust him back into the room.

'*Stay here!*' Tye shouted, then he dashed back out, locking the door behind him again. Kian heard him run down to the cellar, talking to the operator.

'Tye, please just tell me what's happened!' Kian shouted through the door. *Fuck.* He could feel Tye's pain in his own throat, his jaw, chest. He slammed against the door with his whole body. There was no use. All he could do was listen. He threw himself on the floor, ripping the carpet away from the floorboards, tearing it back and pressing his ear to the crack between the wood. He could hear shuffling, dragging, Tye's heavy breathing.

'It's my dad,' Tye said, 'he's had an accident. There's lots of blood…'

The blood drained from Kian's limbs.

'We need you here now, right now, please – I've tried to stop the blood but... it's his head... I think he's cracked his skull, I don't know what's coming out... a drill, it was a drill – he has mental health problems, I don't—'

Kian turned and retched. The last thing he saw was the yellow-brown vomit spreading over the pink carpet, then everything went black.

CHAPTER 3
LYNNE

'Do you know how to make any of these, Barb?'

Lynne slid a handwritten list across the table. Barbara scanned it. She squinted and mouthed some of the words silently to herself. Lynne stirred her tea and sighed. Barbara looked up, shaking her head.

'Sorry, duck. No idea.'

'No. Me neither. I have to try though. Feel awful for them.'

Barbara nodded and patted Lynne's hand. 'It's the thought that counts. Come on. Drink up and we'll go have a look.' She pointed past the cafe exit to a sign above one of the aisles beyond. 'Look – *World Foods* – I bet half that stuff is there.'

Lynne pushed the trolley slowly, hovering at the end of the aisle, watching a woman wearing a headscarf put a tin in her basket. The lady looked up and smiled. Lynne smiled back and thrust her hand out for the nearest packet before throwing it in the trolley. She pushed along to the other side of the aisle and stared at the shelves.

'Lynne, that's Polish – that's not what you're after, I don't think?' Barbara said.

'Shhh!' Lynne hissed. 'Don't make me look daft. I'm just trying to blend in.'

The woman wearing the headscarf made her way to the next aisle and Lynne exhaled.

'Barbara, I'm in over my head here. Let's just get what we can and get out.'

At the bakery counter, Lynne picked up three bags of doughnuts and put them in the trolley. She eyed the cookies.

'They both have a sweet tooth. I can get that right, at least.'

'Lynne, you'll be great. All those boys need is some stability, some love.' Barbara put her hand on Lynne's arm.

'Like I gave Sian?' Lynne said quietly. They stood in silence. Barbara looked at the floor.

'What happened with Sian wasn't your fault,' she offered. 'You know that. She's a law unto herself. Her dad was the problem there, love, not you. You did your best.'

'I didn't. She should never have ended up in care,' Lynne's voice cracked, 'and now look what's happened—' She broke off, dragging the tears away from her mascara with the backs of her fingers.

'Oh, come here, love,' Barbara soothed, grabbing her in a hug. The pair stood, clinging to each other while the chiller unit hummed behind them.

'It's true, though. If I'd been a good mother to Sian, she'd be a good mother to them,' Lynne said, pulling away from Barbara and shuffling in her handbag. She retrieved a tissue.

'David was a nasty, nasty piece of work,' Barbara said firmly. 'And Sian… she was always a wild one. Some children are just born that way. You did your best,' she repeated, 'you gave her chance after chance. Right up until the last time, before she left them again. You did everything you could. There comes a point where someone is just a lost cause… that's Sian.'

Lynne nodded, wiping her nose and folding the tissue away into her bag.

'Now you have a chance to really help those boys, Lynne. While Ray's in hospital, you'll be there for them. They have so much more sense than Sian ever did. Look at the way Tye looks after Kian. And Kian – he's so clever. They're good kids. And you're a brilliant nana. If Ray's there for a long time, they won't end up in care – and that'll all be down to you, yeah?' She searched Lynne's face.

Lynne nodded. 'I'll see them right,' she said, straightening up and taking a deep breath.

'You will,' Barbara said, smiling. 'Come on, let's get through this bloody list.'

***

'Nan…' Tye called through from the kitchen. 'Where's all the stuff I wrote on the list?'

She appeared in the doorway.

He pulled the tins and packets out of the carrier bag onto the work surface, frowning.

'They're all there, I think?' Lynne asked. The kitchen was a narrow, long room with units on one side and a raised leaf table with two stools tucked under on the other. The beige tiles on the walls had illustrations of bread baskets and wheat sheaves on them. At the end of the room, a door with peeling paint and opaque glass panels led to an outhouse where the fridge, freezer and washing machine lived. Tye gripped the handle of the door to open it to go out to the fridge. He stopped, looking at the things left on the work surface.

'Where are the scotch bonnets?'

'Scotch bonnet peppers?'

Tye nodded.

'Well, I couldn't find those, but I got peppers, look—' She picked up the bag of mixed peppers.

'They're not the same – at all. What about the plantains?' he eyed the bunch of bananas.

'I thought that was just the Jamaican word for bananas...
I saw them on *Come Dine With Me* once—'

'Fuck's sake,' Tye sighed. Lynne looked at the floor and
fiddled with her rings.

'Oi, don't be a dick,' shouted Kian from the living room.
'She tried, all right.'

Lynne smiled.

'Shut up, Kian, you're just glad because we'll be eating
potato waffles and chicken fucking dippers.'

'What is *wrong* with chicken dippers?' Kian replied,
emerging into the hall and squeezing past Lynne through the
kitchen doorway. 'If the food I eat is so bad for you, how come
I get straight As and you're thick as shit, hm?'

'I'd rather get Ds than be socially fucking retarded like you—'

'Boys!' Lynne shouted. 'Stop swearing. My house, my
rules!' She folded her arms.

'Whatever,' said Tye, shoving past them both. 'I'm playing
FIFA.'

'No, you're not, I'm on *Battlefield*!' Kian called after him.

'My bedroom, my rules,' Tye shouted back.

'It's OUR bedroom! And I got the fucking camp bed so you
should be more grateful!' Kian ran upstairs after him.

Lynne shook her head and carried on putting the shopping
away.

'Nothing wrong with bananas,' she muttered.

The doorbell rang. She tucked her hair behind her ear and
made her way through the hall.

'Oh, shit.'

The mottled glass in the door blurred the outline, but she
knew who it was. She looked up the stairs. The bedroom door
was closed. Muffled voices were still arguing. She took a deep
breath and put the chain across before opening the door. The
cold hit her.

'What do you want, Sian?'

'Oh hi, Sian, lovely to see you, how are you? Come in, have a brew,' Sian said, her hand on her hip. Her leggings hung loose around her thighs. Lynne looked at Sian's collarbone, the hollow between her cheekbones and jaw on either side, the missing teeth.

'What do you want?' she repeated.

'Take the fucking chain off, I'm not going to rob you.'

'You did last time.'

A shout came from upstairs. Someone had scored a goal. Sian peered past Lynne.

'Who's here?'

'Nobody—'

'They're here, aren't they? Let me see them,' she said, pulling the door.

'No, Sian – they don't need to see you right now. It's not good for them.'

'They're *my* fucking kids!'

'All right,' Lynne sighed. 'How much?'

'Fucking bitch,' Sian said, shaking her head. 'I just want to talk to them…' she trailed off as Lynne reached for her purse on the sideboard.

'How much?' she repeated.

'This is your fault, you know – I'm in this fucking state because of you!'

Lynne dug her nails into the purse and waited.

'Fifty quid,' Sian said, folding her arms and staring at the door frame.

'You know I don't have fifty quid.'

Sian eyed her sideways.

'Yes, you do. What about that drawer?'

Lynne thrust her hand into the purse and nearly tore the notes ripping them out.

'Here, take it – that's thirty. It's all I have and it's more than you deserve!' she shouted, shoving the notes through the gap in the door. Sian grabbed them.

'You're an evil cow, d'you know that?' Sian asked, pointing at her. Lynne slammed the door and leaned against the frame. She heard Sian spit at the door, then walk back down the path. Lynne sank to the floor, holding her hands over her mouth and nose to muffle her sobs.

CHAPTER 4

KIAN

Kian squinted, one eye closed as it was squashed into the carpet. The other strained to see in the dark.

'What are you doing?' asked Tye.

'This was Mum's room, wasn't it? I'm looking for her stuff.'

'I don't think there's anything left. And if there is, it won't be under the bed.'

Kian flicked the flashlight app on his phone on and held it under the bed.

'Wrong again, derr-brain,' he said, pulling out a dusty box.

'Ha! *Derr-brain*?! Are you five? Classic.'

'Shut up,' Kian smirked, 'derr-brain.'

Tye smiled.

'What's in the box, then?'

'Dunno. Let's see.'

Kian lifted the cardboard flap.

'Ha – school books – look...' He lifted the tattered remains of a green exercise book with "SIAN HUGHES" in huge letters, ignoring the lines laid out for them. There was a heart above the "I" and daisies dotted around the other letters of SIAN. Kian smiled, running his finger across the word.

Tye took the book and flicked through the pages.

'God, she was worse than me,' he said, tilting the book so Kian could see the mess inside. Kian stopped the cascade of pages with his hand.

'Look – "MR PRICE IS A BELLEND",' he read. They both laughed.

'Aww. Teddy.'

Kian reached into the box and grabbed a brown, fluffy bear toy. The pads on its paws and around its muzzle were grubby grey. One of its black eyes was scratched dull. Kian felt tears rising in his eyes.

'Come on. Let's go down for tea,' Tye said.

Kian nodded, letting the tears fall onto his hands, gripping the bear.

'Kian – come on, mate. It's not good for you. We have to get on without her. We're fine.'

Kian said nothing, wiping his eyes.

'Look,' Tye continued, 'we just need to focus on helping Dad get better.'

'How? We can't even see him. And anyway, Mum needs help too.'

'She's beyond help, Kian. Dad will get better when—'

'He's not *my* dad!' Kian shouted, kicking the wall.

'*Oi!* Don't you dare say that. He *is* your dad,' Tye grabbed Kian's arm. 'He raised you. He's done more for you than Mum ever has and a fuckload more than whoever she got knocked up by when she ended up with you!'

Kian pushed against Tye and tried to hit him, but Tye blocked his arm. The pair grappled and fell to the floor, struggling against each other.

'You don't know anything about my real dad!' Kian shouted.

'Neither do you, and that's the fucking point!'

Kian felt Tye's arms trying to surround his neck in a headlock, but he pushed against his ribs to keep clear.

'PACK IT IN!' Lynne shouted. She appeared in the doorway, watched them for a second before lunging into the fray to try and pull them apart.

'I said... STOP!' she shouted, clipping them both across the backs of their heads. They stopped, staring up at her from the floor.

'Nan! What the fuck?!' said Kian, rubbing his hair.

'Oh, don't be such a big girl's blouse. Get up, the pair of you. This is ridiculous. How old are you? Hm? Are you still three and five?'

The boys got to their feet.

'Good. Now, Tye, I know it's not what you asked for, but you'll get what you're given. Fish fingers, chips and beans. Come and get it, both of you.'

***

'This place is so fucking boring. Nan is like the youngest person in the village, I swear,' Tye said, sighing.

Kian had stopped listening to him. He was trying to read his physics textbook. It was Friday night, past midnight. The springs of the camp bed were digging into his side. He turned over, causing the frame to creak and screech.

God I hate this place.

'I mean, there's only so much Xbox you can play. I'm going insane.'

'Why don't you ask your friends round?' Kian asked, still reading. *Please shut up.*

'Are you kidding me? It takes an hour to get here. Nan doesn't drive, there's like one bus a week – how would that work exactly?'

'I don't care. All right? I was just trying to say something to make you stop moaning. You never stop.'

'Me?! You're the one who won't shut up about your precious bloody "Nerds United" or whatever that sad little club you belong to is.'

29

Kian turned over to face Tye.

'It's called *Gifted and Talented* and it was the only thing that made my life worth living, actually, and now I can't get there or do any of the shit I'm supposed to be doing and I'm going to end up wasting my life.'

'Oh, Jesus. Don't be such a drama queen. You think you're so much better than everyone else and now you're not hanging round with those snobs you're just worried you might not be so special after all.'

That hurt, dickhead.

'Funnily enough, you're right actually, Tye. I'm worried I might turn out like *you*. Oh, I can't wait to fail all my exams so I can finally get kicked out of school and sign on the dole.'

'Fuck you. I'm not even *close* to being kicked out.'

'Oh sure – that's why the Mr Clark phoned Nan yesterday to ask her to come in and discuss your behaviour.'

'So fucking what?' Tye balked. 'He's a twat. He's got nothing on me.'

'He's not a policeman, Tye, he's the head teacher. He doesn't need to build a case to charge you – every staff member wants rid of you. Except Miss Dornan, but that's only because she fancies you.'

Tye smirked. 'She does fancy me.'

For fuck's sake. Kian dropped his book on the floor and put his hands over his eyes.

'I can't live in the same bedroom as you anymore,' he said. 'I'll lose my mind. I'll turn into a fucking nutbag like Dad.'

Tye sat up. Kian watched him pick up the mug on his bedside table.

'You're a nasty little shit sometimes, Kian, you know that?'

'Don't—' It was too late. Kian was covered in cold tea, as was his bed.

'Fucking bellend...' Kian muttered, taking off his glasses.

'Never call Dad anything like that again,' Tye said quietly, turning the bedside lamp off.

Kian took off his T-shirt and wiped his face with it. He threw it on the floor and lay back down. They both lay in silence, staring at the ceiling.

'I'm moving back to Stoke,' Tye said.

'How?'

'How the fuck should I know?' Tye asked. 'You're the clever one.'

He listened to the silence. *I am. I wish I wasn't.*

'Sorry about the tea,' Tye added.

Kian smiled in the dark.

'It's okay.'

CHAPTER 5

TYE

Tye checked his phone. *Midday. Should get up.* He turned over to see if Kian was asleep. He was, with a book still in his hand. Tye sighed. The door opened.

'Right, up. Up!' Lynne shouted, striding over to the window. She flung open the curtains. Tye squinted. Kian pulled the duvet over his head. Lynne grabbed it off him.

'Up! Both of you. It stinks in here.'

She opened the window.

'Nan—'

'No – "Nan" nothing. We're having a family meeting now, in the kitchen.'

'Family what?'

'Downstairs!'

She marched out.

'We best go,' said Tye. 'She's really got one on her.'

Kian nodded.

They shuffled downstairs. The living room took up the whole of one side of the house, from front to back. The bay window at the front housed porcelain ladies in ballgowns and two Cavalier King Charles Spaniels, sat either side of a carriage clock. The front of the room was taken up with a small table and chairs and a bookcase, all pine. The back housed the sofa and armchair, dusky pink and slightly worn. The TV sat in the corner on a plastic side unit that was made to look like dry stone wall. To the left of that was the fireplace, a grey and brown electric bar heater set in an orange tile border. The hearth had a bowl of potpourri on one side and a coal scuttle on the other. Tye remembered Lynne buying it from a car boot sale years ago, when he was bored out of his brain. She said it didn't matter that they had no coal to scuttle.

He sat on the sofa, resting his feet on the coffee table.

'Off!' Lynne snapped, swatting his toes.

'Jesus—'

'Don't "*Jesus*" me,' Lynne said, pointing at him. Tye caught Kian's eye and stifled a laugh. He saw Kian trying to straighten out his smirk.

'You two,' she said, pointing first at Tye, then Kian, then back to Tye, 'are in trouble.'

'Me?! What did I do?' Kian asked.

'The head teacher called me yesterday, and he's concerned about both of you. Your attendance is shocking, the pair of you. And your attitudes are even worse. Now, I know things have been hard, but you can't let this bump in the road throw you off at such an important time. How you do in your GCSEs and A Levels—'

'I'm not doing A Levels, Nan, I'm doing—'

'I don't care what they're called these days, Tye,' Lynne held her hand up. 'In my day you'd have just got a job by now, but these days you have to be there until you're eighteen, so there it is. I know it doesn't suit you, but you have no choice. Just get through it. Your dad doesn't need to be worrying about you on top of everything else, does he?'

Tye looked at his feet. He knew she was right.

'Don't you want to make him proud?' she asked.

'Of course I do, but…' he trailed off.

'But what?'

Don't make me say it out loud. Not while Kian is here.

'I'm just not… I'm not good at it. Any of the written stuff. The coursework. The practical is piss-easy, but I just hate the rest of it.'

'Don't you think it'd be easier if you turned up from time to time? You're so far behind, Tye, it's no wonder you find it hard. When your dad is out of hospital, do you want Mr Clark harassing him like he did me yesterday? Making him feel like he's a shit dad because you're being a shit student?'

'No.'

'I'm not asking you to get fantastic grades. I just want you to do your best. Turn up. Try. If you come out of it with a pass, then that's time well spent. You have it under your belt and you never have to do it again. And your dad will be so proud.'

Tye nodded.

'Good. Now, Kian – Mr Clark was very worried about you, too. Don't you roll your eyes at me!'

'Nan, he's a tool,' Kian said. 'He's just pissed off with me because my grades are really good even though I don't go—'

'Ah, so you are skiving!' Tye interrupted.

'Don't laugh, Tye this is serious, Kian,' Lynne said. 'You're wrong. Your grades *were* really good, but they're starting to slip.'

'Bullshit.'

'Oi! Don't swear at me. Mr Clark said you're missing deadlines, not handing things in. You refuse to take part in group work. It's not just all about exams, Kian. You're always on your own. You don't talk to anyone, don't have any—'

'He can't have a go at me for not having friends!'

Tye winced. *You told Dad you'd look after him.*

'You don't have friends because you cut yourself off, if you just—'

34

'—just what? Start kissing the arses of all the people who have made my life hell since year seven? Be a doormat? Just let them beat me up and take my stuff, because at least it's company?'

'Kian, I'm sorry – I didn't realise you were being bullied...'

'Oh please, come on. I might as well have "loser" written on my forehead. I'm used to it, Nan. Don't worry about me. I don't care. You shouldn't, either.'

'Why haven't *you* done anything to stop this?' Lynne asked Tye.

Tye opened his mouth, but didn't know what to say.

'It's not his fault,' said Kian quietly. 'He's always rescuing me. I just hate this place and everyone in it. I can't wait to leave.'

Lynne sighed and rubbed her hand over her face.

'Things all went wrong for your mum round your age,' she said. Tye watched the tears start to fill her eyes.

'It's just like reliving it all over again. I can't do it, boys. I just can't.' She shook her head. 'You're both good kids. You could make a go of life, you know? I can't bear the thought of either of you ending up caught in the wrong crowd, making those bad decisions... I can't—' She started to sob. 'I can't lose my grandkids too!'

'Look, Nan,' Tye said, 'We'll try. Won't we?' he looked at Kian. Kian frowned at him. Tye dug his elbow into Kian's side.

'I promise my grades won't deteriorate,' Kian offered.

'We promise,' said Tye, eyeing Kian, 'that the head will not have to ring you to tell you anything bad about us again. Okay?'

Kian exhaled and nodded.

'Good,' said Tye, and then looked at Lynne. 'And I promise... I promise I will try to make Dad proud.'

Lynne grabbed him in a hug and carried on sobbing.

'You will!' she cried, muffled by his shoulder. 'You both will.'

35

Join the army 17, Tye googled on his phone. He scrolled through the pages and played the videos. *I'd be good at that.* The door opened. He quickly switched the screen off and put his phone in his pocket. He looked up. It was Kian.

'Nan wants me to have a tutor,' he said, shaking his head and smirking. 'No fucking way.'

'Why not?'

'Why?! Because I don't need one! I'm top in everything, except PE, obviously. It'd be a monumental waste of money. And time. If anyone needs a tutor, it's you! But I don't think you can get tutors in plumbing coursework,' Kian said, laughing.

'Fuck off.' Tye threw a rolled-up sock at Kian's face.

There must be a good reason Nan wants him to do it.

'Do you want me to speak to her?' Tye asked.

'What? No. I've already told her I don't want one.'

'Maybe she wants to keep you busy. Stop you moping about. She'll probably ask me to do more hours at Tesco. She might just want us out of the house. Fair enough, I suppose.'

'No, it's not *fair enough*, Tye, she's not our keeper. I wouldn't let Dad dictate my life, so why should she?'

'Just think about it. I'll speak to Nan.'

'Have you just ignored everything I said? Jesus Christ. I give up. I'm going online,' he said, putting the Xbox headset on.

Downstairs, Tye found Lynne covering the outhouse floor with newspaper.

'Defrosting the freezer,' she said. 'Can't fit a bloody thing in there because there's a foot of ice round the edge.'

'What's this tutor idea about?'

'He went straight to you then,' she said, smiling. 'Nothing changes.' She wrenched open the freezer door and switched it off at the plug.

'I've thrown away the stuff that we won't have time to eat. The rest is in the fridge. See if there's anything you want for tea.'

'Nan – the tutor – why bother when he's top of everything? Except PE, obviously.'

'He needs to be challenged. I have a feeling he's too clever for that school, you know.'

She chiselled at the wall of ice with a butter knife and the heel of her hand.

'But how much would it cost?'

'Don't you worry about that. Your dad wants me to put his benefits towards it, while he's in hospital. It should cover it. It'd only be once a week. Forget the gym,' she laughed, wiping her forehead with the back of her wrist, 'all you need for a workout is a neglected freezer.'

'When did you speak to Dad?'

Lynne put the knife on the floor and looked at him.

'Just today.'

'How is he? Why didn't you put me on?'

'You were asleep. He's... fine. Listen, Tye. Now he's at the different hospital, he's on a new treatment regime. And what they think is best, for a while... is for him not to have any visitors, for a bit. These are the specialists, now – they know what they're doing. He's healed his body, now he has to heal his mind. It's the next step.'

'What? How is not having visitors the next step? Surely that's a step backwards?'

'To be honest, love, he needs a lot of help. Once they'd dealt with the injuries, they realised how ill he was. In his head... he needs—'

'Why are they telling *you* this and not me? You're not even related to him! This is fucking shit.'

'I'm his next of kin, they need an adult to—'

'*I'm* an adult!'

'You're not eighteen yet.'

'Fucking ridiculous. How long is he not allowed visitors for?'

'I don't know, they don't know – it all depends on his progress. It's very complicated.'

'No, it's not. It's not complicated at all. He needs his kids. We need him. He's not well. We want to help him get better. He'll get better faster if he sees us. He'll get worse if he feels alone, I know he will. I know him.'

'I know you do, sweetheart, better than anyone, but… we just have to trust them. It won't be for long.'

'Bullshit!' Tye shouted, walking out of the back door. He slammed it behind him.

He ran down to the bottom of the garden and kicked the stone wall. *Fuck*. He looked into the field beyond it. Nothing. The wall only came up to his hip. He vaulted over.

'Tye!' He heard Lynne shout behind him. 'Tye, you're trespassing!'

He didn't care. He would carry on walking until something or someone stopped him. He fixed his eyes on the abandoned mill at the top of the hill. He'd seen it from the bedroom window before. He'd never been up there, but he had thought about it. He thought about going up there in the dark and setting fire to it. It was still daylight now. Sunny, in fact.

Not for much longer, though. He felt the lighter in his pocket.

CHAPTER 6

TYE

A bird flew out from the top floor of the mill as he looked up at it. It was a stone-built, two-storey building. Wide and squat, like a stable or an old coach house. One black wooden door at the bottom right and a few small windows dotted here and there were all that broke the stone. *Hollow*, he thought, *maybe like a barn.* Tye could just see the top of the wheel behind it – a thin crescent of wooden slats, peeking over the roof.

He couldn't wait to feel the heat. The thrill was like nothing else. Watching a tiny spark spread, creep, leap and dance up and across everything it touched. The light, the heat… the sound. The temptation to stay in the flames until the end. The power. All in his hand. With one flick, he could stand back and watch the world burn. His heart beat faster in anticipation of feeling that high again.

Calm down. It might be locked up. There could be CCTV. He scanned the building.

The sun still caught it. At the highest point of the valley, the mill was always the last to be cast in shadow. The village was back to grey, but the mill was still blood orange. Here at the top of the hill, there was even a hint of gold in the long grass, shimmering through the net of leaves cast above the trees to the right of the mill.

Fuck off. He was angry at it all. Angry with the peace, the beauty, the calm. *Nothing has the right to be okay. It's not okay.* He scuffed the grass with his feet. Hot tears ran down his face. He brushed them off and picked up a handful of stones from the path, throwing a few into the distance as hard as he could. He threw another at the trunk of one of the trees. It smashed through the bark, sending a piece flying to the left as the stone span out to the right. He heard a bird's caw, harsh and urgent, from the canopy. *That bird from the mill. He's telling me to fuck off.* He picked up another stone and threw it at the tree again, harder. It stuck in the bark. The raven looked at him, but stayed where it was. *You win.*

Tye turned to the mill. There was just one window that still had glass, as far as he could see. He found a rock the size of his palm and picked it up. *Fuck it. If I'm burning it down, I might as well have some fun smashing things.* He hurled the rock at the glass pane. It made a satisfying smashing sound – different to the sound of the car windows he smashed in Stoke. Cleaner, lighter. He wished there were more.

'Oi!' A shout came from above. His heart skipped.

'Jesus!' He took a step back. There was a girl leaning out of the gap where another windowpane would've been, up above him. His age, maybe a bit younger. She was pale, with a huge mane of coppery-blonde hair that needed brushing. Her plaid shirt was crumpled and baggy over her small frame. *What's she doing up there?*

'That was the only window left with glass in it, you dick!' she shouted.

Damn. He felt the lighter in his pocket. He needed to do something, anything, to vent his anger. *This would've been perfect. Not going to happen now.*

'What do you care? It's not your bloody house,' Tye said. 'Some fucking dump that's been here a hundred years, should've been knocked down ages ago.'

'It *is* my house, actually. And you've just damaged it. I could call the police.'

'Bullshit. Nobody lives here. And definitely not you.'

'Why am I here then, shouting at you for breaking my bloody window?' she said, smirking. 'And anyway,' she frowned, 'what do you mean *definitely not* me?'

What is she on? Weird girl. So posh and bolshy. Must be the daughter of whoever owns the land, maybe.

'Okay.' He folded his arms and planted his feet. 'Number one – you don't get tramps and squatters in the countryside. Number two – even if you did, you're too posh to be a squatter.'

'What?! I'm not posh! How do—'

'Oh no, I'm not posh, dahling,' he mimicked. He couldn't help it – it was too easy.

'Fuck off, I don't sound like that. You don't know anything about me. You don't even know my name.'

'I bet it's something well fancy like one of those *Made in Chelsea* types – Henrietta… Jemima!' he laughed. He liked her. *Finally, someone my age in this shithole.*

'It's Ria. My name is Ria and I'm not posh. I'm just not from round here. Do posh girls drink Frosty Jack's?'

'Definitely not.' He shook his head.

'Want one?'

'All right.' He definitely liked her.

She disappeared from the window. He waited.

Okay, so I can't burn it down, but maybe I can get shitfaced in it.

***

41

'Come on,' she said, walking round the side of the mill. 'We need to chill it first.'

He followed. She was shorter than he'd expected. Definitely his age though. She smelled like grass, soot, cinnamon. They turned round the corner and emerged at the edge of a huge pond that lapped right up to the mill, drowning half the wheel. She carried on a few steps further onto a wooden jetty that took them out over the water.

'Here we are,' she said as she stopped and turned round.

Wow. The light, the trees, the water, the wheel. It's beautiful. He thought the words, but didn't say them. He didn't want her to think he was impressed. *The countryside is boring. Not for me. Still, glad I didn't set it alight.*

'Pass me that bag,' she said, pointing at a plastic carrier bag tied round a wooden post that marked the join between the jetty and the bank. *Okay... what's that for?* He untied it and handed it over. She laughed, taking it off him.

'Don't worry, I'm not going to suffocate you.'

'That's good to know,' he said, nodding his head.

He watched her put the cider cans in the bag, kick off her shoes and roll up her jeans to the knee. She sat on the edge of the wooden boards and turned to look at him, squinting in the sun as she tied the handles of the bag round her ankle.

What... is she doing?

'Come sit,' she said, swinging her legs over the edge and plunging the bag into the water with them.

Ahh – an improvised fridge. Clever. Bit weird though. And she must be fucking freezing.

He bent down and squatted next to her, looking into the murky water. *Don't want to get mud on the arse of these jeans – they're the only decent pair I brought to Nan's.*

'You're too tall for that, you can't be comfy. Just put your legs over the edge,' she said.

'I'm not getting these wet!' He pointed to his trainers. *God. I sound like such a girl.*

'Take them off, obviously…'

'Yeah I know, but then I'll have wet feet going back inside them and they were £200—'

'What?! £200 for trainers? Jesus Christ. You're wearing £200 trainers in Talvern Pitts… you do realise the average age round here is seventy, right? Unless you count the cows, who would bring it down a fair bit. But cows aren't impressed by trainers. Especially if they're leather.'

'You're weird,' he said, taking the trainers off. *She's right. Who am I trying to impress round here?*

'I'm not the one dressed for the MTV Awards afterparty in a field in Talvern Pitts.'

'I think I'd rather look like this than you do right now with an Aldi bag of Frosty Jack's tied round your ankle in a lake.'

She was right though, he felt like a dick. He was grateful she had her leg in the water. He needed a drink.

She shrugged.

'At least I'm practical.'

Come on. Stop being a wuss. Just do it. When did I last cut my toenails? Shit.

He took off his socks and shoes and pulled up his jeans to the knee. *I look like a toddler going paddling. This is excruciating.* He sat down and swung his legs over the edge, slowly lowering his feet in. *Shit!*

'Fuck, that's freezing!' he shouted, whipping his feet back out and onto the deck as fast as he could.

'Jesus Christ, it's like an actual ice bath!' he said, and shuffled backwards on the wood so he sat with his legs stretched out and his feet jutting over the edge, well away from the water.

She was staring into the water.

'Get your leg out, I don't need my cider *that* cold – you'll get hypothermia!'

'What?'

'I said, how do you still have your legs in there? They'll drop off!' *Christ. I sound like Nan.*

'I like being numb,' she said quietly, then leaned forwards and reached into the pond for the bag.

'Cold enough,' she said, and handed him the can.

'Thanks.'

It dripped over his fingers. They cracked open the cans and sipped in silence, listening to the wind through the branches above them. Tye exhaled. He wished it was something stronger. But as far as cider went, it was pretty damn strong.

Dad is alone. Ill. Scared. He needs to see us. He needs a reason to get better. Something to get out for. He needs to keep in touch with the real world, or he'll disappear. It happened before.

'You never said what your name was,' she asked.

'Tye.'

'As in tie-a-knot or Thailand?'

'T-Y-E.' *How else would you spell the name Tye?*

'Oh. Why were you throwing stones at my house, anyway?'

'Come on, it's not your house.'

'I don't own it, but that's where I live… most of the time.'

'Most of the time?'

'My great-aunt lives in the village. She's half lost her marbles but she remembers who am I still. I stay there when the weather's bad, charge my phone there, shower. That kind of thing. She gives me money now and then.'

'Where does she live? My nan is on Brindle Lane.'

'Other side to that. Up the hill going out towards Silverton.'

'Where are your parents?'

'They died. In a car crash.'

'Jesus Christ, I'm sorry – that's awful. When did it happen?' *That'll be why she's weird then. Poor girl. That would screw anyone up.*

'Last year...'

'Shit. How did you... I mean... don't you have any other family?'

'None.'

If Nan had dementia, would we have been taken into care? Probably.

'Didn't social services—' he started.

'Well, I do have a sister,' Ria interrupted. 'She's a lot older than me. So they let her adopt me, then they left us alone. But I don't see her. She emigrated.'

'She just left you here alone?! How old are you?'

'Seventeen.'

'Still, that's...' he trailed off, taking a swig. *I would adopt Kian. Even if he was seventeen. And I wouldn't leave him. Not in a million years.*

'It's not her fault,' she continued. 'I made her. She had a job offer in America... I told her I'd got a job with boarding... at a stable. I didn't want to hold her back.'

She must be a really good liar to pull that off. Kian could never get one past me like that. As if she went, though. How could she leave her younger sister to fend for herself with nobody except a mad old aunt to look out for her? Jesus.

'So she has no idea you're sleeping rough?'

'I'm not *sleeping rough,* I just... spend a lot of time outdoors.'

'And you don't go to school or college, or have a job?'

'Like I said, my great-aunt gives me money now and then. I might go to college next year. Or I might just stay here. I like the moorland. Feels like home.'

'So all your stuff is in there?' he said, pointing back to the mill. She nodded.

Fuck me. That's mental. Still, though, I bet she pretty much lives at the old lady's house and just comes here to hang out. You can't live in a building with no windows on a hillside. I mean, unless you're homeless. She doesn't seem homeless. Not properly.

'D'you want to see? We need another drink anyway.' she said, shaking the last drops of her can out onto the grass.

'Okay.'

He smiled, shaking his head slightly. *I came up here to burn the place down, now I'm going to have a tour from the squatter. Well, part-time squatter.*

'How did you find out about this place?' Tye asked, as they stepped over the threshold. Inside, an empty stone-walled space stared back at them. The only features were a pile of rubble in one corner, a chimney breast surrounding a hearth and a wooden ladder at the far end. The ladder leaned up against a hatch in the ceiling. *Smells kind of like the outhouse at Nan's. Damp, brick and soil.*

'I live up here,' she said, walking over to the ladder.

She beckoned him to follow her up.

He hesitated. *Is she asking me up there like that? No. Don't be daft. You've only just met her. But what if—*

'I'm not a serial killer, I promise,' she said, stopping halfway up the ladder.

No, but are you a bit mad?

'Never mind,' she said, lowering herself back down.

Stop being so scared of everything, Tye, it's not like you.

'No,' he stepped towards the ladder. 'I want to see.'

He followed her up the ladder. It didn't seem to cope well with his weight. It bowed and creaked. *Go faster, it's about to snap!* Finally, she climbed out and he followed, scrambling up to his feet on the solid floor.

'It's not much,' she said.

'Wow…' He looked round. *She really does spend a lot of time here.*

'It's just bits I've collected. Nobody comes here. Not that it's worth stealing. It's all junk, really.'

There was a bookshelf that looked like someone had put it together from bits of driftwood, some half-burned candles in old glass bottles and a stack of hay in the corner with a sleeping bag laid on top of it. *This is… strange.*

'Jesus. You really do live here… where are your clothes and stuff, though? How do you cook or wash or like… do anything except sleep and read?'

'I don't really have much stuff… and I don't need to cook. I have food in here.'

She opened a wooden barrel in the corner and lifted out a multipack of crisps. She put it back and got two more cans of cider out.

'I'm all right, thanks,' he said. *She's weird. She spends a lot of time here. Does she actually know anyone in the world except her mad old aunt? Does that aunt even exist? Is she going to keep me here forever just for someone to talk to, like a dog, tied up?* He laughed inside, but part of him really meant it.

There's definitely more to this than she's letting on.

'The rest of my stuff is at Marjory's house. That's my great-aunt's name. I stay there when the weather is shit, if I'm ill, that kind of thing. Get showers, charge my phone. Like I said. I do things for her round the house, keep her company. She doesn't have anyone else.'

Tye didn't say anything. He felt sorry for her. *She probably doesn't have many friends, whatever's going on. If any. This place has no young people.* He turned round, looking out of the window.

'I can see my nan's house from here,' he said, pointing at it.

'Which one?'

'The one with the red fence at the back. There.'

He looked at the wall he'd jumped over. There was a bull in the field he'd stomped through now. *Shit.*

She murmured. He turned round. She was looking at the floor.

'"Ria and the ravens",' he read. It was written in capital letters in the dirt on the floorboards.

'Is that like the name of your band or something?' he asked. She laughed.

'What?' he asked.

'Oh, nothing – just the thought of me in a band. I can't play a thing.'

'Oh. So what is it then?'

She looked nervous. *Is it the name of a cult she's going to try to get me to join?*

'The ravens live here too. Well, they don't live here, they just visit…' she trailed off.

'Okay…' he said, moving towards the hatch. *Yep. Okay. She's mad.*

'No don't – I promise, I'm not insane. Look—'

She unzipped her pocket and pulled out a bag. He squinted. It looked like it was full of chunks of raw chicken.

'Fucking hell. I'm sorry, I'm going—' He started to step down the ladder. *I feel bad for the girl, but this is just too much. Who carries raw meat around? Is that what she means by the ravens? They live here, cut up in bits in a bag, with me? She needs medication like Dad has.*

'Wait! It's for the ravens! Just wait one minute, I'm not crazy – you'll see!'

He stood still, halfway down the ladder. He could still see the top half of her. She rifled in the bag and drew out a slimy gobbet.

Eurgh.

She held it out of the window, balanced in the nook her thumb and forefinger made when she rolled her hand into a fist, as though she were about to flip it like a coin. She looked at Tye and whistled. He watched her hand. Nothing happened.

He waited. Still nothing. *I don't know what I'm expecting to happen. She's nuts.* He started down the steps. She held up her other hand in a "stop" sign. He watched again, from one step further down this time.

'Shit!' he shouted, nearly falling backwards, catching himself on either side of the hatch. A raven clattered in, like a half-open black umbrella thrown through the window. *Is that the bird from the tree earlier? Shit – he'll be pissed off with me—*

'Don't be scared – he's no harm,' she said.

'Are you sure?' Tye asked, clinging to the floorboards on either side of the hatch. *As if she's got him to come like that – how did she do it?*

'I was talking to Bertie...' She looked at him, smirking.

'Oh... right.' *Fuck me. This is the strangest hour of my life. Fun, though.*

She stroked the bird's neck with the back of her finger.

'Now do you believe me?'

CHAPTER 7
RIA

He believes me. Shit. What now?

Keep it up. Keep it up and you can be that girl. Start again, as her. Never see any of them again. Never see your dad again. Never think about him again. That never happened. You never knew him.

She watched Tye climb back up the ladder and slowly walk towards her. He stopped, seeing the raven shift its weight from foot to foot.

'It's okay,' Ria whispered to Bertie. She turned to Tye.

'That is mental,' he said quietly. 'How do you—'

'It takes a long time. My granddad taught me, before he died.'

'How many of them are there?'

'Two. Betty and Bertie. They're a pair. They mate for life.'

'Have they got chicks?'

She nodded.

'They did, earlier in the year. They just left last week.'

'Did you name them, too?'

'No. They never came here. I'd see them in the trees but I didn't try to train them like this one. Or Betty. It might've interfered with them leaving home.'

Ria gave the bird another chunk of chicken, then folded the bag away into her pocket.

'Go on, then,' she whispered.

Tye stepped back as the raven took off, out of the empty window. He ran to the ledge and leaned out, straining to follow the line of flight. Ria smiled. He looked so different to when she first saw him.

'What were you so angry about?'

'Hm?'

'When you came up. I saw you, stomping up the hill. Kicking the grass. Chucking stones. Breaking my window.'

'Oh. Nothing. Just my dad. He's in hospital and I can't see him, that's all.'

'Oh, that's shit.'

She tried to empathise. She couldn't. When she thought of her own father in a hospital bed, she thought of all the ways she could kill him. *Smother him with a pillow. Too kind. And boring. Switch off the machines? Inject him with something? Might not work.* What she really wanted to do, what she'd dreamed of for so many years, was to stab him. Slit his throat, maybe. But to look into his eyes and stab him in the heart, the stomach, the neck – the thought of it made her fingers twitch with anticipation.

'Why can't you see him?' she asked, trying to pull her thoughts back.

'He's too ill.'

'Will it make him worse?'

'Maybe.'

'Jesus. What happened to him?'

She saw his mouth open, but no words came out. He looked out of the window. It was going dark now.

'Don't worry – you don't have to tell me.'

She went over to her makeshift bookcase. On the top sat a box of matches and a pack of antibacterial wipes. She wiped the chicken off her hands and picked up the box of matches.

'He's not in a normal hospital.' Tye's voice was quiet, behind her. She turned round. He was still at the window, looking out. She struck a match and lit the candles, dotted around the room.

'He's in a secure unit. It's in his head, that he's not well.'

She blew out the match.

'Did he try to kill himself?' she asked.

Tye looked at her. His face looked like it had when she first saw him again. Like he wanted to scream and punch someone but sink to the floor and cry at the same time.

'He did. Yes,' he said, his voice cracking.

She saw the first tear fall. He wiped his eyes.

'I'm sorry – I shouldn't have—' she began.

'It's okay. I have to go now.'

He rubbed his eyes with his sleeve and started down the ladder.

'Wait!' Ria shouted. He stopped and looked up.

'Do you...' she started, not knowing how to finish. 'Do you want my number?'

He put his hand to his pocket, then stopped.

'No, no. Sorry about the window.'

Then he was gone.

Shit. Why did I ask that?

She knew why she asked it. Because she always wanted to know about it. Suicide. She obsessed over it. There was one suicide in her family that she knew of. Her uncle killed himself. Ria only found out by mistake, at her granddad's funeral, when her aunt got drunk and shouted at them all. She said she'd married into the seventh circle of hell. The family was built on cruelty and deceit. They were all to blame for her husband's death and she wished she didn't have kids, so that she could kill herself too. Ria remembered it word for word. She was eleven.

Never, ever again. Do you hear me? her mum's voice echoed in her head.

You don't ask about him anymore. I've told you everything I know. You're too young to understand, so stop trying. And why do any of the details matter? Why do you want to know every little thing? The fact that your father's brother hanged himself isn't something we like to talk about, strangely enough. Normally people don't like to go over the minutiae of that sort of thing. But you're not normal, are you? I don't like how morbid you've become, Ariadne. It's unhealthy.

I'm not normal, no. Still not normal, Mum.

She stared into the flame of the candle on the floor. It was a square, fat, short one with a deep hollow in the centre and four curling, twisting horns in each corner, bending over the flame, bleeding drops of wax into the pool surrounding the black wick.

You're not normal. It was her dad's voice this time. She put her finger in the pool of wax to feel the searing burn, but it was over too soon. The reflex to withdraw it meant that the wax solidified around her skin and nail, cooling fast.

You're disgusting, don't you dare threaten me like that, his voice continued, *who would ever believe you? Who would ever want you, if you told anyone? They'd hate you. Your mother would hate you. She'd be so, so angry with you. Disappointed in you.*

Ria peeled the wax off her finger and scanned the room, desperate for something better.

Shut up. Get out of my head.

All she had was paper. She took a sheet and splayed her fingers out, dragging it across the thin curve of skin that stretched between each finger where they met her hand. She bled, but not enough. He carried on.

This stays between us, because you wouldn't survive if it didn't. The lowest of the low. How could you degrade yourself like that? And yet you have, because you're weak, and you need me. You made me do this, it's your fault. You made me. I hate you for it, but I still love you. Despite it all. I'm the only person that loves you. I'm the only one who can protect you from the world. You know that I'm all you have. The only one who will stick by you, even though you're sick in the head.

'Shut up!' she shouted. She ran to the window and sat on the ledge, her legs hanging over the outside wall. The ground seemed distant in the dark, but was it far enough? Her tears blurred her vision. She wiped her eyes and looked straight ahead, out to the silhouette of the hills and houses against the indigo sky. Her house was there. Her real house. Her mum's bedroom light was on. Would she care? She'd probably be more worried about what people would think. Ria looked at the ground again. It seemed closer this time. Not far enough. She breathed in the cool, dark air and closed her eyes.

CHAPTER 8
TYE

The house was dark when he got back.

'Kian?' he shouted up the stairs.

'What? I'm revising.'

'Where's Nan?'

'She's gone for a drink with Barbara.'

'Oh.'

Tye walked through the hall into the kitchen and put the light on. He opened the cupboard where Lynne kept her spirits and turned round two of the bottles to see what they were. *Cinzano. Sherry. Half a bottle of brandy, sat at the back. Old lady drinks. Probably just for Christmas. Pernod. Pernod? He picked up the bottle. Forty per cent? That'll do.*

He unscrewed the cap and sniffed it. *Wow.* He could smell something that reminded him of his dad. His cooking. He smelled it again. *Aniseed, mint. No, there's something else, underneath.* It was earthy, green, peppery, sharp.

'Coriander,' he said it out loud. He suddenly felt self-conscious and leaned backwards to see beyond the door into the hall. Kian was still upstairs.

Coriander. He could see his dad's hands, scooping up the pile he'd just chopped. Soft and spiky at the same time. So intensely green and wet where the knife had broken the leaves, they stained the palms of his hands.

The door to the outhouse was open. He put the bottle down and walked over to it, putting his hand on the textured glass. He remembered being scared of that glass when he was younger. Only at night time, when it was black. It felt wrong, somehow – an inside door that looked like an outside door. Even in the kitchen with the light on, you couldn't escape the fact night was there, in the house. Cold, drafty, damp – it was more than just the dark, it was the night. No other room was like that, even with the lights off. He used to dread being sent in there to get something from the fridge, before he was tall enough to reach the light switch. It always felt like something was behind him, behind the fridge door, on the other side of the window.

Tye pushed the door. He found the smell of damp comforting now. It was the smell of old tennis balls, bikes, soil. The freezer door was still open. All the ice had gone. He stepped onto the soaked newspaper to look out of the window, down the garden.

'Ha,' he said to himself, looking up across the fields and up the hill. She was still there. Or she'd left the candles burning, anyway. One little square of pale orange in the top right corner. He looked at his phone. *22:45. Fuck it.*

He walked back through the kitchen, grabbing the bottle of Pernod on his way past.

'Kian? I'm going out again. I'm at a friend's house if Nan asks.'

'Right. And where are you really?' Kian called down.

'Don't know yet. I've got my phone.'

He stepped out into the dark and locked the door behind him.

So much here was totally different to back in Stoke. There were barely any street lights in Talvern Pitts. When it went dark, it was true darkness. On a cloudy night Tye could hardly see his own hands. Nobody was ever out after midnight, until the first dog walkers at around 5:00am. He was used to sirens, cars, kids, dogs, dealers – but here there was nothing. In the city it was never really quiet, like it was never really dark. This place was so quiet sometimes that he felt like he could hear strands of his own hair brushing against each other when the breeze blew through them. Tonight, the only sound was the Pernod, sloshing with each step.

She's weird. Definitely weird. He turned left and started up the lane leading to the old mill. *But cool. Different.* She seemed totally fearless to him. Slightly wild. Posh, though – he was sure she was posh, despite what she said. He could just tell. *A bit mad, maybe. But then, Dad's mad. Dad's the best. Why did she ask that? Morbid curiosity. I shouldn't have run away.*

Was she pretty? Maybe. Not in the way his ex was. Or the girls at school were. No makeup or long colourful nails. No jewellery. No curling tongs or straighteners through *that* hair. Maybe not even a brush. He smiled. She had piercing eyes, though. There was something about the way she looked at him. It made him feel exposed.

Tye suddenly felt nervous. He was halfway up the hill. Turning to see the black lane behind him, he thought about going back home. *Come on. Girls don't normally do this to you.* He opened the bottle and took a swig.

'Christ!' he coughed. *Yep. That'll do it.* He took another swig.

Looking up the lane at the mill, something caught his eye. *Is that?*

'Ria!' he shouted, starting to run. She was sat, halfway out of the window he'd looked out of earlier, with her eyes closed. She started, opening her eyes. She saw him and smiled.

'Are you okay?' he asked, panting as he slowed to a stop under the window.

'I'm fine – just get a better view this way.' She gestured out to the horizon, then pulled her sleeves over her hands. 'Bit cold though.'

Jesus.

'Do you want a drink?' he asked, lifting the bottle up. She squinted at it.

'Whatever it is, yes.'

CHAPTER 9

KIAN

Come on. You know this. Kian stared harder at the page. The equation started to swim around the paper. He took off his glasses and rubbed his eyes. His phone said 23:17. *Dammit.* He leaned his forehead on the edge of the desk and looked at his feet. His eyes scanned across the floor to the gap under Tye's bed. *Mum's old bed.* It was just in view – the box of her old things.

She's still my mum. I should be able to see her if I want to.

He put his glasses back on and got up.

'Nan?' he shouted at the top of the stairs. *No reply. Still out.* Downstairs, he searched through the drawers of the phone table in the hall. *Buttons. Receipts. Takeaway menus. Hairpins. Wow!* He picked up an envelope full of notes. *Two, four, six…* he counted £280. *Jesus.* He carefully replaced the notes and put the envelope back exactly where it had been, between the Chinese and the pizza menus.

Finally, he found the book. He knew Lynne could barely use her mobile phone and still kept all her contacts in an address book. He flicked to S: Sainsbury's, Selwyn, Sam, Steve, Santander, Sian! He took out his phone and photographed the page. *Please still be the right one.* He started to copy the number into his contacts too, in case the photo wasn't clear. He jumped – Lynne's key was in the door and she was through before he could get rid of the book.

'Why are you still up?' she asked, then looked at the address book. 'What are you doing with that?'

Fuck. Think.

'I'm revising, and… I got stuck – I thought I'd find that tutor's number you mentioned. She was called Christine, right?' He flicked to C.

'Yes – but you can't call her at midnight, Kian!'

'Well, obviously, no – I just wanted to get the number so I can call her tomorrow. Ah, here it is.' He typed the number into his keypad and saved it.

'Okay…' Lynne took off her coat and locked the door. 'I think you should call it a night, Kian. It's late. You look knackered.' She put her hand on his shoulder. 'I'm really pleased you want to give this tutor thing a go though, I think it'll do you no end of good. Where's Tye?'

'At a friend's. I think he's staying over.'

'In Stoke?'

'Not sure… think so. He's got his phone if you want to call him.'

'I'll not embarrass him. I'll just text him. Show me where that is again on here, will you?'

***

'Where the hell were you?' Kian asked as Tye shut the bedroom door behind him.

'Shhhh,' Tye whispered, 'don't wake Nan.' He stumbled over to the bed and fell face-first onto it.

'She's already awake, it's 10:00am – you're lucky she's out doing that Sunday thing.'

'Church,' he said, muffled by the pillow half in his mouth.

60

'It's not church. It's a charity thing. You reek – what were you drinking?'

'Perlow. Per… permow. Per-no. No.'

'You smell like a hospital corridor. Where people are dying.'

'Cheers. Could you close the curtains? The light…' He pulled the duvet over his head.

Kian sighed. He dragged the curtains together, making the rings screech over the pole. He saw Tye flinch under the duvet and smiled. He emptied out the bin and banged it down on the floor next to the bed, near Tye's head.

'If you start chundering, do it in there.'

'Thank you,' Tye croaked.

Kian picked up his books off the desk and carried them out, shutting the door behind him. *I should take him some water. Maybe in a bit.*

In the living room, he got his phone out and looked at Sian's number. His thumb hovered over the call button. *What do I say?* He stared at the blank TV screen. His distorted reflection stared back at him. He felt as though he was sat there for hours, arguing with himself. He half-hoped Lynne would walk in like she had the night before, so he had a solid reason for not calling, but she didn't. He was alone. *Maybe I'll text her. That way it doesn't matter if she's busy… or if she doesn't know what to say to me. She can answer in her own time, yeah?* he agreed with himself. *Okay.*

Hi, it's Kian here – I found your number at Nan's. I hope this is still your phone. Dad is in hospital so we're staying with Nan. Do you want to catch up sometime?

He added, *I miss you*, but deleted it as soon as he saw it on the screen. Send. He exhaled.

He turned the TV on and paced the room, looking out of the window on his way to the front and then back to the TV on his return. The sky was overcast. Spots of rain started to tap at the window. There was nothing to see out of the front of the house. Just a road, a steep verge beyond and a grey fence with a string of barbed wire trailing across it. His phone buzzed. *Shit. It's her.*

'Hello?'

'Kian? Is that you?'

He hesitated. He hadn't heard her voice in years.

'Kian?'

'It's me.'

'Where are you?'

'Nan's.'

'Are you okay? It's – it's so good to hear from you, Ki.'

'You too… I'm fine. Just, a bit shit about Dad, but—'

'What happened?'

'It's a long story. Do you – erm… do you want to catch up… in person? I won't tell Nan.'

'I'd love that, Ki. Don't tell your brother either – it'll just upset him.'

'Okay. Are you still in Stoke?'

'Cobridge. Can you get to the shopping centre?'

'Yeah. Today?'

'Why not? Two o'clock inside the main entrance?'

'I'll be there.'

***

Kian hated Hanley. It was always full of people. Crowded places tested him. The shopping centre was the worst. The noise. Men, women, children, babies – talking, shouting, whispering, screaming. Singing. Cash registers. Scanners. Footsteps, wheels. Clothes hangers, shoe boxes, plastic bags, ripping paper. He could hear people crunching, chewing, slurping, swallowing. The music each shop played spilled out into the walkway and fought with the next in mid-air. The neon strip lights, the flashing TVs, the signs in capital letters, the endless bodies pushing past one another. It was too much. He felt sick.

He stumbled to the exit and pushed his way through the heavy glass door. Air. There was still noise, but it was carried away into the ether instead of ringing round a tin box he was stuck inside. Air. Space. Daylight.

He suddenly felt as though he should walk away. Run, even. *Shit*. He checked his phone. Still a few minutes. He looked at his call list. His thumb hovered over *Tye*. *No. You can't tell him. He'd go mad. But then... she's his mum too. Maybe he'd like to see her? Maybe he knows what I should say to her?* He pressed the button. It rang and rang. Kian realised he was digging his toes into the end of his trainers so hard they'd gone numb.

'What do you want?' Tye sounded like the call had woken him up.

'I'm in Hanley, at the Potteries centre...'

'...and?'

'And I... I'm... I just wondered—'

'Kian, I'm trying to be quiet because Nan has just come back and I've told her I'm sleeping off a headache but I'm hungover as fuck and I don't need you dicking me about—'

'I'm meeting Mum.'

'WHAT?!' he shouted, then hissed, '*What the fuck are you talking about?*'

'I found her number in Nan's address book. I just... missed her.'

Kian waited. He could hear Tye breathing, maybe even swearing under his breath, but he didn't reply.

'Tye?'

'You know what, Kian? On any other day, I'd run out of here and get the bus down, give you a bollocking, drag you back. But today, I'm not. It's time you learned to fight your own battles and deal with the consequences of your fucking terrible decision making. Just don't expect any sympathy from me.'

It was Kian's turn to be silent. He swallowed. He opened his mouth, but no words came. Tye exhaled, then spoke again.

'Look. I'm staying out of it. Just two things. Don't tell her where we are, and don't give her any fucking money.'

Kian heard the line disconnect and looked at his phone. Call ended. The word *Tye* disappeared.

Shit. What if he's right? He's always right about this kind of stuff. Okay. Just go. He took a deep breath and started walking towards the bus station.

'Ki?'

The voice came from behind him. *Too late.* He turned round.

'Mum, hi,' he said quietly. 'How are you?'

They hugged. He already felt like crying. She felt so thin. *That smell. Marlboro and blackcurrant Tunes. Still the same.*

'You've grown!' she said, reaching up to pat his hair. He smiled. He wanted to say, *You've shrunk.* She was smaller, sharper than he remembered. The shadows and lines on her face were darker, deeper.

'What happened to your…?' He pointed to his mouth.

'Oh, my teeth? Just an accident. Is it dead obvious?'

'No, no.' He shook his head. *You can't lie for shit.*

'Can't do anything about it, love. Dentist cost shitloads. You look after your teeth – don't end up like me!'

She reached into her coat and took out cigarettes and a lighter.

'Shall we—' He gestured towards McDonald's.

'Oh right, yeah,' she said, lighting up. 'Just give me a minute.'

CHAPTER 10
RIA

'You know you're supposed to call me if you're staying out, Ariadne.'

'It doesn't really fit in with your *no rules* parenting though, does it?' Ria asked, watching her mum snip at a bonsai tree on the windowsill with nail scissors.

'It's called *free range* parenting, and it's not my parenting style. Any more. I adopt a blend of free range and holistic parenting principles—'

'Fucking hell. Listen to yourself. And you wonder why I'm never here? Jesus Christ. I preferred it when you were a battleaxe.'

'I was never a *battleaxe*. That is a misogynistic concept. Authoritarian? Yes. Misguided? Yes. But I have been on a journey since then.'

She put down the nail scissors and looked at Ria.

'You mean since I was expelled?' Ria asked. Her mum's silver hair was tucked behind her ears, just touching the top of her shoulders. Her huge wooden jewellery clanked every time she moved her head, the earrings bashing into her necklace from the lady she sponsored in Zambia.

'I mean, since we reached our crisis point. Together. We

have grown since then. And I feel like this works better. Don't you? How is this conversation making you feel?'

'I'm going to bed.' Ria turned and walked into the hall, kicking off her shoes on her way up the stairs.

'That's not an answer, and it's three o'clock in the afternoon,' her mum called after her. 'But if this conversation is making you tired and frustrated, then perhaps that is a good idea.'

Perhaps it is. Perhaps I couldn't care less. She shut her bedroom her behind her. *Perhaps I need to move out. Properly. Need a job first.*

She sighed, falling face-down onto the bed. She thought of Tye and smiled. *We kissed. Did we? Or was that a drunken dream? No. I think we did. He tasted like liquorice. Did anything else happen? I don't think so.* She couldn't remember. *It'll come back to me. In pieces. It always does. You need sleep.*

She turned over to face the wall. There it was, the ladder. She stroked her fingertip across the lines. The room had textured wallpaper. No discernible pattern, just random darting lines and wandering streaks of raised paper scattered across the flat.

A long stretch of raised paper was right in front of her eyeline as she lay on her side, and always had been. Like a snake on a snakes and ladder board. Since she was eight years old, every time something bad happened to her, she would put a stripe on the snake's back. She would keep the bad thing with her all day, then when she got to bed, she would put the bad thing in the end of her thumb and press her thumbnail into the paper. It was such a satisfying feeling. It had just the right amount of give. She would push her thumbnail against the paper, feel it yield, and watch her nail disappear into the wall. She'd roll the nail from side to side, maintaining the pressure, to widen the dent. She liked the feeling of pressure in her nail bed. She loved it in the summer, when it was still light so she could see the pink blanche then flood back when she released it. In winter, she did it all by touch. Sliding her finger up the notches, finding the fresh blank sweep, then stabbing it.

She knew the exact moment when the snake became a ladder. It was when she was lying there, and he was there, and she was trying to escape, in her head. She watched the wall, and each stripe became a step. A rung, on a ladder. A ladder up, out, away. She closed her eyes and imagined climbing the ladder, up into a bright, warm sky where she could fly. Even when he made her look at him, she tried to see her sky instead. Sometimes she could, sometimes she couldn't.

Ria didn't need the ladder in the same way now, but she wouldn't let her mum strip the wallpaper. She pressed the duvet corner to her face to dry her tears and turned over, closing her eyes for her first indoor sleep in days.

***

'How are things?'

'Same as ever. You?' Ria asked.

'This rotation is killing me. It's just too depressing, it really is. If that ever happens to me, please shoot me.'

'No problem.'

She's so beautiful. Even on FaceTime, which is impossible. And she's sane. And she's a doctor.

'How come you got all the luck?' Ria asked.

'What?'

'I know I was a mistake and everything... clearly they had their perfect daughter already and twelve years later just forgot to use protection—'

'Ew, please—'

'But why did they have to do such a shit job with me?'

Dee answered. She watched her roll her eyes and shake her head, the way she always did. Ria wasn't listening, but she knew what she was saying. Dee never allowed her to feel sorry for herself. *Mum did the best she could with a bad marriage and a messy divorce. She trounced Dad in the courts, got a great settlement. She knows he was a shit, but she's spent all her time since then trying to make it up to us.*

'She even volunteered to homeschool you. That's dedication. It really is. You're a fucking nightmare,' she laughed. 'She deserves an OBE for that.'

'I know she means well. Meant well. She just infuriates me. And Dad...' she trailed off.

'Dad shouldn't have had kids,' said Dee. 'He's not the right type. He's one of those corporate psychopaths, I think. But lots of kids have divorced parents and absent fathers and they don't get expelled. You can't blame it on him. So he was never there, so what? His loss.'

'He was there too much,' Ria said quietly.

'What?'

She wanted to ask her. She'd wanted to ask her for so long. But she couldn't. *If it had happened to her too, why was she so normal? Why could she talk about him without flinching? But then, maybe it did, but she's just a better person. More resilient. Or not. Maybe it's all a carefully maintained act. Maybe I would ruin her life if I made her talk about it. Acknowledge it. I can't be responsible for that.*

'Nothing.'

'I'm sorry. I didn't mean to be harsh. I know things were worse with them after I'd gone to uni. You had to deal with them on your own.'

I was eight. You were eighteen, I was eight. You left me. That's when it started.

'Remember that time when I turned up at your student house with all my stuff?' asked Ria.

'Your stuff,' Dee laughed, 'was a black bin bag with some teddies and a bird's nest wrapped in kitchen roll. Nothing practical, like, you know, clothes.'

'I also brought crisps.'

'That's true. In lieu of rent. Anyway – I have to go get some sleep before I'm on again. I'll see you Saturday.'

'Saturday? Why?'

'Mum's birthday. Don't tell me you haven't got her anything again?'

'Shit. I'll make her something…'

'I've bought her a spa day. We'll say it's from both of us.'

'This is why I love you best, Dee. Out of everyone in the world. Mwah,' she kissed the phone.

'I know, I know. Except your bird friends.'

'They don't count. They can't buy spa days.'

CHAPTER 11
TYE

Why did I say I'd do this again? Keep Nan happy. Make Dad proud. Fuck.

'One more, come on!'

Fuck off. The sun kept up its relentless glare. His vision blurred with the sweat running into his eyes. His muscles felt like they had been stuffed with burning hot coals, ready to sear through the skin and burst it open.

'I can't.' He shook his head, letting it drop between his shoulders onto his chest. His arms remained up on either side, clinging to the bar above.

'One more and you get to jump in the cold water. Just try.'

Tye strained upwards but his arms gave out, letting his fingers loosen just a fraction, enough for him to fall.

'Well done, Tye – I knew you could do it! Now get in the water then up onto the nets.'

Why did I choose this one?

He dragged himself over to the murky pool of water dug into the field.

I could be strolling around the woods with a map and compass now. Or learning how to make a bridge out of warehouse pallets. It's not useful, but it's easy. He took a deep breath and jumped in, holding his nose. *Jesus fucking Christ!* He shook his hair as he emerged and tried to shout, 'Fuck!' but the cold took his breath away. Instead he just gasped. He could hear the instructor laughing. *Dick.* He hauled himself out onto the grass and lay for a few seconds, coughing.

You know why you chose this one, he told himself. *Because you think you're shit hot. You're actually just* shit. He spluttered, getting to his knees.

'Come on, Tye, Daisy is ahead of you, man!'

For fuck's sake.

***

'How was Cadets? Have they made you join the army yet?' Kian asked, taking a soapy plate from Tye and rubbing a tea towel round it.

'No. They won't do. It's not like that. I'd be more likely to join the Scouts at this rate.'

'Isn't Scouts the same as cadets?'

'Fuck off. I'm not in the fucking Scouts. Cadets is more like the army.'

'But you just—'

'Haven't you got revision or some shit like that to do?' Tye scrubbed at the base of the pan, sending fragments of black crust and non-stick coat floating up to the surface of the water. The bubbles had all burst, leaving a flat, oily sheen.

'Probably. I'm going to that private tutor tomorrow.'

'Even though we're in the summer holidays now? That's a bit much.'

'Not like I have anything else to do though, is it?'

'I suppose. You could come to cadets with me—'

Kian laughed. Tye shrugged.

'There are a load of geeks there too, it's not like action man central. To be honest, I'm relieved we're too far away

71

from college for anyone I know to be there, I'd never live it down.'

'Oh great, thanks.'

'No, I don't mean… well… you know what I—'

'I know exactly what you mean. You're actually far too cool for it. It's full of dweebs and therefore I'd fit right in. You have a reputation to maintain and friends to impress, I don't. It's fine.' Kian threw the knives and forks back into their tray in the drawer and picked up more to dry.

Oh, God. Here we go. Come on. Get him back.

'My friends all think I'm a dweeb too now, so you're in good company,' Tye tried. Kian kept rubbing the cutlery and clanking it into the tray.

'Did I tell you Josh got arrested?' Tye continued. He knew that when Kian was really angry, he walked away. The fact he was still there meant he'd probably come round.

'No.'

'Fight outside Spoons in Hanley. It was his fault, they've got it on CCTV and everything. He's eighteen now, too, so they won't go easy on him.'

'Hm.'

'Then there's Callum, who stopped speaking to me when I wouldn't hold on to all that weed for him. Azaf and Dan took his side. Mo and Loz are still all right with me, but they can never be arsed to come all the way out here and whenever I go back there, they're all together. So… I don't have friends to impress, really, after all.'

'What about that girl you're always hanging round with?' Kian asked, smirking.

'Fuck off. I'm not *always* hanging round with her. Just sometimes.' The water was too dirty now. He pulled the plug and watched it drain away.

'Is she your *sometimes* girlfriend?'

'No! I don't know. Maybe. No… no.'

'Sounds confusing.'

It is. He ran another sink full of water and squeezed too much detergent in. He wanted clouds of bubbles.

'What's her name?'

'Ria.'

'What school does she go to?'

'Don't know.'

'She lives here though, doesn't she?'

'Yeah. She lives with her aunt, or great-aunt, or something like that. Her parents both died in the same car crash.'

'Jesus. Maybe that's why she's strange.'

Tye was about to tell Kian more, but stopped. *She's an orphan who lives in the abandoned mill. She's a semi-feral raven whisperer.* No. *It didn't seem plausible. Is it plausible? You've seen her with the birds. She can make a fire, too.* The right-hand corner of his mouth raised in the start of a smile as he remembered the other night. *The fire out on the jetty, the water, her skin.*

'She is a bit weird, though, isn't she?' Kian interrupted Tye's daydream. 'I've seen her up at that mill, hanging out of the window. And she climbs trees. She's a bit old for climbing trees…'

'Look, I don't know anything about her. I can't explain why she does the things she does. I think what happened to her would screw anyone up. Anyway. Are you coming to cadets with me at some point or not?'

'I'll think about it.'

'You're not still seeing Mum, are you?'

'No! I told you, it was just that one time. I just wanted to let her know we're okay. And she does, now, so… that's it.'

Tye didn't believe him. He needed to keep Kian busy over the summer. *You know what will happen otherwise.*

'Just remember what I said, yeah?'

'Jesus Christ, Tye—'

'—and come to cadets next week,' Tye interrupted. 'If you keep it up, make a decent go of it – you can have the proper bed and I'll have the camp bed.'

'Really? Are you serious?'

'Yep.'

'I'll do it.'

CHAPTER 12
RAY

Thursday 22nd July. Still here. I'm working on it. Those two on the TV though. They want me here. And the clock. The people who watch me through the clock – they won't let me leave. I don't trust the nurse. He tells me this, that. It's bullshit. The doctor is worse. She lies, all the time. To help the two on the TV. In the mornings. They're always there in the mornings. I have to sit in that room. They don't let me stay here. They lock it once I'm out of bed. I hate that room. Bad things always happen in that room. The TV is there. The clock is there. The little girl in the corner who plaits and un-plaits her hair is there. She makes me sad. Just a child, trapped with these dangerous people. Plating and un-plaiting her hair. They ignore her, but she's scared of them. She cries when they get too close. She just wants to go home. I keep asking the watchers in the clock. How can I help her? They won't tell me. They tell me some things. Sometimes they tell me what will happen and how to stop it. Today they told me Gino would die if he went outside for a fag. He'll drop his lighter and when he bends over to pick it up he'll have a heart attack. So I stopped him, on his way out. I held him back and he was pushing, pushing. Then the men came. They have red eyes and bald heads. They're white.

They have no mouths, but they get their voices from their head into mine anyway. Black suits. Black gloves. The watchers send them. When I fail. They hold me down, so many of them all on top of me, my face is on the floor and I can't breathe, they're crushing my skull and I'm trying to kick my legs but they kneel on the back of my ankles I'm shouting, shouting, shouting, screaming for help, but nobody hears me. So many, all on top of me and all I can see is the patch of floor in front of my eye and the foot of a chair leg. The man knelt in front of me opens his legs and shoves them either side of my head, holding my head with his thighs and knees like a clamp. Then nothing – black on both sides. It's so hot. So dark. I try to lift my head, but someone has their arm tight down across the back of it. I can't breathe, I shout. I can't hear myself. My face is wet. I'm drowning in sweat and saliva and the horrible smell of this man. Next time, they say, you do what we ask, and you do it right. You know who we work for, you know we will kill your boys if you defy us. You know we can. And we will, if we have to. So I promise.

CHAPTER 13

RIA

'Are we going out then, or what?' she asked.

'I... um...'

'I don't care, or anything... I just thought we should probably decide. So we know where we stand. Are we just sleeping together, or is there more to it?'

Ria started to get dressed, leaving Tye under the sleeping bags on the hay in the corner. She stared out of the window. The clouds raced past the sun, dimming the daylight in and out. The willow that bent over the hillside swept back in the wind, like silver-green plumage on a bird caught in a storm.

Why is he here? Why did you drag him into your mess?

'I guess,' he faltered. 'I mean, I don't know – but, what do you think?'

Ria dug her nail into the back of her hand. *Five. You've had sex with me five times now and you're still scared of me.* She wanted him to tell her how he felt about her, so she could decide whether to feel guilty about lying to him or not. If he liked her, she'd feel bad. If he didn't, she wouldn't. That's what she told herself.

It didn't matter whether she liked him or not. She couldn't decide, anyway, so it was easier not to try. *Of course I like*

him. Like a friend. Like I like my sister, but we sleep together.
The sex didn't matter. It never did. She couldn't let it mean
anything, after what happened. Since then, she tried to make
it meaningless, worthless. Before she got expelled, she was *that*
girl. The girl who all the boys went out with, because they
knew they wouldn't be a virgin for much longer if they did.
Then they'd dump her, or she'd dump them. Move on to the
next one. The more she did it, the less it meant, the easier it
became. It numbed everything.

But do I like him like him? *Like, love-like? No. Maybe. Yes.
No. You don't know how that feels. It's easier to say no.*

'I think we're friends with benefits. Yeah?' she asked,
turning from the window to look at him. As soon as she did,
she knew she was wrong. His face, so open and kind. He
looked disappointed, crestfallen. Shit. She *did* like him. But
that didn't matter. *It doesn't matter. You don't matter.*

'Yeah.' He scratched the back of his neck, sitting up. 'Yeah,
that's fine. That's what I was thinking.' He grabbed his clothes
and pulled them on. She turned back to the window, wishing
there was still glass in it, so she could tell if her attempt to
thumb away her tears had worked or not. *Fuck.*

'I should go,' she heard his voice behind her. 'Stupid
training. I promised Kian I'd take him.'

She wiped her face with her sleeve then turned round.

'Sure, no problem. I've got to get back for my mum's stupid
thing anyway.'

'What?'

Fuuuuuck. Fuck fuck fuck fuck fuck.

'It's my mum's birthday. Or would've been, today. My
great-aunt likes to do something to mark it still, cake and all
that…'

'Just for the two of you?'

'Yeah.'

'That sounds… kind of sad… do you want me to—'

'—no, thanks. Thank you.' *You* do *like him.* 'She's pretty mad to be honest. I don't know if she even remembers Mum is dead sometimes. I just go along with whatever she's thinking that day.'

'Oh, okay. Well, I hope it's all right.'

'Thanks.'

He left. She took a deep breath in through her nose and out through her mouth.

You have to stop this. Tell him the truth. How can you, though? How can anyone say that and come back from it? They can't. You can't. Stop seeing him. That's the only way.

She whistled. The dead mouse she found on the path had been waiting in the corner since yesterday. She picked it up by the tail then laid it on her palm. It was stiff, but not rock-hard like they sometimes were. There was still a bit of give. She looked at its face. Its eyes were half-closed. She felt like it was a girl, somehow. It looked into the middle distance. The fur was smooth, flat to its cheeks and forehead. The tiny feet tickled her palm, as though someone were dangling ribbons over her skin. It had that smell. The same smell all dead animals have after a bit. Not too strong, though. It was still quite new. Just a hint of that plasticky, fishy smell – like when a fuse blows, or a cat yawns in your face.

Here she is. Betty landed on the windowsill, her feathers blustering against the wind. She lowered her head and tilted it to the side, eyeing the mouse. Ria rolled it onto the stone. Its other side had become flat, like the bottom of an ornament. The beak jabbed at it. It rocked on the uneven surface. Ria stepped back. Please take it away. The beak stabbed again, this time open, securing the body in its vice. She closed her eyes, willing her to take it back to Bertie. She could only hear the wind, no wings. Opening her eyes, she exhaled. Betty and the mouse were gone.

'Did you pre-heat the oven?'

'Check.'

'Right. The potatoes can go in.'

'I'm on it.'

Ria loved cooking with Dee.

'You're like the mum I never had,' Ria said, laughing.

'Ria, shhhh!' Dee whispered. 'She's just through there!'

Ria smirked.

'You're so harsh,' Dee said quietly, shaking her head.

'You think I should be more grateful?' Ria asked, chopping cucumber a little too hard.

'Well, yes, actually, I do. Look at this place.' She gestured around the kitchen with the spoon she was mixing redcurrant sauce with. 'You live in a beautiful house. Mum has given up work to try to make sure you get some qualifications and have some kind of future, despite your best efforts.'

'Just because the furniture is from John Lewis and the food is from Waitrose doesn't mean we're winning at life, Dee.'

'Well, it kind of does, actually—'

'—and what do you mean by *my best efforts*? If I really wanted to hit the nuclear button I'd be *so* much worse than this. Believe me.'

'What the hell does that mean? Who the fuck do you think you are? Donald Trump? The world doesn't revolve around you, Ria. What is it that you want from her, exactly? Blood?'

I don't know. I don't know what I want. An apology. For doing nothing. For letting it happen. Did she know? No. I don't think so. But then…

Ria shook her head.

'Nothing.'

'Well give her a fucking break then. You don't have to *like* her, you just have to love her. I'm sure that's what she tells herself about you.'

That's probably true. I doubt she succeeds in either, though.

Dee put down her spoon and flicked some of the sauce onto Ria's cheek. She half-smiled.

'For the record,' Dee said, putting her arm round her. 'I love you *and* I like you. I—'

Ria grabbed her and hugged her, crumpling her face into Dee's chest. Her jumper soaked up the tears.

'I'm sorry,' Ria mumbled. 'I just miss you, that's all.'

'Shhhh.' Dee stroked Ria's hair.

They stood in the smell of pastry and stock, silent. *Come on, Ria. Pull yourself together and get through tonight. For Dee.*

'Ri?' Dee asked quietly, still holding on to her.

'Hm?'

'Don't hit the nuclear button when I'm around, will you?'

***

Make. An. Effort.

'Sorry?' Ria asked. Her mum's friend, Valerie, was asking her a question.

She's the only guest. Be polite. Don't be honest.

'I was just saying – what do you want to do once you've done your A levels? University?'

Ria didn't have anything against Valerie. Some of her mum's friends were so pretentious she found it hard to be in the same room as them, but Valerie was straightforward. Ria only knew three things about her: she was a lesbian, she had lots of dogs, she had common sense. Ria liked the fact that Valerie kept her mum's flights of fancy in check. Whenever she started talking about becoming a healer, or going to live in a kibbutz, Val brought her back down to earth.

'Maybe,' she answered. 'I'm not sure yet. Depends on my results, I guess. Mum's a good teacher, though.'

She quickly glanced at her mum, then at Dee, then back to her plate. She focussed on cutting potato. She knew they were staring at her. In a good way, though.

'Thank you, darling.' Her mum put her cutlery down to mark the moment. 'You're a good student.'

Ria laughed. *If you're wondering where I learned to lie, Mum, it should be obvious.*

'Do you think you'll follow your sister into medicine?' Valerie asked.

'Oh, God, no, no. I mean, I quite like the gore and stuff but—'

'She's always been better with arts, humanities – although having said that, she's a keen naturalist,' her mum said, grinning. 'But not a *naturist*, which is what she told the careers advisor she was when she was in year seven.'

Valerie laughed politely. Ria sighed.

'I don't know, it depends how much she's had to drink,' Dee said, raising her glass and winking at Ria.

'Is everyone done? Can I clear plates?' Ria asked. *For the love of God, please, let's keep things moving.*

In the kitchen she took a deep breath and downed the wine that was left in the bottle on the side.

'Woah, slow down, I was only joking!' Dee's voice came from behind her. 'At least stay semi-conscious for the cake. Pass me the candles.'

Ria emptied the bag of alphabet letter candles onto the table. Dee picked out the letters to spell "happy birthday" and placed each one in the icing.

'Could you go any slower?' Ria asked, opening another bottle of wine.

'I'm trained to be accurate, Ri. I can't help it. You'd be grateful if I was doing your cannula.' She finally struck the match and took it along each wick. 'Well done on the teacher comment, by the way,' Dee said, looking up at her.

'Ha. That's nothing – watch me sing happy birthday like I mean it, now.'

They took the cake in, singing. Valerie joined in.

'Aw, lovely. Do you mind if I put mine in some foil and take it home?' Val asked, shifting her chair back and putting her napkin on the table. 'I need to get back for the dogs. Stussy is still new and he'll have eaten half my furniture by now.'

Dee jumped up and parcelled the slice.

Valerie left with it in her hand, waving the foil package as she said goodbye.

Will anyone notice if I drink Val's wine? Nearly done now. You can go to bed soon.

The three of them sat in the candlelight, eating cake. The only sounds were of forks clinking against china and the wind whistling down the chimney, except for Ria swallowing wine now and then. Her mum broke the silence.

'Now Val's gone, I need to talk to you both.'

What is it this time? Has she decided to sell the house and hitchhike round the Middle East? Dee knows what I'm thinking. She's got that invisible smirk that only I can see.

'I'm... in a relationship,' she announced.

'Ha!' Ria laughed involuntarily. They both looked at her.

'Sorry, that's just not what I was expecting. In a good way, though.'

'Oh, well – I'm glad. The thing is, it's probably not – well, it might be a bit of a surprise...'

'Oh my God, you're a lesbian!' Ria shouted, excited. 'Are you seeing Val?'

Dee laughed.

'No, Ariadne, on both counts. And do you have any idea how offensive that is? To assume, if I were indeed gay, that I'd be going out with Val simply because she's a lesbian? That's

83

like saying you must be seeing the postman because he comes to the house regularly and he has a penis.'

'How do you know?' Dee asked, smirking. Then, seeing the look on her mum's face, added, 'Sorry.'

'Seeing as you both think this is so hilarious, I don't know why I'm bothering to try and save your feelings!' she snapped, then drained her wine glass and replaced it heavily on the table. They waited.

'It's your father. I'm seeing your father. Again.'

'What?!' Dee shouted.

Ria felt as though she was falling. She couldn't breathe. Dee talked. She was angry. Asking questions, maybe. Ria couldn't tell. She couldn't hear anything. The world sounded like it was underwater. Like a dam had burst up the hill and the whole village was flooded. The room they were in was full to the ceiling already. Everything was floating, drifting. She couldn't breathe. White noise. She could still see Dee and their mum arguing, underwater. They were shouting, shaking their heads, pointing. *I can't breathe. The lights are going out.* Everything slowly got darker, fading from the outside in. All she could see was her mum, holding her head in her hands, crying.

I'm dying. This is it.

'Don't bring me back, Dee.'

CHAPTER 14
KIAN

This house is huge. He'd only seen the hall, the stairs and the study – but that was enough to convince him it was the biggest house he'd ever set foot in. *The hall is bigger than the entire ground floor of Nan's house.* It was tiled, with a mahogany staircase sweeping down one side and several rooms leading off the other. One open door revealed a dining room, with a broad oak table and chairs, a fireplace housing a wood burner and the edge of a piano. He couldn't see enough of it to tell what kind. Upstairs, the study was smaller – but still bigger than his and Tye's bedroom. Floor to ceiling bookcases on every wall surrounded a double desk. The two desks and chairs were fused together in mirror image, with a small divider in the middle that housed an inkwell and a grooved edge either side.

This was his third lesson, but he still felt like he was sitting in a museum. He looked out of the window. The garden had a fountain. An *actual fountain. She must be loaded.*

'So, who are your philosophical influences?' the tutor asked.

'My what?'

'What philosophy do you think most closely aligns to your worldview?'

'I… erm… we don't do philosophy at my school.'

'Well, no – nobody does these days. It's no excuse though – don't you read? Outside of your set texts?'

'I revise, all the time – I've got loads of textbooks they don't bother with in—'

'I don't mean textbooks. I mean… the canon – fiction, non-fiction – the great thinkers, the influencers. Their works. Have you read them?'

'I… don't… think so. We're doing Shakespeare, for the GCSE lit paper?'

'Derrida? Kant? Foucault?'

I have no idea what you're talking about. He stared at her.

'Chaucer? Milton? Shelley? Keats?'

You're just saying names now.

'Wollstonecraft? Mill? Bentham?'

'Look, let's just say no. It's a no. To all of them, probably. If school haven't told me to do it, I haven't done it. I don't own a library.'

'But you have the internet?'

Please lay off me. Just accept that I'm ignorant, okay?

'Right,' she said decisively. 'I'm writing you a list. Most of these are out of copyright now and they're available for free online. I need you to read at least one a week, if not two.'

She scribbled. His heart sank.

'But – I'm better at science, maths – I mean, I can do what I need to, to get an A in English, I know I can. But I don't like it, really…'

'Look at that,' she said, pointing to the third book on the list.

On the Origin of Species by Charles Darwin.

'Okay, well—'

'You can't be a good scientist without a basic understanding of the human condition, Kian.'

He gave up. He nodded and folded his arms, watching the list grow.

***

Shit. It's her. His phone buzzed. Lynne looked at it.

'Who's Lucy?' she asked, grinning.

'Just… a girl from school.'

'What?' said Tye. 'Lucy who?'

Fuck.

'You don't know her.'

'Aww, Kian!' Lynne rubbed his arm. 'You've got a girlfriend!'

'Bullshit,' Tye said, shaking his head.

'Fuck off. She's just a friend.'

Lynne beamed.

'Aren't you going to answer it?' said Tye.

'I'll call her back.'

He's onto me. Bollocks.

Lynne cleared away the plates and sat with her cup of tea looking at them both, smiling.

'I'm so proud of you two.'

Tye shifted in his seat, but smiled. *He loves praise. He never gets it.*

'You're doing so well with cadets,' she said to Tye, then turned to Kian. 'And you seem to be getting a lot out of this tutor, Kian – are you enjoying it?'

He nodded. *Get her talking about that instead of "Lucy".*

'It's hard – and different. It's not the kind of thing I've done before,' he paused, trying to think of more to say to keep them off the phone call topic. 'I was a bit overwhelmed to begin with. But it's good, being challenged. There's so much out there I didn't know about. But I feel like there's a lot more out there for me than I ever thought before, too.'

Lynne looked like she was going to burst into tears of pride. Tye rolled his eyes.

'Oh, Kian, I knew it would be the making of you… and you have a *girlfriend*, too!'

Tye laughed. 'You're a normal human being after all!' he mimicked.

'Fuck off,' Kian muttered.

'Tye, that's not what I meant,' said Lynne. 'I'm just pleased for you both.'

'So, how come I don't know this "Lucy" if she's at our school?'

'Well, you're in sixth form… she's in my year…'

'I know everyone in your year.'

'Leave him alone,' Lynne interjected. 'He's embarrassed, bless him.'

You're loving this, you bastard. Right.

'Why don't you tell Nan about *your* girlfriend, Tye?'

'What?' Lynne turned to him. 'Are you seeing that Nina again? She was such a lovely girl. She didn't really wear enough clothes, mind, and a bit too much makeup – but she was so polite.'

Hahaha. He looks so pissed off.

'No, not Nina. Not anyone. Kian's making it up.'

'Well, you spend a lot of time with her, if she's not your girlfriend… and you spend the night with her a lot, too.'

'Tye – you know about being careful, don't you? I don't want you getting into trouble like that now, it's the last thing we need. You should bring her here, introduce us – she's welcome to stay. I mean, Kian would have to stay on the sofa because she'd be on the camp bed, but—'

'Oh, Jesus. I'm going out,' Tye said, standing up. He looked at Kian and added, 'Thanks, dickhead.'

He walked out. *Mission accomplished.*

'Right,' said Lynne. 'I'm doing the big shop with Barbara. Do you fancy joining us?'

'You're all right, thanks, Nan. I've got reading to do.'

He waited until she'd shut the front door behind her and took his phone out. *Why did you save her as "Lucy"? Idiot.* He changed the name to "Ben". *I'm sure Nan's met Ben before. She could believe we're good enough friends to speak on the phone. I think.*

He called the number.

'Hello?'

'Hi, Mum – I'm sorry, I was with Nan so couldn't pick up.'

'No problem, love. Listen, I was just wondering if you wanted to catch up?'

'Oh, erm…'

'You don't seem to want to meet up anymore – I thought we were enjoying spending time together again… has your brother got in your ear?'

'No, no. He doesn't know. I'm just… I've been busy with this tutor, and… okay. McDonald's?'

'Good lad. You're my son, and I'm your mum. Nobody can replace that, you know?'

'I know.' He did know. He missed her. It was hard, not seeing her. *Despite everything, you can't forget her.*

'Now. I've got a favour to ask, love.'

Shit.

'I'm being kicked out. My landlord – he's a dickhead. Says I've damaged the property. I haven't. It was Bez, when he was off on one. Anyway, he wouldn't fix the front door, so I stopped paying him. I owe him a few weeks' rent…'

'Oh… okay.'

'I know you don't have that kind of money, Ki. But your nan does.'

He was silent.

'Ki?'

'Hm?'

'I just need to keep him off my back till I can find somewhere new, otherwise he'll change the locks and I'll be out on my arse.'

'Right… what about Bez?'

'He doesn't live here. He just stops sometimes. He's in the hostel. He can't help out, love – he has to beg as it is—'

'Okay,' he felt his stomach twist. 'What do you want me to do?'

'I knew I could count on you, Ki. There's no stronger bond than a mother and her child. I'd do the same for you, if you needed it. Lay down my life for you, I would, Ki.'

***

He felt sick. It was the first time in his life he'd been to McDonald's and not eaten anything. He clung to the brown envelope and thought about Tye. *He'd murder me. Actually murder me. Fuck. When Nan realises this has gone... what do I do? Pretend someone broke in. Really? You're a shit liar, Kian. You won't pull it off. Fucking hell.*

Here she is. She looks worse. Again.

'Come here, love,' Sian said, arms outstretched. They hugged. She stank of weed.

I'm going to be sick. He swallowed and sat down. He was suddenly hot, shaky.

'You all right, Ki?' she asked, eyeing the envelope.

'Just a virus, I think.'

'I'll get you a brew.'

'No, it's okay. Here—' He handed over the envelope. It was done.

She opened it and counted the money.

'Thanks, love. You're a star. This means I'm not on the streets of Hanley tonight.'

She grabbed his hand with both of hers and held it.

'I'm getting better, you know?' She searched his face. He nodded.

'Are you still, do you still...' he trailed off.

'Methadone. I'm on methadone. It's weaning me off it. I

should be clean in a few months. Then – who knows? I might be able to get a job, a nice place. You could come live with me. It'll be like old times, yeah?'

Kian smiled. He wanted to believe her.

'It meant a lot to me, you know,' she said.

'What?'

'You chose me. When I split with Ray. I mean, I know he's not your dad – but he's a good man. I knew Tye would stay with him. But the fact you wanted to come with me. That's love.'

Kian looked down. *It was a disaster, though, wasn't it?*

'I know it didn't work out,' she continued. 'But I was in a bad way then. You're the only reason I'm trying to sort myself out now, you know?'

He exhaled. *She's got the money. There's nothing you can do about it now. Just enjoy spending some time with her.*

'Do you want a coffee?' he asked, getting up.

'Love one, Ki,' she smiled.

***

'I've read all these,' he said, handing Christine the list. Four titles were ticked off. Since taking Lynne's money, he'd stayed in the bedroom and read, only coming out for meals and the toilet. No matter how boring, confusing or frustrating he found the texts, he wouldn't stop unless sleep forced him. Every time Lynne said his name, he felt sick. He was certain the next words would be, 'Have you taken my cash?' but so far, they hadn't been. He distracted himself with the compulsion to get to the end of the page, the chapter, the part, the book. He blamed his headaches on the endless reading, all done on his phone screen. The four books he'd read that week would've taken months at his normal pace. He was proud of the ticks on that list, but he knew why they were there.

'Fabulous!' she said. 'What did you make of this one?' She pointed to *The Aeneid*.

'Erm… I don't know. It was a bit… repetitive. Some phrases, over and over again. But I liked the underworld bit.'

'My daughter is named after Dido.'

'The one that kills herself?'

'Yes. I suppose it seems a bit strange when you put it that way. But she's a great heroine. I've always had a fondness for tragic characters. My other daughter is named after another classical heroine who gets screwed over by a man. Seems a bit perverse, doesn't it? But I suppose it's my way of giving them the last word. Men may have ruled the world back then – not now.' She shook her head, smiling. 'My two would eat those bastards alive,' she said proudly, lifting a photo frame off her shelf.

'Is that them?' Kian asked, as she turned the frame to face him.

She nodded. 'Dido,' she pointed at the eldest, then across to the younger, 'and Ariadne.'

He squinted. There was something familiar about the youngest girl. *Hang on – is that?*

'Is that a recent photo?' he asked.

She turned it round to scan it.

'Hm – about four years ago, maybe?'

'Dido and Ariadne,' he repeated. 'Didn't they get picked on at school?'

'Ha. Yes, well – they call themselves Dee and Ria.'

Bingo.

'I think I've seen Ria. Up at the mill. She has some tame ravens, doesn't she?'

Christine shrugged and sighed.

'Lord knows. I don't try to keep up with her schemes. But yes, that sounds about right.'

Interesting.

'Did she ever live with anyone else? Or in another place? It's just,' he said, trying for once to lie convincingly, 'when I saw her the other day, I thought I recognised her from somewhere else, that's all.'

'No, no. Her dad lived with us, until we got divorced. But we moved here before she was born. She's never lived anywhere else. We used to live down south when Dido was our only child. Their dad's company opened some offices around the midlands, because it's cheap. So we moved up here, I got a job lecturing at Keele and we had a romantic notion of living in the country. We didn't know the area. It's not exactly the Cotswolds, but we could never afford something like this down there.'

'What school does she go to?'

'She doesn't.' She placed the picture back on the shelf. 'Ria was expelled from St John's. I'm guessing you didn't go there, though. I'm homeschooling her now. Not that she needs it. But don't tell her that. Anyway. Let's start with Marx.'

CHAPTER 15
TYE

'Remember – a *decent go of it*, otherwise, no bed swap!' Tye shouted down the hill to Kian.

Tye tried his best to look as though he wasn't out of breath, stood with his hands on his hips, squinting in the direction of the sun, as though he was enjoying it.

'People,' Kian panted as he hiked up towards Tye, 'people die doing this kind of thing. They die, I'm… not… kidding.'

'It's not SAS training, Kian. It's a hike. We just have to find our way to the pick-up point, then you can sit down.'

Kian was finally next to Tye. His face was raspberry-red and his hairline wet, dripping onto his glasses.

'No,' he said, turning and collapsing on the grass on his back. 'No pick-up point. I won't make it.'

'Oh come on, don't be pathetic. It's just hot. You're not used to it. It doesn't mean you're going to die.'

Kian took off his glasses and wiped his face with his T-shirt, before throwing his arms back down onto the grass by his sides. Tye watched him, waiting for a response. His heavy breathing continued, eyes closed. Tye sighed.

'We're well behind the other teams, now.'

Still nothing. He took off his rucksack and rummaged inside.

'Here,' he said, holding out a bottle towards Kian. 'Have some water.'

Kian opened his eyes and looked sideways at the bottle. He sat up.

'Thanks,' he said, gulping it down.

'Come on.'

Kian sighed heavily and struggled to his feet, replacing his glasses. They walked on.

'The other reason this is dangerous,' Kian said as they finally started a downhill section, 'is that I'm disabled. Technically.'

'What? You're not disabled.'

'According to World Health Organization standards, without my glasses, I'm actually blind.'

Oh, God. Not this again.

'Yeah, but so is everyone who needs glasses.'

'No – only people with a visual acuity of less than 3/60—'

'Oh, for fuck's sake. You're not blind.'

'If these glasses were lost or broken – which they very well could be, out here – I wouldn't stand a chance. I couldn't find my way home.'

'The fact you couldn't find your way home has nothing to do with your eyesight. It's because you have no sense of direction, no coping skills and you're shit-scared of strangers.'

'I'm not scared of them! I just… don't like people I don't know.'

'You don't like anyone you *do know* either.'

Kian stayed quiet.

The sky was cloudless. Only the white ball of sun broke the blue, on its way down to the horizon. Tye tried to ignore the rivulets of sweat running down his neck and the hot, damp patch on his back where his rucksack leaned against him. *Ria would nail this. She can do anything outdoorsy.* He thought of her making the fire. Climbing that tree and sitting in the branches overhanging the lake. Scaling the old water wheel and smiling down at him from the roof of the mill. He loved the way she kissed, the way she talked. The questions she asked him. The way she made him feel. *I don't want to be* friends with benefits. *I like her. Like, really like her. Shit. How do you tell her?*

'Tye, where the fuck are we?' Kian asked, stopping again.

'Just trust me, okay. We're fine,' he announced. *Maybe. I think we are. Hopefully. Change the subject.* 'So anyway,' he asked. 'Lucy isn't real, is she? It was Mum on the phone, wasn't it?'

They tramped on in silence. He knew Kian wasn't going to try to lie anymore. He was so bad at it. Tye unfolded his map and studied their location. *Shit. Maybe we are a bit lost.*

'Just use Google Maps,' Kian said, getting out his phone.

'It won't work, that's the whole point.'

'Bullshit. Google Maps works everywhere,' he said, stopping to type their location in to his phone.

'We're using the map, because it has things on that Google doesn't… is it working?'

'Hang on,' he said, holding his phone up. 'Why isn't it working? This never happens.'

'So I was right, then. And anyway, using Google Maps isn't giving it a decent go, Kian. Come on, it's this way.'

They carried on, over the scrubby grass that had been scorched brown in the sun. It continued over undulating hills, as far as Tye could see. Other than a handful of trees scattered here and there, nothing else marked the landscape. He tried his best to keep his sense of rising panic in check. *We're on track. It's just that there is no track, or anything in sight to aim for. Come on. It'll be fine. Just keep going.*

'I did the wrong thing,' Kian said, his voice far behind. Tye turned round.

'What?'

Kian stood still, eyes fixed on the ground in front of him. The sun was starting to set, casting a long shadow behind him.

'Kian, what did you do?' Tye asked, dropping his backpack.

'It *was* Mum, okay,' Kian said, turning away.

'I knew that already. What have you done?'

Kian looked up at the sky, still facing away from Tye.

'She already knew where we were… she'd been round, but Nan wouldn't let her in.'

'Right…'

'Her landlord was going to kick her out—'

'Oh, fucking hell, Kian. You don't believe that, do you? You gave her money, didn't you?'

Kian looked at the soil in front of his feet again. Tye shook his head and rubbed his hands over his eyes. *I knew it. Why didn't you stop him? How did you let this happen? Dad's going to be so pissed off. How are we going to get rid of her this time?*

'How much?'

Kian opened his mouth, went to speak, but stopped. He took off his backpack and sat down, crying.

'Kian,' Tye's voice suddenly focused, hardened. 'How. Much.'

'£280.'

'Two *hundred* and eighty pounds?! Where the hell did you get that from?'

Kian looked up at Tye, eyes red and full.

'No,' Tye said, shaking his head. 'No – you didn't—'

Kian put his head in his hands and sobbed.

'She… she needed it—' he tried, ripping at his fingernails.

'*Of course she fucking needed it, Kian, she needed it for smack!*' Tye shouted, bending down into Kian's face. Kian shrank away. Tye straightened up, clasping his hands behind his head.

'Fuck!' he shouted, kicking both the backpacks across the dirt. Kian flinched.

'This is my fault. I should have stopped you. That time when you called me, I should have come down. Told her to leave you alone.'

'She's changed, Tye—'

'Don't… don't you dare try to tell me you stole our nan's savings for a noble cause, Kian. I don't believe it for one second. Even if it were – even if you donating it to fucking charity – you don't steal from *your nan*, Kian! It's just one of those things people with a conscience don't do. Are you a fucking psychopath? I mean, I've done some things in my time. Put Dad through a lot. The police know me. But your fucking *nan?*'

Kian got to his feet and started shouting at Tye, pacing up and down.

'I did it because she's my mum, Tye! Because she has no-one and she was going to be homeless! Don't you love her? Don't you care about her at all?!'

Tye picked up his backpack.

'I can't even look at you. I'm going to do something I'll regret,' he said, marching off across the field.

That fucking kid. Nan's savings. Jesus Christ. He could feel the veins in his head and neck throbbing. The blisters on his heels and toes burned. *How could she do it? Heartless. Totally heartless. Dad can't find out about this. Ever. What do I tell Nan? Shit.*

The sun was half-hidden behind the hillside. He stopped and turned round. Kian was following, at a distance. Kian stopped too. They stood, staring at each other from twenty yards away.

'Fucking hurry up,' Tye finally shouted, 'or I'll smash your glasses and leave you out here.'

***

Tye stared at the polystyrene tiles on the ceiling. He could just about see the grid pattern in the dark. He glanced over at Kian. He was facing the other way, but Tye could tell he was awake from the silence. If he were asleep, the camp bed would be creaking with deeper breathing.

'I can get Nan's money back, eventually,' Tye said to the back of Kian's head.

Kian said nothing.

'It will take a while though. It's a zero-hour contract at Tesco, so...'

Kian turned over.

'Don't do that,' he said. 'I'll figure out something.'

Jesus, Kian, stop living in your own world.

'No, you won't. I'm sorry, but you're fifteen, you don't have a job. You don't know anyone except me who could possibly give you the money. What were you planning to do, rob another old lady?'

'Don't be a dick.'

'Me?! Fucking hell Kian—'

'You always do this,' Kian said, sitting up. 'Act like a knight in shining armour saving the day. You make me feel so small, you're so patronising—'

'If you didn't do stupid things, I wouldn't have to—'

'No! My stupid thing was being honest. I should never have said anything. I'm not the stupid one, Tye.'

'But I am, is that it? I'm the thick one. Fine. You get A grades. We all know that. You're academic. But you don't have any fucking common sense, do you? You have no social awareness. I might be a dropout, Kian, but I don't steal from my nan to keep my mum in drugs!'

He felt like strangling Kian. Reaching over and shaking him until he understood what he'd done.

'You want to talk about common sense?' Kian asked, pointing in the dark. 'Your girlfriend, Ria. Her name is

Ariadne. Her parents aren't dead. She lives with her mum in one of the posh houses on Dearne Drive.'

'What the hell are you talking about?' he asked, sitting up.

'She's Christine's daughter. My tutor. They're fucking minted. So maybe I have no common sense, but at least I haven't been taken in by a load of bullshit from the local freak!'

'Bollocks, you're taking bollocks.'

'Look at this.'

Kian took out his phone and opened the photo gallery.

'There. That's her, isn't it?' He thrust the glowing screen towards Tye in the darkness.

It's her. The photo was a school portrait. Seeing her with her hair brushed and neatly plaited, in an ironed white shirt and tie jarred Tye's notion of her.

'Where did you...' he trailed off.

'There was a photo of her and her family, in the study. It was old, but I knew it was her. The next time I was there, I went in the living room while I was waiting and found the school photo. The time after that, I actually passed her in the hall. I swear, Tye, I'm not lying. You know I'm a shit liar. Look,' he said, taking his phone back. 'I'm sorry. I know you liked her.'

Tye was still struggling to process the information. He stared at the skirting board.

'I didn't mean what I said,' Kian continued quietly. 'I don't think you're thick. And I know you really meant it, about getting that money. But it's my problem. I'll just have to tell her. Come clean before she finds it's missing. Pay her back as soon as I can get a Saturday job.'

Tye murmured in agreement. He didn't care. He lay back down and turned to face the wall.

He knew there was something. But not this.

CHAPTER 16
RIA

She's tutoring again. Let her. As if everything is okay.

She breathed deeply and stared up at the ceiling. *Let her. Let her think it's all okay. At least you know now. She couldn't have known. If she's bringing him back into our lives, she couldn't have. She mustn't know. She's just ignorant. Wilfully ignorant? It doesn't matter. It won't matter.*

Let her think you're over it. Be civil.

Her phone rang. Dee on FaceTime.

'Hi.'

'Have you been crying?' Dee asked.

'A bit.'

'You're still not okay, are you? I'm still pissed off. But she's a grown woman. I've said my piece. We have to let her make her own mistakes.'

Ria was silent.

'Look,' Dee continued. 'Why don't you come and live with me for a bit?'

'I don't want to leave the birds.'

'Don't be silly. When is he moving in?'

'Don't know.'

'Come on, stay with me.'

101

Until this happened, she'd have jumped at the chance to live with Dee. She still wanted to, but she couldn't. Not now. There were things to sort out.

'Mum's still tutoring me. Important year coming up. I can't move away now.'

'Well… you change your mind, any time, and there's always a bed here for you.'

'Thanks,' she said, trying to smile.

'I told Mum – the other day – that you'd passed out because you drank too much.'

Ria let out a short laugh.

'I know. She was having a go at me this morning about that.'

'But you had a panic attack, didn't you? Then fainted. Because of what Mum said—'

'I'm fine, Dee. It was just a shock, that's all.'

She has to think everything is fine too. Everyone has to think you're normal.

'Okay… keep an eye on it, though. And if you're that anxious about it, I really do want you to come stay here.'

'Thanks, Dee. I'll bear that in mind.'

'If they start arguing, just go in another room. Go for a walk. Ignore them.'

Ha. Does she think that's the problem? Jesus. She really has no idea. But then, why would she? It was after she left. Let her carry on thinking that.

'I will.'

'And don't expect Dad to suddenly become father of the year. Remember what I said – he should never have had kids. He's still the director, so he won't have changed. Don't expect him to spend any time with you. I mean, when was the last time we saw him? Years ago. He can't expect us to accept he's different now.'

'No, he can't.'

'Are you sure you're okay? You're being… weird.'

'What, weirder than normal?'

'Yes.'

'Oh. I think I'm just coming down with something.'

Make conversation. Ask a question. Seem normal.

'So, after I blacked out – or during, whatever – did she say how this had ended up happening?'

'Sort of. I was shouting a lot, so I didn't listen to much of it but… well, apparently they've met up a few times since he left… but they stepped it up recently. Didn't you notice her being gone quite a lot?'

'I'm never in.'

'I guess. I had a go at her, about what a dick he is. She said she knows that better than anyone, but she never stopped loving him. Love is complicated. All that bollocks. She said they split up because she was a widow to his work. But he's got a load more people on his senior management team now, apparently. So he has more time. I don't know. She seems to believe he's changed. Idiot.'

Ria shook her head. *For fuck's sake. Say something.*

'For an intelligent person, she really has a blind spot when it comes to him.'

'That's it?' Dee asked. 'I thought you'd be raging! Come on – I *never* bitch about Mum. You have my permission to join in. Go for it!'

Ria made a tight, close-lipped smile. She couldn't keep this up.

'I'm sorry, Dee, I'm just feeling like shit. Going to have a lie down. I think it's a virus.'

'Okay. Text me later though, yeah? I'm worried about you.'

'Don't be,' she said, shaking her head. 'I'm fine. Honestly.'

They hung up.

I need to avoid her. She knows me too well.

Not well enough.

'Hey, you two.'

Betty and Bertie were on the windowsill. It was a hot day and the mill was cool.

'I don't have anything for you, I'm sorry. Unless…'

She went over to the barrel and lifted the lid.

'Probably not that good for you, but…'

She opened a bag of crisps and scattered them on the floor. The pair looked at the jigsaw of shards on the floor and flew down to inspect them.

'You'd eat it if you were in a city, I reckon.'

They stabbed at the pieces. The crisps slowly, noisily disappeared.

'You seem happy enough. If one of you dies from crisp toxins, the other one can sue me, okay? Or take vengeance. Come and murder me in my bed.'

Betty looked up at her.

Saying the word made her smile.

'Ria?'

'Fuck!'

The ravens flapped up and out of the window. She turned round. Tye.

'Jesus, you scared the shit out of me.'

He stood on the ladder, his head just above the floorboards.

'Are you okay?'

'Yeah, sorry – you just startled me.'

'No, I mean – you look like you haven't slept for ages,' he said, putting his hand on the floorboard in front of him.

'Oh, great. Thanks. Do you want a drink?'

Tye climbed up and stood on the crisps. He looked down at them and frowned.

'No. Well – what have you got?'

'That's more like it. Frosty Jack's… leftover Pernod—'

104

'No.'

'Okay – ooh, I have whisky? I nicked it from the off-license yesterday.'

'Yeah. Whisky.'

She took a swig then handed him the bottle. He took a long gulp and coughed.

'Ria – do you remember me telling you I had a brother?'

'Yeah.'

'That he's dead smart but a bit of a loner?'

'Mm-hmm. You made him sound like a serial killer.'

'Ha, yeah. Well, Nan was worried about him sort of, turning in on himself. Now we're living here, in the middle of nowhere. And we don't know when we'll move back. He'd started skiving. Which is fine, if you're like me. But not him – he actually has a future.'

She laughed.

'So anyway, she wanted to do something to focus him, to challenge him.'

The eaves creaked. Cooling down after the heat of the day. Ria looked up. She knew the last of the sun was on the roof, the top of the wheel. Just like the day he first came here.

She looked down. He was staring at her.

'He's going to your mum for tutoring, Ria.'

She swallowed. She got that same underwater feeling again. The white noise, the weightlessness.

Breathe. You should've ended it. You got distracted. Fuck.

She held out her hand, motioning for the whisky. He held it back.

'No – not until you tell me the truth.'

'Fine, Jesus Christ.'

She marched over to the barrel and found the Pernod.

'All right,' he said. 'If you're that desperate.'

He handed the bottle over.

She drank. Again. And again. Then coughed.

'I'm sorry,' she managed. 'I'm sorry.'

'I knew you were lying about something. But your parents being dead?! What's wrong with you?'

She drank more. *I don't need this.*

'I don't know. But it's not your problem, is it? We're just friends. Or were. You never have to see me again. It's not like you actually cared about me, is it? So why do you give a shit?'

'Because… because, you lied to me—'

'Oh, grow up. People lie. It's what they do!' she shouted. 'You'll meet lots of girls who lie to you. Lie and tell you you're amazing. Lie and tell you you're a great shag. Lie and tell you they love you. Get used to it.'

She watched his face change. That was the look.

'I don't care… about other girls… I just want to know, I mean, *why*…' he trailed off.

'Look, just do us both a favour and fuck off out of here, okay?'

His face. It tore at her insides. There was a creature in there, clawing at her guts. She turned away.

'Fuck,' she heard him say quietly, in a breaking voice. She heard his footsteps down the ladder. Out of the window, she watched him disappear. Down the path, not the field. He was out of sight in seconds. She leaned with her back against the wall then sank down, sobbing.

You liked him, you know you did.

But it doesn't matter. It doesn't matter. It. Doesn't. Matter. You. Don't. Matter.

She tried to catch her breath, but she couldn't. *In through the nose. Out through the mouth. Come on.*

She snatched up the whisky bottle. Mum's whisky. *Fuck Mum. Fuck them all.* She drank as much as she could then threw it at the wall, watching it splinter off into glittering shards. She felt in her pockets. No lighter. She looked around and grabbed the box of matches. *Empty. Argh!* The urge to set the place alight was too much. *You can make a fire. No. It'd take too long.*

She went round the room, smashing everything she could. She kicked the bookcase, held the planks between the wall and the floor and stamped them in half. Watched the splinters fly. Tore the pages out of the books. Threw them out of the window. She picked up the barrel and threw it down the hatch, watching it burst open on the stone floor below. It was getting dark. *No lighter, no matches, no light. That's okay. I can still do it. Dark is fine.* She climbed down the ladder and ran out of the door, down the path onto the jetty.

The air was warm, thick. It smelled like blossom, bark. The water was black, gently nudging against the wood. She stood on the last plank.

Fuck! She slapped herself across the face. And again. She looked down at the water. The light was fading. It looked like a dream. Like a fuzzy, faded old photograph. *Do it.* She jumped.

The sound of the water breaking, then rushing over her, made her feel calm. She didn't feel the cold. Not in the way she should. It was a relief. She softened to it. She opened her eyes. Murk. Cold, dark, murk. The wheel was there, somewhere to her left. Like a sea monster, massive, sleeping. Blackness below, weeds, tangles of darkness. Sound of bubbles. Fizzing. Cawing. She heard cawing. She looked up. The sky was pale still, light compared to the water. Two black shapes, circling. Cawing. Blurry. *Do I breathe in the water?* she asked them. She stopped moving, sank lower. She felt something against her leg, like a stroking hand. But she still watched them. They got bigger. They stood on the edge of the jetty, looking over, cawing. They spoke to her.

It's not time, they said. *This isn't how it ends. Remember. Remember what you promised yourself. You were so close. You can still do it. It's not time.*

PART 2

EIGHTEEN MONTHS LATER

CHAPTER 17

RAY

'You've come so far, Ray. You really have.'

'It's taken long enough. Two years I'll never get back. Two years of my boys' lives I missed.' His voice cracked. He leaned forward, leaning his forehead on his fingertips.

'But Ray – honestly, I'm not just saying this. People with what you have… who undergo such acute episodes and find themselves in secure… honestly, it takes a long time. I've known people take decades. I've known people who have never come out. They die there. And not in the way you think – I mean people who spend forty years inside. You can't underestimate how well you've done, Ray.'

Ray nodded. He straightened up, sighing. He gripped the polyester seat cover. Dr Thurlby reached for her plastic cup of water and took a drink. He watched her. *My key worker. Getting me out. Into the community. The only person in here I can trust.* She was the one who had convinced him, nearly a year ago, to comply. *It's the only way out.* He started to take his medication. To go to the group sessions. Do some of the things he hated, like escorted leave. It made him feel like a dog on a lead. Or one of those prisoners in America, in an orange boiler suit, with chains around their wrists and ankles, being transferred between vans. But he had to do it.

'How are you feeling about tomorrow?' she asked, replacing the cup on the low wooden table.

'A bit… nervous. My eldest, Tye – he's helping me move in. He's going to Afghanistan at the end of the month. I don't want to…' He shook his head. '…let him down. Embarrass him.'

'You couldn't. He'll be so proud of you. So glad to have you back.'

Ray nodded. He looked out of the window at the swaying trees. *Will he?*

'He's doing well,' he said, looking back at her. 'He was top of the group in training. Class, or whatever. Corps, division, unit, company – I don't know what they call them. I went to see him pass out.' He shook his head. 'So proud. I'm so glad they let me go for it. Meant a lot.'

'That's brilliant. And how about your other boy?'

'He's… he's got his problems. He needs help. But I'm hoping, now I'm out – I can start to give him that help. He's had a rough time. Like I did, his age. I won't see much of him, but…' Ray's head was back in his hands again, resting against his fingertips.

'What kind of problems?'

Ray shook his head, straightening up again.

'I don't want to get into it. But he'll be okay.'

'Don't get too involved, Ray – you don't need any additional stress in—'

He held up his hand. 'I'm fine. Don't worry. I've been there, I know how it works.'

'So it's mental health? Or substance abuse?'

He looked at her. *Don't.*

'Sorry,' she said. 'I won't pry. Just… put yourself first, okay? Tye can look after Kian.'

No, he can't. He tried. It's my turn now.

112

He stroked the starched sheet. Sitting on the bed, the wall of random blu tack patterns faced him. *The wall of my cell. Room. The wall of my room. My old room. Last night here. The third ward you've been on. The* getting out *ward. The* moving to the community *ward. Two boxes. Is that all my time in this place comes down to? Two boxes. Ridiculous.* He shook his head. He looked at the bin. All the screwed-up paper. *My drawings. They aren't coming with me. They can't. They don't belong with me anymore.*

He looked at the small square window in the door. *Why do you still check that? They don't do obs on you now. There's no face coming to check on you.*

He looked at the screwed-up paper again. Reflexively glancing at the viewing pane, he lunged forward and grabbed one of the bits of paper. *Stop looking at the window. No-one is coming.*

He unscrewed the paper and smoothed his hand over the creases.

There they are. The drawing didn't do them justice. He'd only had the pencils the unit provided. He had envisioned a huge, life-sized oil portrait. He was good with oil paints. But they gave him A4 paper and a child's set of coloured pencils. *Still. He had to do it. He'd have drawn it in blood if he had to.* Four, five, six of them. Stood there, watching. Bald heads. Black suits. Red eyes. White skin. No mouths.

Ray stared at the paper. He picked it up, walked over to the sink. *You weren't allowed a sink in the last ward. You got one here.* He smiled. He put the men in the silver basin and turned on the tap. He watched them bleed, stretch, disintegrate. He gathered up the remnants, squeezed them into a tight ball. Red and black bled out of his hands. He squeezed and squeezed, until all the liquid was gone. The damp, flaking ball sat in the palm of his hand. His window only opened a few inches, but it was enough. He dropped the ball into the darkness.

CHAPTER 18
CALLY

'That's me, on the wall. Isn't she beautiful?' the girl asked, pointing at the wall. She sat cross-legged on the bed, rocking slightly.

Cally stood at the side of the bed and surveyed the enormous mural. It took up the whole wall with its swirling black lines. She could feel the girl watching her, waiting for her reaction.

'She is,' Cally said, still searching for a face or a human form in the mass of curling threads and feathery sweeps.

'There,' said the girl, getting to her feet to stand on the bed, pointing to the middle of her work.

'Oh, I see,' Cally said, tracing the outline of a face, neck, shoulders. The rest was obscured by the figure's flowing hair and dress, spread over the wall in all directions.

'Are they wings?' she asked, discerning feathers stretching out on either side.

'Yes. I have wings.'

Cally nodded.

'It's really good. You're a very talented artist.'

The girl smiled.

'Cally.'

The voice came from the doorway. She turned round. It was Dave.

'Cally,' he said again. 'Five minutes?' he asked.

'See you in a bit,' she said to the girl.

'Bye.'

Dave closed the door behind them and pointed to the nurse's station. It was an island in the middle of the wide corridor with windows on every side, like a Perspex box. *Reinforced glass.* She remembered the phrase from her training. He opened the door and pointed inside.

Fuck. I'm in trouble.

Cally entered the box. He closed the door and locked it. She looked at the lock. *What is he doing?*

'You always lock the door, remember? They can't have access to this room,' he said.

'Right, yes. Sorry.'

'I wanted to talk to you about just now,' he said, pointing at one of the two chairs. She sat down. An old computer sat on the desk behind her, which spanned three walls and was otherwise completely covered in paperwork. Filing cabinets and shelves of lever arch files towered over them both, obscuring half the window space.

'You were in that room alone,' he said, folding his arms.

'I wasn't, I was with—'

'I mean staff. You were the only staff member. You should always have one other support worker with you, yeah?'

'Oh, I just thought... I mean, nobody seemed to really follow that, so I just didn't think—'

'But they should. We all should. Especially new staff like you. You're vulnerable.'

'Right. Okay. Sorry.'

'I needed a word with you about Karen, too.'

Cally tried to remember which one Karen was.

'Karen?'

'The one with the burns,' he said.

'Ah, yeah. What about her?'

'Stay away from her. Where you can. Don't be alone with her. She doesn't like you.'

'Oh, right. Why?' Cally asked. *I've barely met her. What did I do?*

'She doesn't like your face.'

'I can't really do anything about that…'

'No. Exactly. So avoid her. She has a tendency to lash out physically and you've not had chance to put your restraint training into practice yet, so just tread carefully.'

'I will… thanks.'

Jesus. Thanks for putting me at ease, Dave.

'Do you have any tips on how I could get around it?' Cally asked. 'I can't totally avoid her…'

'You've had the de-escalation training, haven't you?'

She nodded.

'And MAPA?'

'Yep.'

'Well that's it then. Just remember it. Like you say, you can't change your face, so don't try to be her friend, or her enemy, and you'll be fine.'

Great. Brilliant advice. I'm not scared at all now.

'Don't try to be *anyone's* friend, in fact,' he continued. 'Not hers, not hers either,' he said, pointing to the girl with the mural on her wall. She was in the corridor, running her finger over the wallpaper.

'I'm not trying to be her friend… but she's friendly. She's nice to me. I'm not going to ignore her,' Cally said. 'I think she's lonely.'

Dave sighed and rubbed his eyes.

'Of course she's lonely. She's in a secure unit. Everyone here is lonely.'

He gestured out to the day room at the people sat on the sofas and at the tables.

She stared at them. *They are.*

'Sorry,' he said. 'You're new. And you're not trained. I mean, properly trained. You're not a doctor, or a nurse. You're another psychology graduate who just wants enough experience to do their next qualification.'

She didn't know what to say. It was true, but she didn't realise it was something they were bitter about. Three others on the training were there for the same reason.

'Is... that a problem?' she ventured.

'No, no. As long as you do as you're told and don't try anything stupid, you'll be all right.'

'Right...'

What's his problem? What does he think I'm going to do?

'You say she's friendly. She's nice to you. Didn't you look at manipulation in your degree?' he asked, looking over at the girl.

Cally said nothing, watching her.

'You might want to read her file. In fact, have you read any of the files?'

'Well, I haven't had time, and... seeing as I'm *just* a support worker, not properly trained—'

'Nobody has time. But everyone needs to read them. Read them on your break.'

'But we can't remove them from the station—'

'So? Take your break in the station. Do the next obs round then take your break. Here.'

'Fine.'

Fucking dick.

***

What's so bad about her then? Let's see. Ariadne Wells. Ariadne. Why doesn't she use that? It's a beautiful name.

Age eighteen. Nearly nineteen. She's a child compared to the others. Wonder whether she came from CAMHS. Cally scanned the list of medication. The dates. Hospitals. Wards. Summary. Diagnosis query. Sexual abuse. Expelled. Arson. Theft. *Same old same old.* Stabbed. Slit. Mutilated. Murder. GBH. Court dates. Transferred to forensic psychiatric care. Indefinite. *Fucking hell!*

Shit. She looked up. Ria had gone. *Probably in her room again. Or the yard, if they've let her. She's never in the day room. Only meal times, when we make her.*

A knock on the door made Cally jump. Through the glass she could see Nance. She smiled. Nance waved. Nance was wider than the doorframe and not much shorter than it, with closely-cropped grey hair.

Cally opened the door and stepped out, locking it behind her.

'What's up, Nance?'

'It's tea time – you're supposed to supervise the cutlery,' she said, pointing at the caddy the kitchen staff had dropped off.

'But where's—' Cally looked around. *No Dave. No Tracy. No Faz. No Mara. No staff at all. Except me. Fuck. That's the second time this week. Don't be alone with anyone, he says. How about alone with ten patients? Does that count? This place is ridiculous.*

She went over to the caddy and opened it up. The patients formed a line. She counted the cutlery and opened up the trays.

'Okay,' she shouted down the line. 'We have shepherd's pie, Quorn bolognese or sandwiches. Then fruit or crumble. Bear with me, there's just one of us serving today.'

'Shepherd's pie, please,' said Nance. 'And peas. No gravy. I'll just have a fork.'

Cally spooned out the food, handed the plate over and opened the cutlery compartment. She handed her the fork

119

then grabbed a pen and put a tick in the "fork" column next to Nance's name.

Over the shoulder of the next patient she saw Ria, sat in the corner, picking the paint off the wall. *She won't eat again. You have to try to get her to eat something.* Don't try anything stupid, *Dave said. Does that count?* The patient in front of her coughed. It was Karen.

'Sorry, Karen. What would you like?'

Karen stared at her.

'Shepherd's pie? Quorn bolognese? Sandwi—'

'You're very symmetrical,' Karen said, leaning forwards, close to her face.

'Am I?' Cally asked, letting a short, nervous laugh out. *Fuck.*

'Yes. I'm not though, am I? Look at my face. Feel it.'

She grabbed Cally's hand and put it to her cheek – the side of her face that was scarred.

Cally swallowed. Her fingertips grazed the skin. It felt like it looked. Shiny, ridged, tender.

'Everything okay?' Dave said, walking in through the door from the yard.

Karen dropped Cally's hand.

'Ham sandwich, please,' Karen said, looking at the floor. Cally handed over the sandwich and watched her walk to a table.

She smelled cigarettes on Dave.

'Dave, did you go out for a fag? I'm supposed to be on my break and it's just me on here. Where is everyone?'

'Dealing with an incident up on Huntsman. Didn't you hear the alarm?'

'I did, but—'

'Well then. And yes, I had a fag on my way back. As a nurse, I have to *save lives*. I just had to cut someone down and perform CPR. They're in an ambulance now. I've done four back-to-back nights this week and I'm covering this day shift because we're short staffed. I've done fifty-eight hours this week and counting. Not once have I had a break while I've been here, except to piss. So I had a fag. Walking back. Then I came in and prevented another incident from happening, because you didn't take my advice. Report me if you want. We'll see what happens.'

'Sorry,' she murmured, reaching for another plate. *Dick*.

ONE YEAR EARLIER

CHAPTER 19

RIA

Winter meant days at the mill, nights at home. At night, she watched the door handle in the dark, just as she had when she was a child. He never came. She fitted a lock. She carried a knife. But he did nothing.

It's part of his plan, she told herself. *Well, you fucking snake, I have my own plan.*

Ria knew he was watching her. She knew he followed her sometimes, when she went to the mill. *He thinks I don't know. Let him.*

He didn't follow me today. She sat on the wooden floorboards of the top floor, wrapped in two sleeping bags. The mill clung to the cold in winter. It held onto it, chilled it while it hung there, like a carcass in an abattoir. Her gloves were fingerless, so she could work. She rebuilt her bookcase. Repaired the barrel. Mainly, though, she carved. She found a good knife in her mum's box of art supplies. A Morakniv from Sweden. That's what the blade said. It was the sharpest thing she'd ever touched. It was too easy to cut herself with it.

At night, in bed, she made patterns. Delicate carvings of her skin. The inside of her arms, legs, the sides of her waist – they were decorated with scars, like a bride's henna work. In daylight, at the mill, she carved wood. Wooden ravens, flowers, trees. She carved sticks into spears, to see how sharp she could make them. A row of them leaned against the empty fireplace, from the one that could barely stick in soil to the one that drew blood when she grazed it against her tongue.

Ria kept the knife's blade sharp on a smooth, flat rock. Every time she carved wood, she went down to the pond with her sharpening stone. She sat on the jetty, scooped some water over the rock and sharpened the blade back up again. She knew he watched her doing this. It pleased her. *You watch me, sharpening this blade, and you think it's for you. But I have something different in mind for you. Something slower.*

***

'Ariadne, you're spending too much time outside. You're behind,' her mum said.

'I like being outside. I'm not behind. Test me.'

'Is she always this difficult?' her dad asked.

Ria looked at him. *Yes. And much worse.*

'That's nothing, Anthony. You missed the worst years,' Christine said. 'Another thing you left me to pick up the pieces of.'

Sitting round a dinner table, with Mum on one side and Dad on the other. *Who'd have thought it. You're good at this. Keep it up.*

He finished his glass of wine. *Red. Always red.* She remembered the sour smell, the way it stained his lips and teeth. He caught her eye as she watched the empty glass. She looked at the table.

'Think I'll open another bottle,' he said, getting up.

'I'll just have one more,' Christine said, lifting her glass as he walked past her.

'Ariadne,' she said in a hushed tone as he disappeared. 'It's not just that. You're being rude. It's been two months, and you haven't even spoken to your father. This has to stop. It's childish in the extreme. Are you spending all day at that bloody ruin just to avoid him? He's not an ogre, you know – you need to give him a chance.'

'Really? Do I? Why?' Ria asked, digging her fork into the back of her hand under the table.

'Because he's your father and he loves you. We're trying to make a go of things here, and this cloud hanging over everything… it's not helping.'

She couldn't bring herself to do it. Not yet. It had taken a week just to look him in the eye. She knew she had to do it. To seem normal. Mum will start to suspect. Being in the same room, the same house – the same part of the country, even – was hard enough. He walked back in and stopped to fill up Christine's glass. He sat back down and filled his own.

He's here, in the dining room, drinking wine. Like he belongs here. Like he never left. Like nothing ever happened. She watched him while he scrolled through the news on his phone. *A small, grey man. Balding. Glasses. Beard. Tie loosened after work. His shoes are by the door, his coat is hung up. His feet are under this table, socks with worn heels resting on the carpet. Scanning the headlines. Like any other man on any other evening.*

'Right,' Ria said, suddenly. He looked up. Her mum stared at her.

'We're living in the same house, now,' she carried on, stabbing the fork into her palm this time. 'And you're back together. I don't like it, I don't like you.' She looked him in the eye, fleetingly. 'Or what you did to us.' She looked at her hand when she said *us*. 'And I won't forgive you. But until I move out, I will be civil to you, because Mum wants me to,' she paused, 'so I will.'

She felt the silence creep around the room. Her mum's face seemed pained. She didn't look up. She just looked at her finger, spinning the base of her wine glass around. Ria looked at her dad. He was looking at her mum, too. Searching her face. Finally, he looked at Ria and said, 'Thank you,' with a half-smile, half-nod.

Suddenly, he reached over and put his hand on her shoulder. She froze.

'I hope,' he said quietly, leaning forwards, trying to fix her eyes with his, 'that you can forgive me. In time.'

She couldn't move. He withdrew his hand and sat back, picking up his glass.

'To us,' he said, raising it in Christine's direction, then Ria's.

***

The doorbell rang. She sat up in bed. *This is it.*

'Ria!' her mum shouted up. 'What have you ordered now?'

She pulled her jumper and jeans on and ran downstairs. Her mum stood with a brown package in one hand and a mug in the other, waiting.

'Just stuff for the birds,' she replied, snatching the parcel from her and running back upstairs.

'I'm not signing for any more crap!' her mum shouted up after her. 'Spend your allowance on books, theatre tickets, music – anything! Those birds eat rotting flesh and live in trees, Ria, buying them creature comforts is madness. Utter madness.'

Ria closed her bedroom door and locked it. She slit through the tape and pulled out a bubble-wrapped cylinder. A brown, blurry shape was suspended inside. She sliced through the wrap with her knife. *There it is. It looks like nothing. Like something in the bathroom cabinet.* A small, brown plastic bottle, with a white child-safe lid and a white label. The label was printed in Chinese. She had no idea what it said. All she knew was that it was her best shot.

A knock on the door startled her. She dropped the bottle. It spun across the floor, pills clattering inside. The handle turned, but the lock held. She snatched up the bottle and threw it under her pillow. Ria took a second to breathe. Her heart was still pounding as she drew the lock across and opened the door.

'Ariadne,' her dad said, leaning on the doorframe with one hand. 'We need to talk.'

'What about?' she said, her face blank.

'Can I come in?'

'No.'

He sighed. 'Come for a drive with me, then.'

'I'm staying here.'

He shook his head.

'You know who the victim is, here?' he asked. She stared at him. 'Your mother. I don't know why you are punishing me, but that's fine. Do whatever you need to do to make yourself feel better. Put a lock on your door for the imaginary monsters.' He pointed at the door. 'But your mum – she's been through so much. This behaviour is taking its toll on her, you know.'

'You *don't know* why I'm punishing you?' she asked, trying to stop her voice shaking.

He shook his head, shrugged his shoulders, let out an exasperated sigh.

'Because I left?' he ventured. 'Because I worked too much? Because I hurt your mother? Because I stayed away when you asked me to?'

She felt the blood drain from her limbs. She swayed.

'Ariadne, are you okay?' he asked, stepping towards her.

'Fuck off!' she screamed, slamming the door. It hit his forehead. She heard him swear on the other side of it. She put the lock back across and fell to the floor, gasping. She couldn't breathe. Her heart was beating so fast, she couldn't keep up. Tiny black dots appeared, swimming across her vision. Then darkness.

When she woke up, she was lying on the floor, facing the door. She could see through the gap underneath it. The fibres of the carpet. The painted wood of the bannister base. Her dad's face.

'Fuck!' she shouted, getting to her feet. 'What are you doing?!'

'You passed out, I've been trying to get in. Are you okay?'

'Is she awake? Is she okay?' she heard her mum's voice behind him.

'There's nothing wrong with me. Please just fuck off and leave me alone.'

'Fine,' he said, 'but please eat something today. You're making yourself ill.'

She listened as his footsteps retreated downstairs. *Okay. He said all that because Mum was within earshot. That's why.*

Her mum was still there. She could feel her, standing there, hesitating. *Ask me. Ask me now, and I'll tell you the truth.* Ria stood on her side of the door, knowing her mum was a mirror image on the other side. *Ask me.*

'Ria?' Her mum's voice was soft. *She called me Ria. She's never called me Ria.*

'Yeah?' Ria put her hand on the lock to slide it across. She stopped, listening.

'You know we both love you, don't you? He's trying his best. Please, just give him a chance.' Her mum's voice cracked. Ria pulled her hand away from the lock, leaving it across. She leaned against the door and listened to her mum's footsteps disappear.

She sat on her bed and pulled the brown bottle out from under her pillow. *He's a psychopath. He can lie so well. So*

well. Maybe it wasn't for Mum. Maybe he's convinced himself.
Maybe he thinks he can convince me. Make me think I'm mad.
Make me think it's all in my head.

He'll see what's in my head.

CHAPTER 20

KIAN

'Your dad never taught you to drive?'

'I'm not old enough...'

'I could drive when I was eight.'

'Right. We didn't have a car, so—'

'I'll teach you. I'm your stepdad, aren't I?'

Kian winced. *No, Bez. You're not. This bedsit isn't big enough for the three of us. You're not supposed to be living here.* He sat on the only chair. Bez and Sian were sitting on the mattress, leaning their backs against the wall. They had a kettle and a microwave on the windowsill, a dirty fridge next to the mattress and a TV on the floor by the door. Everything else was clothes, rubbish, shoes. Out on the landing, a door with peeling paint led to a shared bathroom. Kian hated using it. He hardly showered anymore and tried to mainly use public toilets. Theirs was filthy, almost always broken, and the door had no lock.

'You hear that, Kian? Isn't that good of him?' Sian said, flicking her ash onto the carpet.

'Yeah,' he said, chewing his thumbnail.

Bez strode over to the door, putting his baseball cap on. He turned to Kian.

'Well? What you waiting for?'

'Oh, you mean, now? I don't have a provisional license—'

Bez and Sian burst into laughter.

'Good one,' Bez said. 'I don't have my driving gloves either. I think we'll survive.'

Shit. He looked at his mum. *Help.* She sat back against the wall and gestured towards the door, raising her eyebrows.

'Go on, then!' she motioned him away, turning up the TV.

The car stank of weed. He'd never sat in a driver's seat before. It felt strange. Like he was on a ride at a theme park.

'Now,' said Bez, lighting a cigarette. 'Put your left foot on the left pedal and push down. If you can't get it all the way down, move the seat forwards.'

Fucking hell. This guy is teaching me to drive. He's off his head.

'Before we get started, word of warning. If the police pull us up, don't act like it's stolen. And don't act like there's anything in the glovebox. Them wraps will get you two years, straight off.'

Yep. I'm fucked.

***

The McFlurry machine was out of order at McDonald's. Kian was more disappointed about that than he wanted to let on. *Tye's treating you – just get an extra cheeseburger.*

They sat at the window seat, watching the people of Hanley go by. It meant they didn't have to look at each other, which Kian preferred. The less social interaction, the better. This time in particular, because he didn't want to get emotional. He focussed on the smell. It always comforted him.

'I'm telling you, just try. For Dad's sake.'

'Tye, she kicked me out. I deserved it. I'm fine at Mum's. She really is on methadone, you know – it wasn't a lie.'

133

Kian was already halfway through his meal.

'Is there food in the house?' Tye asked, opening a pot of BBQ sauce.

'Enough. You know me – I only eat crap anyway, so it suits me fine.'

'And you're going to school?'

'Yes.' Kian sipped his drink through the straw, trying to slow his eating.

'What about the tutor?'

'No. Obviously. Dad's money was going to Nan, so…'

'Okay. Keep going to school though. Promise me.'

'I'll be fine, Tye. She's not like she was.'

'Her bloke is a proper dick though – just avoid him.' Tye stuffed a handful of fries in his mouth and shook his head. 'Fuck,' he said, through the mash of potato and BBQ sauce. 'I don't like leaving you like this.'

'You said it yourself, remember? I have to fight my own battles and deal with the consequences of my shitty decision making,' Kian said, licking his fingers and wiping them on a paper towel. 'That's what I'm doing right now.'

'I'll only get access to my phone for a couple of hours in the evening. But you know you can call the training centre in an emergency any time – I messaged you the details on WhatsApp—'

'Tye – I'm not five years old any more. This will be the best thing you've ever done and you don't need to be stressing about me. In a year's time, when I'm there at your passing out parade, the only thing you'll be worrying about is the fact I'm stealing your limelight because I got the best exam results since records began.'

Tye laughed.

'All right. I'll hold you to that.'

They were finished. *Time to go. Shit. Please don't go. Don't leave me here. I'm shit on my own.*

'Make the most of it,' said Kian, as they stood up. 'And at the end of it, see if you can get posted in Cyprus instead of Afghanistan, yeah?'

'Ha – I'll try. Are you coming to the bus station?'

'No, meeting Mum. Staying here. You could stay... say bye to her before you go?'

'Nah,' Tye shook his head. 'I don't need that right now. Easier not to.'

They hugged. *Fuck. You won't see him for months.*

'You have the details for Catterick, right?' asked Tye.

'*Yes*, I told you. But nothing bad is going to happen. There won't be any emergencies. I'm a model student now, and Mum is turning things around.'

Kian knew that was bullshit, but it was what Tye needed to hear. *Besides, she is on methadone. It's just that she's on a lot of other things, too. And I'm still smart. I just don't get to school as much as I used to. That's all.*

Tye hugged him again. *Don't cry. Don't cry.*

'Take care of yourself, I'll keep in touch,' he said, and walked out.

Kian nodded and sat back down. He watched him walk past the window. Tye put his hand up and mouthed "bye". Kian waved. Then he was gone. The *Big Issue* seller still paced up and down. The donut van still had a queue. People still buried the bottom half of their faces in their scarves and coats, eyes on the floor, hurrying through the cold. Everything was the same, but it was different. *You're on your own now.*

CHAPTER 21
TYE

I feel bad about how we left things, he said to himself. *No. That sounds shit. I'm going away for a year, and I just wanted to let you know – no. Bollocks.*

'Tye?' Lynne's voice called up from downstairs.

'Yeah?' He finished folding a T-shirt and put it in the suitcase.

'Your dad's on the phone, love.'

His heart skipped. *Dad?* He ran down the stairs and grabbed the handset from her.

'Dad? Are you okay?'

'I'm fine, Tye. I'm good. They let me call. I'm so grateful that you tried to visit, son. And I'm so glad they let me call you before you go. When are you off?'

'Monday.'

'You done your packing yet?'

'No.'

'Ha. Why am I not surprised?'

'How is everything going, Dad?'

'I'm trying. I have a new keyworker – Dr Thurlby. She's so good. Better than anyone I've seen so far. She'll get me out, Tye, before you know it. She knows the system.'

'That's great. I'm made up for you, Dad. You listen to what she says and just do whatever you need to, to get out, yeah?'

'Don't you worry, that's all I'm thinking about right now. That and you! Off to join the army. I'm so proud.'

Tye smiled. If he was a cat, he'd have purred.

'You be careful, though, son. There will be days when you want to quit. People you don't like. Stuff you find hard. But it's all in your head. Your body can do whatever they ask of you. It's the mind that struggles. The mental discipline – that's the difference. You need to be relentless. You fall down, you get up and go again. You see someone fall, you pick them up.'

'I will, Dad.' Tye nodded. *He's lucid. Really lucid.* Tye hadn't heard his dad sound so articulate for a long time. Even before they stopped his visits. *He's better. So much better.*

'And for the love of God, *listen*,' Ray continued. 'Learn to listen. You go off and do your own thing because you think you know best in a war and you'll get yourself killed, yeah?'

'It's just training, Dad—'

'I know, I know. But *listen* and *think*. A boy like you can do push-ups till the cows come home. But if you want to get through it and you want to make something of it, you have to be more than muscles. You're a smart guy, Tye, when you use your head.'

He felt like purring again. He felt like crying, too. Surely he would be allowed to visit soon. *But you're not allowed home for months. Shitty timing.*

'Thanks, Dad.'

'Is Kian there?'

Fuck.

'No, he's... at his tutor's. Having a lesson.'

'Ah, good. Is it going well?'

'I think so, yeah... he's doing tons of reading, so...'

'Tell him I send my love. And tell him to stick with it.'

'I will do.' *Shit. It's a white lie. Just until he's better.*

'Dr Thurlby likes to hear about you two. She... oh, hang on...'

Tye waited. He heard a muffled sound, then a bang.

'Dad?'

'I have to go, son. The clock. The people in the... I have to go.'

Ray's voice was different. Panicked. *He's scared.*

'Dad, are you okay? Who's there?'

'Don't... just... when you go, wear a red T-shirt, yeah? On the coach. Promise me.'

'Erm... okay... I will.'

'Make sure you do, promise me.'

'I promise.'

'I have to go. They're telling me.'

'All right, well, I... Dad?' Tye stopped, he could already hear the dead tone.

Tye looked at the phone.

'Everything okay?' said Lynne, walking in from the living room.

'I don't know. He hung up – I think they were badgering him about the time or something. He was totally fine for most of it. He sounded back to normal. Completely. But then... he seemed a bit... I don't know. Worried.'

'Of course he's worried, love, you're joining the army. But he's so proud. So proud.'

Hm. It's not that. Let it go, Tye. Nothing you can do. You have to trust them.

'You haven't told him about Kian, have you?' Tye asked. 'I just pretended like nothing had changed.'

'Oh, God, no,' she said, shaking her head. 'Of course not. It wouldn't do him any good.'

'He said no, when you asked him, didn't he, Kian?' he asked.

Lynne sighed, nodding.

'I've told him – he can come back, any time he likes,' she said. 'I feel awful. It's just… that's how it started with Sian, you see. Stealing. Money, especially. And it was all I had in the world. I know it wasn't his fault, but I just panicked. That same night I was ringing and ringing him to come back, but—'

'I know, Nan. It's not your fault. He missed Mum. That's what got him into this mess. Maybe after he's seen enough of her, he'll be back. I hope so.'

'Me too. Anyway. You get back to that packing, otherwise you'll be up until midnight tomorrow trying to get your washing done.'

Upstairs, Tye dug through the pile of T-shirts in his suitcase. He pulled out a red one and hung it over the wardrobe door.

He looked out of the window, up to the mill. No sign of her today. *Are you going to see her or not? Tonight, maybe?* He picked up Kian's stress ball off the desk and squeezed it. *Why? What do you want? Forget about it. Forget about her.* His knuckles were white as his nails dug into the foam. He released the ball, placed it back on the desk and grabbed the list that he'd been issued detailing what to bring. *Come on. Focus.*

CHAPTER 22
RIA

You're doing it tonight. Dinner will be at eight. He'll open the wine at seven.

You have to get Mum out. She picked up the landline and scrolled through the address book. Valerie.

'Val? Hi, it's Ria.'

'Oh, hello! I thought it would be your mum. Is everything okay?'

'It's fine, everything is fine. Listen, are you busy tonight?'

'No, not busy. Just in with the dogs. Why?'

'Do you mind if Mum comes round?'

'Er... no, not at all... is she okay?'

'Yes, she just... I need some space. Dad and I have a lot of shit to sort out, you see, I need to talk to him. Without her there. She'd just get upset. We need to clear the air, properly. I don't want her wading in, you know what she's like. I just need a few hours where it's me and him. Thrash it out, you know? Some things we have to talk about, shit from the past. I have to have it out with Dad before we can move on, as a family.'

'Doesn't she need to hear it too, though?'

'Not yet. She will, but not until Dad and I know where

we stand. If she were here, she'd start crying, or go on the defensive, or try to be the peacemaker – and we wouldn't get anywhere. We need to just have it out and get over it.'

'Does your mum know this is the plan?'

'No. But I don't mind her knowing. If you want to tell her, you can. As long as she gives us the space.'

Valerie sighed.

'That man has a lot to answer for,' she said.

Ria waited.

'Okay. I'll call her, see what I can do. I think honesty is the best policy though, Ria, I really do.'

'That's fine. Just… frame it in some kind of therapy-speak and she'll be more likely to accept it. Talk about trust and non-judgement and closure and all that crap. She should appreciate that.'

'I'm her friend, Ria – I'm not going to say anything that's not true.'

'It *is* true, though – she needs this, if anything, more than I do. It's for her I want to do this. She's at her wits' end with the aggro in this place. She must've told you how much it's stressing her out—'

'All right. We'll see.'

'Thanks, Val.'

'I hope you get what you need from it, Ria.'

'Me too.'

She hung up and exhaled, sitting on the bed. *You're doing this. You're doing it tonight. No matter what.*

The sound of her mum's ringtone downstairs pierced the silence. She heard footsteps across the kitchen. Her mum picked up. The conversation was muffled, but Ria knew what was being said. Christine hung up. Steps softly trod up the stairs. Ria took a deep breath.

'Ariadne?' Her mum knocked on the door.

'It's open.'

'Val just called me,' she said, opening the door and stepping in. 'Why didn't you just come to me in the first place?'

'I… I don't know. I suppose,' she shrugged, looking down, 'I thought you might be more likely to agree if she asked.' She looked up at her again. 'Plus, I needed her to give you a place to spend the evening, so…'

'Don't be silly,' Christine said, sitting on the bed next to her. 'I would have given you the space regardless. I'm glad you're doing this.' She stroked Ria's hair. Ria looked down at the duvet. 'Obviously,' Christine continued, 'it's hard for me not to be involved. I want to be part of the conversation. I want to help you both. Keep you from hurting each other. You two can be cruel with your words, sometimes. Dido and I aren't like that. Maybe that's why you clash so much. You're so alike.'

Ria winced. She said nothing.

'But I understand you need a non-judgemental space. You need to know I trust you. And you have to have this honest conversation in order to move on. To get closure on the issues you're working through.'

Thank you Val. Thank God *for you.*

Ria nodded.

'I really think this will help me, Mum. I've needed it for a long time. He needs it, too.'

Christine grabbed her in a hug, swaying them both gently from side to side.

'I'm so proud of you, darling. This is emotionally healthy. You might shout and scream, get frustrated. But it's important to get it out there. It's cathartic. Just try to work towards a solution, hm?' She let go of her and looked at Ria's face. 'See if you can reach a place where you understand one another a little better. You can both apologise and move on. Life will be easier.'

'Yes, it will be, Mum.'

Ria stood in the kitchen and listened. *Dad's in the study.*
Mum's in the bath. Get it now.

She stretched up to the long cupboard above the spotlights
that lit the worksurfaces. It had hinges at the top rather than
the side, meaning it opened like the boot of a car. Lifting the
door up with one hand, she grabbed the mortar and pestle
with the other. She closed the cupboard and sank back down
from her tiptoes to flat feet. She listened again. *Nothing.* She
put the pestle in her pocket and tried to hide the mortar under
her jumper, but it was too big. *Just go.*

She carried it upstairs, quietly and quickly. The study door
handle turned. *Fuck.* She held the bowl behind her back and
leaned against the wall.

'Ariadne,' her dad said, stepping out. 'I wanted to catch
you. We're on our own, tonight, I hear?'

'Mm-hmm.' She nodded. 'Just us.'

'Your mother says you want to talk things through.'

'I do, yes.'

He nodded, slowly, looking her up and down.

'That's good,' he said finally. 'I think it'll do us good.' He
stepped towards her. She gripped the bowl. A noise from the
study stopped him. His mobile.

'Ah. I must get that. It'll be the accountant. Well, dinner
tonight then. Eight okay?'

'Yep. Always is.'

'Great. See you then.'

He stepped backwards into the study, eyes still on hers
until he closed the door.

She closed her eyes and breathed out. *Fucking hell.*

***

Her phone said 18:58.

'Right,' her mum said, walking into the living room. 'I'm off. Good luck, darling.' She leaned down and kissed her cheek. Ria hadn't been in the living room for months. She sat on the sofa, pretending to watch TV, pretending to be normal.

'Thanks. Have a nice night.'

Her mum looked up at the ceiling.

'He'll be done soon, I'm sure. You know how it is on Saturdays.'

Ria nodded, pulling a tight, close-lipped smile.

'See you later on,' Christine said, and kissed her again.

'Bye.'

Ria watched her walk out of the room and listened for the front door.

She's gone. She turned the volume down on the TV and listened for the study door. *Come on.* She checked her phone. 19:00.

There it is. Footsteps down the stairs.

'It's just pizza for tea – hope you don't mind?' she heard his voice call through from the kitchen.

'No, that's fine. I'll put it in if you want.'

'Thanks. I'll be done for eight. Just opening the wine. Let it breathe.'

Ria gripped the remote control. She heard the pop of the cork. *Go back upstairs.*

He went. She heard the study door close.

Now.

She walked up the stairs normally, not trying to be quiet. Just as though she were heading up to get her phone, a book, whatever. She found the bowl under the bed with the pile of white powder sitting in the bottom. She picked it up and stalked back to the door. Craning her neck to see round the corner, she could see that the study door was closed. She heard his voice on the phone. He was talking about shipping.

144

Okay. Go.

She hurried down the stairs and into the kitchen. *Fuck.* Her heart beat so fast and hard she was scared he would hear it. *Stop shaking.* She felt hollow, as though her organs had disappeared and she was just an empty frame made of springs, twitching and bouncing. She went over to the open bottle and grabbed hold of it, taking a deep breath. Her shaking hand raised the bowl to the bottle's neck and leaned the bowl's pinched beak over the opening. She started to tip the powder in, slowly. The grain was somewhere between salt and chalk, coarse but powdery.

I'll have to shake this up.

'What are you doing?'

She gasped and dropped the bowl. It clattered on the counter but didn't smash. The voice came from behind her.

'Nothing—'

She turned round. He was there, in the doorway, frowning, looking at her, then the wine.

'You were putting something in the wine... what's—'

She darted for the back door. *Locked. No key.*

'Ariadne!' he shouted, lunging over, grabbing her arms.

'Tell me what it is!' he shouted, dragging her over to the work surface where the powder lay, half in the bowl, half spread across the black granite. She looked at it.

'I don't know—' she faltered.

'Taste it,' he said, still gripping her wrists. 'Taste it. Tell me what it tastes of and we can figure out what it is, hm?' He pulled one of her hands towards the white dust.

'No!' she shouted.

'Why not? Why are you scared of it? Will it hurt you? But it was meant for me to drink, so it can't be harmful, can it?' He twisted her wrist around until she screamed.

He nodded.

'I thought so. I knew you were up to something. You're sick, Ria. Very, very sick in the head. Have been since you were young.'

145

She was close enough to see the veins in his temples pulse, the skin redden.

'I'm going to show you something,' he said, dragging her out of the kitchen.

He pulled her into the hall. She kicked, shouted, threw all her weight backwards, tried to bite him, but he was like a constricting snake. The more she struggled, the tighter he gripped.

'I'm doing this,' he said, 'for your own good.'

He pushed her against the wall and let go of one of her arms. She tried to run, but he caught her by the neck and held her against the wall, his hand round her throat, crushing her windpipe. *This is it. I'm going to die.* She couldn't breathe. He grabbed his lanyard off the table and let go of her throat. She sank to her knees, gasping. He snapped the badge off and tied the cord around her wrists, pulling them together. She tried to get to her feet, to pull her arms away, but she couldn't focus or lift her limbs. Her throat felt like it was pooling with blood, haemorrhaging on the inside, swelling up and out.

Ria's mind was blank. Frozen. She knew she was going to die. Her veins were coursing with adrenaline, but it did nothing. She was unable to convert the energy into anything other than terror. She felt like an animal, stood in the road, staring at the blinding lights bearing down on it, waiting for the impact of the car to hit.

Her wrists were lashed together tight. Her breath came back, slowly, as he dragged her out of the front door into the darkness.

'Help!' she managed to croak. 'He—' He smothered her mouth with his hand as he pushed her into the passenger seat of his car. She bit as hard as she could. She hated his hands being on her. Near her nose and mouth, it made her feel sick. His hand in her mouth was the worst – but she had to hurt him somehow. He cried out, pulled his hand away and shut the door, locking her in. She saw the blood on him, but already knew he was bleeding. She could taste the metallic tang and feel the warmth of it. She spat it at his face as he got in the driver's side. It hit his cheek and slid down. He looked at her, locking the doors again.

'Nobody can hear you. Nobody is coming for you. This,' he held up his hand to show the bite wound and pointed to the bloody spit on his face. 'This is why you need help. You're ill. And I'm the only one who can help you. If you scream, you know what will happen. I'm going to show you something.'

She hadn't heard that phrase in so long. *If you scream, you know what will happen.* He used to say it when she fought him. *I'll kill your mum, then I'll kill your sister, then I'll kill you.*

One night, when she fought too hard, he said he'd show her what he meant. The next day, after they did the supermarket shop, he told Christine to unload the boot and he'd park up in the garage. Her mum got out. Ria moved to open the car door and follow her. She heard it lock.

'The door's locked,' he said. 'You stay there and watch Mum.'

Christine stood behind the car, trying to open the boot.

'Anthony,' she started, looking in through the rear window. 'Anthony it's lock—'

The car lurched backwards. Ria heard a thud and saw the terror on her mum's face, as though she was being dragged underwater by a shark, as she disappeared down behind the window and then another thud, heavier, on the floor. She screamed.

Her dad turned in his seat and for the briefest second caught Ria's eye.

'You see? This is a warning,' he said, then spun round and jumped out of the car.

'Oh my God, Christine! I'm so sorry, are you okay? Don't move. I'm calling an ambulance. Oh Jesus, I think you've broken your wrist! I'm so sorry. I put the damn thing in reverse by mistake!'

She believed him then, she believed him now. She didn't try to scream again.

'Where are we going?' she asked, tears streaking down her face.

'Your favourite place,' he said, reversing the car out of the drive and pulling off down the lane. 'We'll be there in two minutes. You thought you had a private place, didn't you? Somewhere you could be yourself. Alone with the voices in your head.'

She watched the road ahead, the car headlights throwing white over the grass verge on the left and the pavement on the right. Up ahead she saw a figure. A man with a dog. They were about to drive past. She leaned forward, urging him to look at her. *Help. Help me.* She held up her wrists to show they were tied. Her dad saw and batted her hands down just as they were nearly level with the man. The man looked up, looked right at her. Her dad sped past. The dog barked. *He saw me.*

'That was stupid. Utterly stupid. What did I tell you?'

'I didn't scream.'

He looked in the rear-view mirror.

'It didn't work, anyway. Look, he's just gone back to walking his dog. He didn't see you. Even if he did, why would he care? Nobody cares about you. I'm the only one, remember?'

Ria started to sob. *He's going to kill me, then he's going to kill them. I knew this was how it ended. I knew it.*

'See,' he said. 'You're upset. Because you're ill. You've got a lot worse since I left, Ariadne. You need me, you see. You never cut yourself when I was here, did you? Because I wouldn't let you. Your mum told me all about the things you do.'

He parked the car at the bottom of the path that led up to the mill. The orange light above the mirror blinked on, then slowly faded over them both.

'I think that's the thing that angers me the most,' he said, turning to her. 'Because you have no right to do that. Your body is *mine*. Always has been. That perfect, porcelain skin.' He stroked her arm. 'It's ugly, now. You've grown into an ugly young woman, Ariadne. Disgusting, really. And not just on the outside.' He ran his hand up her thigh.

She swung her bound fists at his head as hard as she could, then elbowed him in the face.

'Fuck!' he shouted, grabbing her arm.

She struggled and lifted her legs to kick the door, but it didn't open.

'Stupid, stupid girl!' he said, wrestling her away from the door and then dragging her out of the car on his side. As she struggled to her feet, she suddenly felt a weight smash against the side of her face. She fell towards the ground, but he hauled her up. The night spun around her, little sparks flickered at the edges of her vision. Her face throbbed. She could feel him there, stood, sweating, panting, gripping her by the arm, in the darkness.

'There. Now you do as I say, hm? Come on. Show me your little Wendy house, then.'

She stumbled in the dark through the wet mud as he dragged her up the path.

'No,' she managed, throwing her weight back as much as she could, digging her heels into the mud. 'No, please... just kill me. Kill me now, but leave mum and Dee. Please—'

He carried on dragging her. Her limbs were exhausted. Her throat felt crushed, her eye socket and cheekbone glowed hot with pain. Her wrists were raw where the cord had sawed itself against her skin again and again.

Still dragging her, he laughed.

'What makes you think I'm going to kill you? You'd be no use to me then, would you?' They reached the door and he kicked it open, turning to face her.

'But it's always an option, isn't it? If I get sick of you.'

He pushed her inside and slammed the door shut behind them. His phone lit up the room. The familiar smell, the cold in the air, the brick-dust and damp. The silence. It could do nothing for her now.

'It's up there, isn't it? Your hideaway.' He pushed her towards the ladder. 'Up. Now.'

She stood at the bottom of the ladder as he flashed the light onto the steps.

'I can't.' She held up her wrists. 'I can't—'

'Don't be pathetic,' he said, kicking the back of her leg. 'Move!'

She stumbled onto the first step and leaned her wrists on the one in front of them, pushing with her fists as she lifted her feet to the next step. *Throw yourself out of the window,* she thought. *When you get up there, just run. Jump out of the window. If you do it fast enough, you'll die.*

She got to the top and stepped up onto the floorboards. She turned to see the two hollow squares in the stone where windows used to be, letting the indigo night pour into the black room. She could see the stars in the sky. *Run to them,* she told herself. *Run.*

She tripped. Something had caught her foot, her leg. It fell under her. She smashed down onto the floorboards in the dark, unable to break her fall with her hands. It was him. He was holding her ankle. She turned onto her back and tried to sit up, shuffling backwards to lean against the wall.

He stepped up onto the floorboards, shining the light in her eyes.

'You have candles here, don't you?'

She didn't answer.

'I know you do. Ah, there we are.'

He pulled a lighter from his pocket and flicked on the flame. He turned his back to light the row of candles on the bookcase. *Do it now.* She lifted her wrists to her hip. She knew, in her front pocket, she had the whittling knife. It had a cover on the blade, but if she could at least pull it out…

He stopped and turned round. She clasped her hands together and froze.

'You know why you're here, don't you?' he asked, holding the wheel of the lighter down, still lit, the flame flickering in front of his chest.

She said nothing.

'Because you're too far gone,' he said, turning away from her, taking the flame to each candle wick. She thrust her hand into her pocket and got the knife, pulling off the safety cover and putting it in her other pocket. He turned to her again. She hid the knife in her fist, the blade flat to her palm, the tip piercing her fingers. *You're okay. Soften to it. The pain will help you focus.*

'Something happened, when I left,' he carried on, pacing the room. The five flames cast a glow over him, over her hands and legs. He picked up one of the sticks that leaned against the fireplace and felt the tip. He pushed it against his palm, then put it back. He paced to the window, tracing his finger over the wooden carvings she'd left there.

She drew her knees up to her chest, keeping her hands hidden. She let the blood trickle from her fingers as she released the knife, turning it to cut the cords around her wrists. It was wet with blood, slippery. The knife was so sharp it cut through the cords and caught her wrists. More blood. She didn't dare look down. *It doesn't matter.* She kept her eyes on him.

'You became wild,' he said, bending down to inspect the wooden raven. 'Your sister kept you quiet, when she was here. Then she left, and you were a law unto yourself. She always knew when to stop. You never did. Your mother tried to keep you in line. Groundings, time-outs, no dinner. All the old favourites. But it took more for you. Something only

I could provide, because I'm the only one who understood you.'

He straightened up and turned round. She held her wrists together, as though the cord were still tied, and tried to soak up the blood on her jumper, still hiding the knife by closing her fingers around it.

'I knew coming back would be hard,' he said, stepping over to the barrel in the corner. 'I'd need to re-establish myself. My authority. Remember that time when I broke your mum's arm with the car?' he asked, his hand on the barrel lid. She nodded. He lifted the lid and reached inside, keeping his eyes on hers. He pulled out a black shape and tossed it at her feet.

'Just so you know I mean it,' he said, smiling.

Gripping the knife, she leaned her knees to one side to see the heap at her feet. She straightened up.

'You fucking bastard!' she shouted. 'Fucking shithead!'

Bertie lay, dead, broken and tattered, on the floorboards. His eyes were open. His beak was slightly ajar. She went to grab him, but stopped, keeping her wrists together. The candlelight flickered over the feathers, the black shining eye. *Fucking bastard.* She bent over him, her tears falling on his plumage.

'You're crying again,' he said. 'You see? You're not okay. You need me.'

She looked up at him. *Oh, I'm okay. I'm great. You'll see.*

He stepped towards her, undoing his trousers. He knelt down in front of her. This had happened so many times. So many times she'd seen him like this, unzipped, that thing there sticking out like a Nazi salute. *Fuck you. Fuck. You.*

'Aren't I a bit old for you now?' she asked. The rage boiled up through her blood to the surface of her skin, every nerve ending sparked for a fight.

He narrowed his eyes.

'No. You never will be.' He pushed her backwards, down on the floor and climbed on top of her. She kept her wrists together, gripped the knife against her palm. He kept his eyes on hers, undid the button on her jeans and pulled down the zip. Finally he looked down, grabbing the sides of her jeans. He saw the blood on her hands and paused. *Now.*

In his neck. The knife was in his neck before she even knew she'd lifted her hand. His eyes. Shock. She stared at him. He lifted his hand towards hers, shaking. She threw her weight forwards and fell down on top of him, her hand still gripping the handle of the blade in his throat. His mouth opened and closed, a gurgling, choking rhythm came from it, with dark blood spilling from the corner. His eyes stared at her, his hand still grasping at her arm. He tried to sit up, to turn over, but she gripped his torso with her thighs and held his shoulder down with her hand. He was getting weaker. She wrenched out the knife and watched the blood spurt, black in the darkness, up in the air like a fountain, dappling the floor like rain.

'Fuck you!' she shouted in his face. 'Fuck… you.'

She leaned in, close to his face. All the times he'd been that close to her. The terror she'd felt. The guilt. The worthlessness. His blood was shooting up, soaking her hair, the side of her face. She grinned.

'Just so you know I mean it,' she said, and plunged the knife into his chest, right where she knew his heart would be. And again, and again. She shouted with each stab of the knife, screamed in his face. His movement became slower, weaker. His eyes rolled back in his head.

'No,' she said. 'We're not done yet.'

She stood up, smeared the blood away from her eye with her sleeve. He twitched, the guttural cracks and rasps still reverberating in his throat. She looked down at him.

'What's the matter? Your cock's gone soft. Tell you what. I'll sort that out for you.'

She knelt with one knee on either side of his legs and pulled the sides of his zipper apart.

'There,' she said, looking at his glazed eyes. 'I can see it all now. You know, this was the first knob I saw. I've seen a lot since then. And it's the most pathetic, disgusting thing I've ever seen in my life.'

His body jerked, a sound came from his mouth, like a plughole draining. His eyelids blinked.

'Oh good. I'm glad you're still awake.'

She grabbed his penis and pulled it tight, until the base was thin and white. A low growl sounded from his throat, his head shifted a fraction, then it fell back to the side.

It was tough. She hacked away, watching each sinew snap and rip apart from the base. Blood wept over the wiry hair and wrinkled testicles, pooling in the seat of his trousers. She pulled it taut and finally made the last slice, severing it totally from his body. The bloody stump left behind continued seeping blood. He'd stopped moving entirely now, just a shallow rasp left, rising from his throat.

She gripped the penis, contemplating what to do with it. *You ruled my life. Ruined my mind. Damaged my body forever. Hideous, ridiculous thing. So much power from something so shitty and small. Stuff it in his mouth. Up his arse.*

No. You know what to do.

She went to the window and whistled.

CHAPTER 23

TYE

He stared at the suitcase, zipped, lying on its side. *That's it. You're done.* He paced to the wardrobe and held the hem of the red T-shirt. His eyes flitted to the window. It was black outside. Proper black. Except for the mill. His feet took him over to the window. Part of him didn't want to look. *It's lit, though. She's there. Candlelight. No. Go to bed, Tye. If you still want to see her in the morning, go see her tomorrow.* He drew the curtains.

In the bathroom, he looked in the mirror as he brushed his teeth. *They'll make you cut your hair.* He looked at the perfect frame around his face. *I've not had short hair since year seven.* He smoothed back the firework curls from his forehead, his temples, trying to guess what it would look like. *I look weird. Bare.*

'Night, Nan,' he said, passing Lynne on the landing.

'Night, love.'

She grabbed him in a hug and rubbed his back.

'Don't be nervous,' she said. 'You'll be fine. I'll do us a nice Sunday roast tomorrow. Set you up right.'

He smiled.

'Thanks, Nan.'

Tossing and turning. *You knew this would happen.* He threw back the duvet and sighed. His phone said 22:35. *Of course you can't sleep. Why did you go to bed so fucking early?*

You know why.

He turned his head to look at the shaft of moonlight falling through the gap between the curtain and wall. Clouds must've cleared. He unlocked his phone and opened his messages from Ria. The last one was from before they argued.

Bring booze xxx

He smiled, resting his phone on his chest. He took a deep breath and swung his legs over the edge of the bed, sitting up. The shadowy form of his T-shirt on the wardrobe looked like a man standing over him. He stood up and opened the curtains, letting the moonlight flood in. The moon was full, low in the sky. The blue-grey mottling over its surface was so clear, he felt like he could see mountain ranges, spreading across the shell white sphere. Still, he couldn't stop his eyes tracking down to the mill. Still lit.

'Fuck's sake,' he whispered.

Get dressed then. You know you're going.

'Nan,' he said quietly, with a gentle knock on her bedroom door. 'I'm going for a run. Can't sleep.'

'You be careful – stay close by. Have you—'

'Yep,' he interrupted. 'I've got my phone.'

'You won't be long, will you?'

'No, don't worry. Just need to tire myself out.'

'Don't put your headphones in – you can't hear cars.'

'I won't.'

Why do you feel more nervous about this than joining the fucking army? Get a grip.

The night was cold. He remembered that first night when he walked out up to the mill, with the bottle of Pernod. He

156

smiled. His heart beat faster. *Calm down. You just want to see her. Smooth things over. Part as friends.*

Something about her stuck with him. The things she said, they hurt. The lies she told were horrible. Sick, really. But he knew there was so much more to her than he'd seen. Something told him she had a story, a life he knew nothing about. Maybe it excused her, maybe it didn't. All he knew was, he couldn't leave without seeing her again.

Just tell her you're sorry. You didn't mean to rush to judgement without the facts. Whatever has happened to her, that's her business. She was a good friend, when you were alone. You'd like it if you could stay friends. Benefits not necessary. You wanted to say bye before you go away. Part on good terms. Stop rehearsing. You'll be fine.

He was halfway up the road that led to the mill. A car was parked at the bottom of the path. He frowned. It was parked askew, sticking out into the road. He looked around. Nobody. He looked up at the mill. The light flickered, but he couldn't see anyone in the windows. He quickened his pace.

It's probably nothing. Someone just left their car. Ran out of petrol. Could be stolen. Joy riders. They've left it. Could just be someone down the road. Walking a dog. He passed the car, peering in through the windows. Nothing.

On the path through the field he looked at the troughs and furrows in the mud. No sound from the mill. He put his hand on the black door and then leaned his head against it, listening. *Is that her?* He pushed the door, shining his phone into the darkness. Singing. He could hear singing. Candlelight glowed down the ladder from the hatch. The notes were intermittent, absent-minded. It was her, though, he was sure.

'Ria?' he shouted up from the bottom of the ladder, looking up at the eaves above. The singing stopped.

'Ria, it's me, Tye.'

Silence.

'I'm sorry, I didn't want to disturb you. I know I've not seen you for months, but I just wanted to say bye. I'm leaving on Monday—'

'That's okay,' her voice answered. 'You can come up.'

He took a deep breath and grabbed the ladder. It swayed a little under him. He could smell something new. Something other than the damp, the candles, the wood. Something metallic. Sour.

At the top of the ladder he looked over at Ria and nearly fell off, down into the dark.

'What…' he started, then trailed off. She sat cross-legged, turned her head towards him and smiled. Her hair was matted on one side, damp, purple-black. Stuck to her face. Her face, which was spattered with a bright red. Her clothes were saturated, hands glistening, covered in blood.

'What the hell… are you—' he started, climbing up out of the hatch.

She held her hand up.

'I'm fine. It's not mine.' She pointed over to the corner. He saw a body. Ripped, bleeding.

'*Fuck*—' he shouted, stumbling to the window, leaning out to retch.

The vomit fell away from him into the dark. He pushed himself back up and turned, shaking, to look at the body again.

A man, maybe in his fifties, sixties, with grey hair and glasses, lying on the floor. His eyes were open, blank. His neck was torn, a gaping slash, letting the night in and out. The dark blood was a perfect mirror glaze under him, stretching out away from his side, down to his feet. His sweater was darkened and torn in two patches, stab wounds to his chest. His trousers were undone, zip down, pulled apart. Blood covered the crotch and thighs. The testicles hung, congealed in blood, under a crater, a dent of raw flesh, torn tubes and ragged muscle. *It's been cut off. Ripped off.* Tye retched again, staggering back against the wall, steadying himself.

'I don't know what to do with him,' she said, looking at her fingers. 'I don't think I can get him down the ladder. Could shove him out the window. I was going to weigh him down, roll him off the jetty into the pond.' She looked up at Tye. 'I don't think there's any point though. It's a lot of effort. They'll find him anyway.'

She shrugged, peeling the sticky hair away from her eye.

Fuck. Fuck. Fuck. He stared at her, motionless, pressing against the brick behind him with his fingertips.

'You...' he said, pointing at the body. 'You did that?'

She nodded, looking at the corpse. He couldn't read her face. There was nothing. No anger, fear, despair – just nothing. It was as though she were reading a bus timetable. Tye pushed away from the wall and slowly stepped sideways, towards the hatch.

'Don't worry,' she said, turning back to him. 'You go if you want to. I'm fine. I'm not going to hurt you, though.' She smiled faintly, looking at her feet. 'I wouldn't hurt you.' She looked up at him again. 'You said you wanted to say bye, before you leave?'

He nodded, sitting down at the top of the ladder.

'That's sweet. Thank you. After everything. The lies. All that. I was horrible. I didn't mean it. What I said.' A tear sprang from the corner of her eye, streaking a clear path through the bloodstain on her cheek. She wiped it away.

'I really liked you, you know?' she asked, letting more tears fall. She sniffed. He said nothing.

'Where is it you're leaving to go to?' she asked, wiping her face with her sleeve.

'Army,' he said. 'I'm joining the army. Ria...' he struggled to finish the sentence. He didn't want to look at him again. It was impossible not to see him.

'Who… who is he? Was he, I mean. Did you… did you know him?'

'He's… he was my dad.'

Okay. Get out. Call the police. Don't look back.

'He killed one of my ravens – Bertie,' she said, pointing to the tattered black heap next to her. 'But that's not why I did it. I was going to do it anyway. At home. Tonight. But it didn't work out how I wanted it to. Then he drove me up here. To show me Bertie. And to do what he always does.' She shook her head. 'I told myself I wouldn't let him do it again. So I didn't.'

'What did you do with the… his…' He couldn't bring himself to say it, staring at the concave stump where it had been.

She smiled.

'I gave it to Betty. Bertie's partner for life. She ate it. She's widowed now, it's the least I could do.'

The room started to swim. Tye swayed. He suddenly felt weak, the candlelight flickered and extinguished. All black. He heard a small noise, maybe his name, then nothing.

***

'Tye?' He heard her voice above him. Everything looked blurry. He rubbed his eyes and tried to focus.

'Tye, are you okay? I think you fainted.'

He could see her face, hair, above his left side. The blood was all still there.

I didn't dream it, then.

'I called the police. They're on their way,' she said. 'So you might want to go. Or stay. Whatever you want. You've got blood on your T-shirt,' she said pinching the fabric between her fingers. 'Because I had to grab you, to stop you falling down there,' she pointed down the ladders, 'you fell forwards.'

160

He sat up, looking down at his T-shirt. He swallowed. The tang of sick clung to the inside of his mouth still. He looked at her. She was still kneeling there, inches away from him.

'You don't… you don't seem like—' he started. He didn't know how to finish.

'Good luck. In the army. You'll be great,' she said, with an apologetic smile, then leaned forward and kissed him. He closed his eyes, wishing they were back on the jetty, with their cans of Frosty Jack's. *Things could've been different. Couldn't they?* He pictured her there, her messy hair and plaid shirt, pale legs in the water, sparkling eyes on him. Smiling. He opened his eyes. She pulled away slowly, sat back cross-legged. The purple-black blood was still matted into her hair, the dark red smears were still down her cheek, her clothes and hands still soaked. Her eyes still sparkled, though, and they were still on him.

'What will you do?' he asked, trying not to let the tears rise up and out.

'Prison, I guess. Depends if I stick around or not.'

'They're coming, though, aren't they? The police?'

'Oh, no – I don't mean *here*. I mean, in general.'

'What… like… disappear?'

'In a way.'

He watched her. *She doesn't mean it. Does she?*

'Whatever he did to you, he can't do it anymore—' He looked over at the body, then quickly looked away.

'I know. I'm not sure if it matters, though. I nearly drowned myself, a few months ago. After I told you to fuck off that time, remember?'

He nodded.

'I just didn't want to be here anymore. Couldn't do it anymore. I jumped in,' she pointed in the direction of the pond, 'stopped moving, sank down. It felt like a relief. It was the ravens that stopped me.'

Ria walked over to the body of Bertie and picked him up. She stroked its chest with the back of her finger.

'They told me it wasn't time. They knew I had unfinished business, you see.' She glanced over to the body. 'I had to do it, so he couldn't hurt anyone else. And,' she said, kissing the head of the raven before placing it back on the floor, 'because he just didn't deserve to live. I know I lied to you, before, and there's no reason for you to believe me now. But he didn't deserve to live. He didn't. He ruined me. There's no coming back from it. I know that's the truth, and it's good enough for me. If they don't believe me – and they probably won't – the girl who cried wolf, the compulsive liar who got expelled, lost all her friends, disgraced the family... so be it. I've done what I had to do. I don't care what happens now. There's always a way out. They can watch me twenty-four seven. They have no idea who they're dealing with,' she smiled. 'I could kill myself with thin air. They'll see.'

Blue lights. He saw the flashes, faint at first, then the sound of engines, the blue became brighter. She turned to look out at them, then back at him.

'You can still go – that back window will get you onto the wheel.' She pointed to the black hole in the back wall.

He shook his head, looked at his T-shirt, then at her.

'I'm staying.'

PART 3

CHAPTER 24

KIAN

'Tye gets to come back for a bit at Christmas. Do you want to see him? I mean, if he wants to see you?'

'I'd love to, Kian, but I don't think he wants to see me. Your nan has already told me not to go near him when he's back.'

She sprinkled tobacco across the Rizla and then crumbled over the grass. He looked at it. She caught his eye.

'I don't mind, you know,' she said, rolling the joint. 'I know you've smoked a few with Bez.' She licked the paper and sealed it up.

He shifted on the mattress. *A few? How about every day for the last few weeks.*

I didn't want to. I had to. He wouldn't let me go until I smoked it. Now it's just a habit. Like drinking tea.

'What do you think of it?' she asked, lighting up.

He shrugged. At first, he didn't like the taste, the feeling in his throat. The smell. It reminded him of bad times, years ago, when that smell was always in the air. He got used to it again, though. He liked the feeling it gave him. It was like a lightness, a detachment. Different to alcohol. He'd only been drunk twice, on Sian and Bez's Skols. The weed didn't make him clumsy and confused, like that did. It didn't make him hyper, braver, angrier. It just made him thoughtful. Relaxed. Lighter. He laughed more. The things that he struggled with – crowds, loud noises, strangers – they were still there, but it seemed to turn the volume down on them, somehow.

'It's all right,' he said, rubbing his eye. 'Not fussed really.'

She nodded and took a long drag, holding it in before eventually exhaling over her shoulder.

'Yeah,' she nodded. 'It depends what you get. Here, try this.'

She held out the joint by the middle so he could take it from her.

'It's fine,' she said, grinning.

He took the joint and felt his phone vibrate.

'Hang on,' he said, then checked his phone screen. Tye.

Shit. Don't answer it. He'll be able to tell. I don't know how, but he will. Hear it in my voice. Smell it through the phone. He put it back in his pocket and looked at the joint. His first memory of a joint was when he was eight. The last time he lived with her, in the flat at Penkley Court. *God. That place was like a mansion compared to this. Two bedrooms. Its own bathroom. A radiator that worked. Sometimes. But then, there were needles everywhere. Strangers round all the time. The man with the knife who came to stab Mum. Bez is dodgy. Dense. But he doesn't hit her. He loves her, in his own weird way.*

He took a drag and let it sit at the back of his throat. He coughed.

'It's more pure,' she said, reaching to take it back. He handed it over.

'Does your dad still do it?' she asked. He shook his head.

'He's a good guy, your dad. Ray, I mean.'

'Do you—' he stopped. He could tell the weed was working. He felt philosophical.

166

'Do you think it matters,' he carried on, 'that I don't know my real dad?'

'No,' she answered, instantly. 'I knew mine, and I wish I hadn't.'

He nodded.

'But... it's not just that I don't *know* him... it's that I don't even know who he is. I mean, you don't either. He could be anyone. He could be dead. Could be alive. It's like... Schrödinger's Cat...'

'Who?'

'He was an Austrian physicist—'

'Let me tell you something,' she interrupted. 'There are a lot of people that could've got me pregnant with you, but I think I can say for certain, none of them were scientists. And why would it matter if he had a cat?'

He laughed. Once he started, he couldn't stop. He laughed until he was short of breath. He reached for the joint and took another drag, coughing out the smoke as he sniggered, wiping tears from his eyes.

'I'm Schrödinger's baby!' he shouted, collapsing into fits of giggles. 'Am I alive or am I dead? Or am I simultaneously both? Nobody knows!' He held his stomach. His muscles ached with the spasms of laughter. He struggled to catch his breath.

'You're mental,' she said, frowning and smirking at the same time. 'Don't ever do Spice – you hear me? It'd fucking ruin you.'

'Oh, God,' he sighed, rubbing his face. 'Schrödinger's baby.'

'I mean it,' she said. 'I'm serious. Weed is fine. Bit of weed never hurt anybody. But Spice, smack, crack – no son of mine is doing that shit. And don't touch Monkey Dust, for the love of God. I don't want that for you. Look where it's got me.' She gestured round the room, then up and down her body. 'Too late for me. But you've got your whole life ahead of you—'

'So have you,' he said, finally managing to breathe without laughing. 'You're not on it anymore, right?'

'Methadone. For now. But I've been here before, Ki. I know how it goes. Something fucks up in my life and I'm back on it. It's a cycle, and it'll just repeat till I die. And anyway – maybe no needles, for now – but those pills. They'll probably kill me quicker.'

He didn't want to know what they were. He knew Bez gave them to her. He knew how she got the money for them. He didn't like thinking about that. Especially after he'd smoked. If he started thinking about negative things, it was hard to come back from. Sometimes if his thoughts got away from him when he smoked, he spent days in a downward spiral. Skiving school, smoking down at the underpass, nursing a coffee in McDonald's for hours on end. If Bez was about, he let Kian sleep in his car, because it was warmer than the flat. He helped him change the number plates. He liked having access to a car, even if it was stolen. Nobody in the family had ever had one before. He liked driving. He was still bad at it, but Bez didn't mind. He let him drop them off and pick them up from places sometimes.

'You know, Ki,' she said, putting her hand on his shoulder. 'I don't think this is the right place for you, love. You should be at your nan's. We haven't got heating, any food… I mean, we share the mattress…'

'Top and tail though, it's fine—'

'You've got your exams. Your nan's been on at me about school, she's doing my head in. Plus… you need your own space.'

'You mean *you* need your own space,' he said, folding his arms. 'You want Bez here instead of me, don't you?'

'That's not it. Look, the minute the social services realise you're here, they'll make you move back anyway. I don't get anything for you being here, because they don't know. But if they did know, you wouldn't be here. So—'

'I'm a burden. I get it. It's not just that you don't want me cramping your style, you don't want me here when you could be subletting to some scrote.'

He snatched the joint off her and took another drag.

'It's not that, Ki, this isn't a good place for a kid—'

'I'm not a kid! I had to grow up really fast, really young, if you remember? In on my own all night while you were out. What's for tea, Mum? Oh yeah, you're not here. There's nothing in. The door's locked. I'll see what's in the bin then, shall I? There's a man trying to kick the door down, Mum. What do I do? Oh yeah, you're out again. That's okay, I'll lock myself in the bathroom and piss my pants.'

She shook her head and bent forwards, leaning her forehead on her hands. He could see her screwed up face, the tears. It just made him more angry.

'If you regret it, why did you do it? If you knew it was wrong, why did you let it happen? I chose to live with you. I chose you over Ray because you were my real mum and he wasn't my real dad. I didn't want to leave him, I didn't want to leave Tye. But you were *my mum*. I couldn't just let you go.'

She sniffed and wiped her eyes.

'You should've done, Ki. I shouldn't have taken you. I shouldn't have had kids, at all. I'm sorry.'

She looked across at him, her eyes bloodshot. She leaned her cheek on her knuckles, tears still running down her face. He knew she was right. Looking at her, it was obvious. She was so thin. Her nails were bitten so far down, her fingers looked like worms. She had puncture wounds all over her arms, hands. Her bones stuck out of her skin. The translucent, grey-white skin. Her teeth were half-missing. The ones left were brown, broken. The dark bags under her eyes looked like fat, grey slugs. She only dyed her hair once every few months, so the first inch was grey, the rest a dark reddish-brown. It was scraped back so tight, he could see where it had started to come away at her temples. He looked away.

'You have to stop trying to make this work,' she said. 'I'm a bad person, and a shit mother. I want to see you. I'd love to see Tye, too… but I can't look after you. I just can't. You deserve better.'

'I don't need looking after now,' he said, quietly. The fight had left him, though. He knew she was right. She was a shit mother. More than that, she was a barely functioning human being. He wasn't making her life any easier being there. He knew she felt crowded. Inhibited. She couldn't be herself around him. He could tell she felt ashamed. She took her drugs in the bathroom. Wouldn't allow Bez's friends up. *Maybe there's something in what she's saying about my exams and stuff, too. Maybe she does care.*

'I'll go back to Nan's. If that's what you want. It's late now. I'll go tomorrow.'

She nodded, starting to cry again, leaning over to hug him. *Marlboro, blackcurrant Tunes. Never changes.*

Someone knocked on the door.

'That'll be Bez,' she said, getting up off the mattress. She wiped her face with her sleeve and opened the door.

'All right?' he asked, stepping in. He zipped up his grey tracksuit top. 'Colder in here than outside!'

She opened a can of Skol and sat back on the mattress.

'You okay?' Bez asked. Kian looked at his feet.

'Fine,' she said. 'Kian's going back to his nan's.'

'Ah, mate! Why? We get on, don't we?' he asked, laughing.

'Leave it,' she said. 'Just leave it.'

'Fucking hell, all right! Calm down.' He looked at his phone, then at Kian. 'Listen son, you want to do a drive for me?'

Don't call me son. *But fuck it, why not.*

'All right.'

170

He caught himself, eyes closed, falling towards the steering wheel. He jerked his head backwards with a sharp intake of breath and looked round. Still nothing. *Come on, Bez, it's 2:00am.* Kian looked at the entrance of the block of flats. The neon strip light in the stairwell blinked. He sighed and rubbed his eyes. The air was stale. He turned the engine on, flicked the blowers on and wound down the window. The rain pattered in. He watched it land on the inside of the door, his sleeve, his joggers.

'Kian!'

He looked up. Bez was running towards the car, hood up, eyes fixed on the car as though it was his last chance to escape an advancing tidal wave.

'Kian! Start it up!'

His fingers fumbled with the keys before he realised it was already running. Bez flung the door open and hurled himself in.

'Go, go!' he shouted, slashing the air with his hand.

Kian put his foot down and steered off, sending the wheels spinning on the wet road as he turned. He could see two men running down the stairwell and out of the entrance to the flats. They ran towards the car as he sped up.

'Fuck – what did you do?' Kian asked, looking in the rear-view mirror. Bez craned his neck round to see them.

'Shit, they're following! Black Golf. Lose it!'

'What?!' Kian asked, his heart thumping. 'Which way? The light's red—' He slowed the accelerator, his legs and feet shaking. The junction was empty. Only the streetlights to the sides and the red light up ahead hung in the air.

'Fuck that – run it!' Bez shouted, grabbing the wheel. 'If you brake now, we'll roll – get your foot down!'

'Shit!' Kian tried to grab the wheel back but took his foot off the brake and onto the accelerator, obeying the command in blind panic. They swerved to the right onto the main road, but went too far and carried on turning until they were spinning onto the other side towards the kerb. Everything slowed down. They were moving in slow motion. Roaring, crunching white noise blasted into his ears as the impact came from one side, then the other, then from behind, then from the front. His stomach felt weightless, as though he was levitating – but he had no control of his limbs, his neck and head – they flew around in all directions, crashing against unknown surfaces and snapping back. He could see it all unfolding, but could do nothing. He watched as lights bore down on them, smashed into their side, flung them up on the pavement and into two black shapes, then into the wall.

CHAPTER 25
TYE

'This is the best Christmas ever,' Tye said, folding his arms. 'Come back from army training to visit Dad in a secure unit and you in youth offenders.'

He shook his head and sat back in the plastic chair, shuffling his backside forwards so he could slouch down and look up at Kian across the table. Kian said nothing, chewing his fingernails.

'There a lot of gear here?' Tye asked.

Kian nodded.

'You use it?'

Kian shrugged. Tye waited. Nothing.

'Well, this was really worth the 150-mile trip.'

'I didn't ask you to come.'

'Great. I'll just go then, yeah?' He shook his head. 'Nan wanted me to give you a present, but she doesn't understand how prison works—'

'I'm not in prison,' Kian interrupted.

'Kid's prison. You're in kid's prison. *I* didn't even make it here, Kian, and I was a little shit when I was your age. In and out of trouble with the police. But I never...' He stopped, sitting up, leaning forwards. 'I mean, what *the fuck* happened?'

'You know what happened. I killed two people. Injured a third.'

'Yeah, I get that. But how did you *let* it happen?'

'*Let it happen?*' Kian frowned, staring at him. 'I didn't let a lion into a crèche, Tye. I crashed a car, it was an *accident*!'

'A stolen car. Without a license. Or any lessons. Driving one drug dealer away from two other dealers. While you were stoned. Jesus Christ, what happened to the Gifted and Talented group? The straight A student?'

'It was called Nerds United, actually,' Kian said quietly, smirking.

Tye wanted to say, *It's not funny Kian, grow up.* But he couldn't help smiling. He looked up at the ceiling then down at Kian, shaking his head.

'Do you get a Christmas dinner here then or what?'

'Yeah. I don't want it though. The dining room is like purgatory.'

'You see, Kian – that's why you don't belong in a place like this. I don't even know what that word means.'

Kian laughed.

'Listen… please… just try to keep your nose clean, yeah?' Tye looked him in the eye.

'I will. I'm trying. It's…' Kian paused, rubbing his eyes. 'It's hard though, when you're awkward, anxious… like me. I'm different. To them. They know it. They don't like it. I get stressed. Paranoid—'

'You know what'll make that worse though, right? The gear. All of it. You might think it makes life easier. For half an hour, maybe. But it will ruin your life in the long run. Look at Mum.'

'I know, I know. Are you… seeing her, too, while you're back?'

Tye looked down at his hands. They were gripped together.

'I don't think so. I don't know where she is.' He was lying. He knew where she was, what she was doing, now that she was on her own. But Kian didn't need to hear it.

'She'd be really proud of you,' Kian said.

Not any of her doing, Tye wanted to say.

'Anyway, I have to be going soon. Dad's visiting hours are pretty tight.'

'Tye…' Kian didn't carry on.

'What?'

'What happened to her?'

'Who? Mum?'

'No… Ria.'

'What? Where'd that come from?'

'I just… that was the last time I saw you, just before that happened. Then you went off to training and we never really talked about it. I just wondered, that's all. She always seemed weird. But the stuff that was in the news—'

'I'm not sure,' Tye interrupted. 'Her sister messaged me a while back but I've not heard from her in ages. I think she might be somewhere like Dad is. But more like prison.'

He looked out of the window and ran his finger across his bottom lip.

'Fucking hell, what's wrong with me? Everyone I've ever cared about is locked up.'

'Well,' Kian raised his eyebrows, 'you're the common factor, Tye. You just have that effect on people.'

Tye half-laughed. *It's true. Maybe it is me.*

'Out of everyone, I always thought it would be me, you know? Not hospital so much but… prison, definitely. I'd have put money on it being me.'

'Funny, that. You're the only one who's free… but you've signed your freedom away.'

'Nah. I'm a free man. I just have to do what the government tells me. Isn't that the same as everyone else?'

'Oooh, political,' Kian laughed. 'The government can't make *me* cut my hair.'

'True,' Tye smiled, rubbing his hand over his close-crop.

'You look like GI fucking Joe.'

'I'll take that. Anyway. Merry Christmas,' he said, getting up. 'Keep out of trouble. You have a problem, go write something. Read something. Do a load of sit-ups. Anything. Just don't get into fights and don't get off your face, yeah? Fucking hell. I can't believe I'm having to tell *you* that. I mean it, though.'

Kian nodded, following Tye's lead to stand up. They hugged.

'See you at Easter.'

CHAPTER 26
RAY

25th December

Tye came to visit today. He's doing so well. I'm so proud. Kian couldn't come. I was really sad about that. Tye said he was ill. Flu. Can't get out of bed or anything. Lynne didn't want to talk about him. I think they're hiding something from me. Dr Thurlby would say I'm paranoid. She'd tell me to let it go.

I'm taking my medication. It makes me so bloody fat, though. I feel enormous. I could see it on his face when he saw me. The shock. I look like shit. I know I do. He's so tall. So fit. You'd never believe it, but I used to look just like him. Twenty-eight-inch waist. Cheekbones to cut ice with. I could do 800 metres in two minutes. No problem.

He gave me a card. It's on the wall. I couldn't give him anything. They had a "craft session" making Christmas cards, but how ridiculous is that? I wouldn't do it. I'm not a child. Grown men, sat round with glitter glue and plastic scissors. It was so pathetic I nearly cried. Just awful. The little girl enjoyed it though. Her name is Mia. She told me, the other day. She's happier now. Most of the time. It depends what's going on. Dr Thurlby says I can keep talking to her, but I shouldn't worry about her. If I get better, so will she. So I'm trying.

Dr Thurlby told me to talk to the people in the clock. Question them. Stand up to them. Not like what I did to the old voices, though. I tried to get them out by drilling a hole in my head. It made sense to me, at the time. Didn't work though. They just got replaced by the voices in the clock. The only way I can get rid of them is by getting better. They only exist because of me, she says, so I'm the one with the power, really. If I get better, I'll get rid of them. So I'm trying.

If I keep this up – keep taking the medication, keep doing what they say – she says I could move to Spencer in a few months. Weeks even, maybe. Then on to Harrison. That's the one before you get to leave, forever. I'm trying.

PART 4

CHAPTER 27
RIA

Cally's the one. I know she is. Finally. Nearly a year in this place, waiting for the one. Now she's here.

Ria sat in the corner and watched Cally mark down Nance's cutlery. *Poor thing. All on her own for feeding time at the zoo.* Cally looked right at her. Ria looked away, stroked the uneven plaster on the wall. When she looked up again Cally was talking to Karen. *She looks nervous. She knows she hates her.* Suddenly, Karen had Cally's wrist, she pulled it to her face and made Cally stroke it. *Interesting.* Ria watched Cally's face. *Terror. I can save her. Do it.* She sprang up off the sofa, just as the head nurse came in. He asked what was up. Karen dropped the hand. Ria flopped back down.

There were two others who didn't eat. They made them stay in the day room at meal times. Jenny played solitaire. She didn't speak much. She had an interpreter sometimes, for the ward rounds. Jenny was her English name, she told Ria. Her Chinese name was Li-Ling. Ria liked Li-Ling better. She wanted to be friends with her, but she didn't know how. She knew nothing about her, except her names.

'Li-Ling?' Ria asked, sitting next to her.

'Jenny,' she said, shifting over in the other direction.

'Can I play, Jenny?'

'Solitaire,' she said, pointing at the rows of cards. 'It's one person.'

'Yeah, but... do you know anything else? Blackjack... snap, even. Snap?'

Jenny stared at her.

'Maybe if—' Ria reached for the cards. Jenny swatted her hand away.

'No, please. Don't touch.'

Jenny scooped up the cards and got up. She walked down the corridor, out of sight. *You can't get in, Li.* She came back, tears in her eyes, and sat over on the opposite side of the room from Ria. She wiped her eyes and started laying down cards again.

Leave it. For now. You need to give her something she likes. Wants. Needs. Get it to her, somehow.

Ria turned to Kerry. *Kerry likes me. Kerry is one of the good guys.*

'Guess she didn't want to play,' Ria said, shrugging her shoulders.

'Snap?' Kerry asked, one eyebrow raised.

'Fuck off,' Ria laughed. 'Just trying to make an effort.'

Kerry put her hood up and sat back on the sofa, arms folded. Her bare feet rested on the coffee table.

'What does that mean?' Ria asked, pointing at the tattoo across the front of Kerry's foot.

She twisted her ankle sideways to view the writing.

'It's from *The Handmaid's Tale*. Have you read it?'

Ria shook her head.

'You should. I'll lend you my copy.'

'Thanks.'

'It means: *Don't let the bastards grind you down*. Worth remembering in this shithole.'

Ria nodded. She looked at the clock. Still half an hour left.

'I'm going to escape from here,' she whispered.

'When?' Kerry asked, looking at her.

'I don't know yet.' She looked over at Cally. 'I need some time. But I'm going to get out. Finish what I started.'

'Well *that* sounds ominous,' Kerry said under her breath. 'You're not planning to shoot up a shopping centre or some shit like that are you?'

Ria threw her head back, laughing.

'No, don't worry. You won't see me on the news. Well, you might – but not for that.'

Kerry shook her head and laughed.

'Going for a fag. You coming?' she asked.

'If they'll let us,' Ria said, eyeing Dave.

They stood up. Doling out time was over. The patients sat at the tables, some eating, some ignoring the food. Cally was in the off-shot utility area, filling up the kettle. Ria could only see her top half. The door was like one on a stable – the bottom kept closed and locked at all times, unless it was open for staff to get in or out.

'Weird, isn't it?' Ria said to Kerry, 'They won't let us near the kettle or the toaster, but they'll give us hot drinks. I mean, I could chuck that over someone and burn them, if I wanted.'

'Yeah. They won't give us proper boiling water though. If you notice, they leave it to cool before they'll give it out. That's why hardly anyone bothers. Who wants a lukewarm cup of tea? Makes me want to vom.' She turned round to Dave as they reached his seat by the door. 'Can we go for a fag?' she asked, putting her hands together in a mock prayer.

He looked at them and sighed.

'Not time yet.'

'But we don't eat – this is like, instead of food for us.'

'You know what? I can't be arsed with arguing today. Fine.'

He lifted his fob to the sensor next to the door and the buzzer sounded. They pushed through.

'Thank you!' they called as the door shut behind them.

Ria laughed.

'What?' asked Kerry, pulling her packet of cigarettes out.

'They'll all kick off now because we've been let out.'

'Hah. Yeah. Poor Dave. I think he's given up.'

She pulled out one cigarette and gave it to Ria, then drew out another for herself. They wandered over to the wall lighter and Ria waited while Kerry held the button down. She held her cigarette in the heated gap, sucking air through the filter, then kept it pressed down for Ria.

They both let out contented sighs as they turned to lean against the wall, inhaling the smoke.

Smoking, drawing – they were the two things that kept Ria out of trouble. Mostly. She looked at the same walls every day, saw the same faces. One piece of toast in the morning, one banana in the evening. Water from a plastic cup. Sometimes, she let them think they were winning. She'd eat a sandwich. A muffin or a cookie, even. Crisps. Nothing that involved a plate, a bowl or cutlery, though. Or sitting down.

The TV was always on. Ward round. Meds. Meal time. TV. Yard. Meal time. Meds. TV. Yard. Ward round. Meal time. Yard. TV. Meds. TV. Bed.

She hated the fact that the yard's concrete flags and high chain-link fence would always be under the same patch of sky. Next to the same line of trees. She hadn't touched, smelled or tasted anything different for a year.

She heard the outside, now and then. Cars, birds. There was a bus that stopped on the road behind the trees. She heard people laughing, chatting. Moaning about the bus being late. She saw the outside too, sometimes. Not the outside that was always there, but the outside that came and went – the weather, the wildlife. The clouds that lingered, raced, gathered, disintegrated. She watched the birds flitting between branches, preening, singing. Magpies. Pigeons. Blue tits, cola tits, blackbirds. Crows, sometimes. Never ravens.

The outside was its own master. She had no control over when it appeared or what it did. That made it interesting, at least. Inside was so predictable. She lived for the moments when things went wrong. She enjoyed it when someone kicked off. When the alarms went. When staff piled on top of patients. Even if it was her. Just for something to do.

Drawing was getting harder. All her wall space was taken up. The paper they gave her wasn't big enough for what was in her head. The pencils were always blunt. No sharpeners allowed. The pens were dry. Her big, beautifully black marker pen had been confiscated. Smoking overtook drawing as her hobby when that pen was taken away.

Smoking was a reason to be outside. A reason to stand and stare. A reason to close her eyes and feel her lungs. Something to buy, something to consume at her own discretion. Sometimes, if she felt like she needed to remind herself that she could change things around her, she stubbed one against the wall, gently, when it was only half burned down. She'd place it back in the box, saving it for another moment. *You decide.* It helped her. She couldn't cut herself like she did before. It was hard to get hold of something sharp enough, but that wasn't the reason she'd stopped. She could always harm herself if she wanted to. There were so many ways she'd learned since being there. If she wanted to get out, though, she had to convince them she didn't do it anymore. So she kept busy. She smoked.

'Go on then – what's your big plan?' Kerry asked.

Ria glanced over to the door, then back at Kerry.

'Play the system. Make them think I'm fine.'

'Right... but... if you can convince them you're fine, isn't that because you *are* fine?'

'Exactly. I *am* fine. I know I'm not crazy. They're the ones that think I'm mad. So I just have to make them see it.'

'That's not playing the system, Ria, that's just, well, recovery – isn't it?'

'Mmm, not really. You see, I think their interpretation of *fine* and my interpretation of *fine* is a bit different.'

Kerry nodded slowly, exhaling a white plume of smoke.

'And then what?' she asked, flicking ash on the floor.

'Once I get my unescorted leave, I'm off,' Ria whispered, 'for good.'

Kerry laughed, shaking her head.

'Just like that,' she said. 'Easy, eh? Do you know how long it takes to get unescorted leave? The hoops you have to jump through? Let's say if you get it, if you do manage this magical transformation into the model patient. Then you do a runner. They'll track you down in no time. You'll be back here, with no privileges, worse off than you are now. Or – maybe you do such a good job of convincing them you're sane, you go back to prison?'

Ria shook her head.

'No. that's not how it works.'

'How do you know?'

'I just do. They think – they know I did what I did because I was mad. That's what they decided. In the end. I can't go to prison just because I'm not mad anymore. It'd be like... I don't know... being done for drink driving when you scored zero on the breathalyser.'

Kerry raised an eyebrow. 'Well. What do I know? I'm not getting out of here anytime soon. The woman I assaulted sent me a letter, you know? Forgiving me. She said God would heal me. Hearing voices means I'm special, apparently. They were demons – the voices – when I got her. But she's been praying, and asking everyone at her church to pray for me too, and now they're angels. They'll guide me to the light.'

'Christ.'

'Exactly,' Kerry nodded, laughing. 'Damn right.'

'Ladies.' Dave's voice emerged as he pushed the door open. 'In. Meds.'

***

'Mum won't ever come to see me, will she?' Ria asked, leaning her cheek on Dee's shoulder as they hugged.

'Not yet. Give it time.'

'It's been a year.'

Dee pulled away and sat down.

She's pissed off with me already. Get her back.

'How's the GP life treating you, anyway? Better than the wards?'

Dee nodded.

'I get to sit down, at least.'

'That's something. Are the hours better?'

'Yeah. Long, still. But I can have food at semi-regular intervals and I've not had a UTI from never drinking water and never getting chance to piss either, recently, so that's good. Speaking of which – you're horribly thin, Ria.'

'Oh, thanks. Is that how you're supposed to talk to anorexics, as a GP?'

'You're not anorexic. You're just... distressed.'

'Right. Did you bring me that chocolate I asked for?'

Dee looked around at the other tables of patients and visitors, then at the support workers, then back to Ria.

'No, I didn't.' She lowered her voice. 'I can't get it, and you know I can't get it. Stop asking me for it.'

No smartphone today, then. Balls.

'You're the one who thinks I'm painfully thin, so I just thought...'

'Don't be facetious, Ria. You're here for treatment, for help. I'm a *doctor*. I think you should—'

'You're also my sister,' Ria said, crossing her arms and leaning back.

Dee's face crumpled. She put her hands over her eyes and leaned her elbows on the table, shoulders shaking. *Shit. I'm sorry.*

'Dee… I didn't mean to…' Ria leaned over and put her hand on Dee's forearm. 'I'm sorry, I—'

Dee batted Ria's hand away. She shook her head, blotting the tears from her cheeks with her sleeve.

'Do you even care?' Dee asked, narrowing her eyes, focussing on Ria's. 'Do you even care about what happened?'

I knew it. I fucking knew it.

'You don't believe me, do you? You're another one. You don't believe that he did what I said he did. You don't—'

'It's not *about* that, Ria. Mum nearly died. She lost her husband, the father of her kids, the love of her life, in the most horrific…' She closed her eyes, frowning, then opened them, staring at Ria again. 'Then she loses her daughter, too. Hears the worst things… blames herself…'

'She hasn't *lost* me. I'm not dead. And of course I care about her. I want to see her.'

'She *has* lost you. You don't get it, do you?' Dee gripped the table edge and cast her eyes up to the ceiling. 'Fucking hell, Ria, you make me so angry! I—' She let go of the table, took a deep breath and closed her eyes. She took another breath and opened them. 'I'm sorry. I know you're ill. You need help. It's just… it's been hard. It's hard. And when I come to see you and you seem so… nonchalant… it just doesn't sit right, that's all.'

'It's a front, Dee. You should know that by now,' Ria said, replacing her hand on Dee's forearm. *Is it? Maybe. I don't know. It doesn't matter.*

'I know, it's your way of coping,' Dee said, putting her hand on top of Ria's. 'I'm sorry. I miss you. Mum misses you, too. She's just… not there yet. You know?'

Ria nodded. She felt heat rising in her throat and behind her eyes, a fullness bursting out that she didn't recognise.

'Don't cry,' said Dee, welling up again. 'I didn't want to upset you – I'm sorry.'

I'm crying. That's what this is. Ha. The tears fell. She felt them streak her hot cheeks. She had to sniff, to stop her nose running. She was breathing faster, shallower. *When was the last time you cried?* She couldn't remember. She felt as though she was stood next to herself, watching. This alien creature doing the strangest thing. The world suddenly seemed completely two dimensional. As though everything was made of cardboard, stuck to a paper background. All grey-brown. People were stickmen. A child's drawings. No facial expressions. Lines and dots for mouths and eyes. Dee's face was just a circle of card, with a straight black line for a mouth and two dots for eyes.

'Dee!' She reached out and grabbed her shoulder. It was sharp, thin. It was card. Then she saw her own hand. It was paper. She screamed, holding her hands up, turning them round, looking down at her paper body. She tore at it, ripped it up, pulled out her hair and saw it was shredded newspaper, falling to the floor.

CHAPTER 28
CALLY

Alarms. She jumped up.

'Which one?' she asked, running into the day room, looking at the flashing wall panel.

'Visitors,' said Mara. 'They're short down there. Come on. Faz – stay here.'

Cally ran behind her, stopping for each door she had to unlock with the fob. Down the stairs, up the corridor. *Please don't be a bad one. No suffocating, no bleeding, no breaks. Please.*

'Hope it's not a spitter,' said Mara, putting her fob to the last pad. 'Or Nance. She weighs a fucking tonne.'

The door opened and they ran in, scanning the room. They stopped.

'Already got her,' Mara said, as they watched the girl be pinned to the floor by three staff.

Ria. She was writhing under them, screaming muffled cries into the space between her face and the floor. The support worker was struggling to hold her head still. Ria smashed her face down onto the floor, again and again until the support worker clamped either side with her thighs.

'Stop it!' shouted a woman stood behind them. 'You'll suffocate her!'

'It's all right,' Mara said, stepping forwards. 'It looks bad, but it's safe. We're trained.'

The three support workers on Ria looked at Mara and Cally.

'She's one of yours, isn't she?' the staff member holding Ria's legs said.

Cally nodded.

'We can take her back,' Mara said, then turned back to the woman, who stood sobbing. 'Were you visiting her, sweetheart?'

The woman nodded. She looked older than Ria. *Thirty, maybe. Nice hair. Well turned out. Cousin? Older sister?*

'Just stay here, sweetheart,' Mara soothed. 'And I'll be back in ten minutes. I'll get you a glass of water, okay? She'll be all right. It's just an episode. It looks worse than it is.'

Everyone in the room was staring at them. The woman sat down, hands over her face. Ria stopped screaming. She breathed heavily.

'We're going to get you up,' the support worker across her back said, slowly and loudly, in the direction of Ria's head. 'Don't do anything silly. Mara and...' He looked at Cally.

'Cally. It's Cally, Ria. I'm here.'

'Mara and Cally are going to take you back to your room. Okay?'

Ria's breathing became softer.

'Three, two, one,' he counted down. Two of the support workers dragged her up by her arms while the third stood poised behind her. She didn't struggle. She stood straight, craning her neck round to see Cally. She smiled. Her nose and mouth were bloody.

'Have you bitten your tongue?' Cally asked. Ria didn't answer. The two support workers shuffled her towards Cally and Mara. They made the handover, transferring one arm at a time to link with Mara on one side and Cally on the other.

'What has she done?' the visitor asked, getting up and moving towards Ria.

'Stay seated, please,' said Mara, holding her hand out in a "stop" sign. 'It's just where she hit her face on the floor. It's not broken. She'll be fine.'

The lady sat back, hand over her mouth, still crying. Ria stared at her, then started to pull Mara and Cally away.

'All right, slow down, we're coming,' said Mara.

Cally walked, her left arm linked through Ria's right. It felt like a coat hanger – thin, hard. She felt the glow of heat from Ria's body, like steam. Her hair had escaped from its loose plait and sprang out like wire wool in all directions, grazing the side of Cally's face. In her peripheral vision, she could see blood dripping from Ria's chin.

'We'll clean that up,' Cally said quietly.

They reached the bottom of the stairs.

'Are we okay to let go?' Mara asked. Ria stared ahead. Mara motioned for Cally to carry on. The three of them walked up, arm in arm, Mara counting the steps out loud. At the top of the stairs, Ria stopped and swayed.

'Low blood pressure,' said Mara. 'She needs to sit down. Come on, let's get to your room.'

'I want to sleep,' Ria said. 'I want to go to sleep.'

'No problem, my love. You can go to bed now. Look,' she lifted her fob to the pad on the wall next to the ward door, 'we're here now. Let's get to your room.'

'I'm all right,' Ria said, lifting her arms against theirs, gently.

They let go of her and let her walk through the door. It was tea time. All the patients were sat around tables with their food, except Kerry and Jenny, who sat on the sofas. Everyone looked over at Ria.

'Oh, shug!' cried Gwyn, rushing over. 'What've they done to you?'

Cally didn't know Gwyn. She'd just been transferred from another ward. She guessed that she was about fifty. She had grey roots and an auburn bob which was almost the same colour as her skin. *Aged with the sun, maybe*, Cally thought, looking at the dense network of freckles across her chest and arms.

'All right, Gwyn,' Mara said. 'She's fine, leave her be.'

'I'll look after you,' Gwyn said, reaching out and grabbing Ria's arm. Ria snapped her arm back and elbowed Cally in the ribs. Cally winced. Ria mumbled an apology.

'I said *leave her be*,' said Mara, grabbing Gwyn and pushing her back into her chair. 'Now you stay there and mind your own business, all right?'

Gwyn looked at the floor.

'Good,' Mara said, walking over to the corridor of bedrooms and gesturing at Cally. 'Come on, let's get her down.'

In Ria's room, Cally looked at the mural while Mara unwrapped the sterile wipes. She felt Ria's eyes on her, sat on the bed, motionless.

'It's really good,' Cally said. 'Like that urban street art you get in the big cities.'

Ria smiled. Mara rolled her eyes and cleaned Ria's face. She pulled down Ria's bottom lip.

'Open up.'

Ria opened her mouth, impassive. Mara held her front tooth, then the one next to it and the ones along the bottom.

'Nothing loose. You're lucky. Just the lip. And the nose. But it's not broken. No stitches either, it's all minor. Keep it clean, hm?'

Ria gave the faintest nod, staring at the wall. She turned and pulled the duvet back on her bed, then crawled under it.

'Can you do the light?' her voice came from under the cover.

Mara packed away the first-aid kit and got up.

'Cal,' she said in a hushed voice, stepping over to Cally. 'One-to-one I think. Until handover. Are you all right to do it? Faz is on her own.'

'Yep, that's fine. I'll get the record.'

Cally walked into the office and exhaled. *I get to sit down, for hours. She won't give me any trouble. She never does.* One-to-one observations meant sitting on a chair in the open doorway of a patient's room, watching them constantly in case of self-harm. Sometimes it meant watching someone sleep, try to sleep or pretend to sleep for hours on end. Ria was one of those. With some patients, it meant very intense conversations that Cally didn't feel qualified to have. Being called the worst names, being threatened with all manner of retribution. Having things thrown at her. Being spat at, grabbed, hit, scratched, bit. Wrestling knicker elastic out of a patient's hands before they could strangle themselves with it. Pulling them away from the wall when they banged their head against it repeatedly. Pleading with them to stop ripping their hair out. Having to pull her alarm, again and again, for help to de-escalate the same situation over and over.

She sat on a plastic chair in Ria's doorway, hoping she'd stay in bed. A clipboard rested on Cally's knee – the grid of times, tick boxes and comments empty for now. The light from the corridor crept in to the room, touching the top of the bed. Ria was buried under the duvet.

I wonder if she knows I'm here. Unusual for her to kick off like that. Maybe it was to do with the visitor. She looked nice, though. Could be guilt. Memories. Bad news from home, maybe.

She took a deep breath and let it out slowly, quietly. Most of the patients were in bed. She could hear one or two were up still, watching TV in the day room. The ceiling lights were off, the TV volume low. It gave the whole ward an eerie glow and a low, static buzz. Cally listened, trying to guess the programme. There was a live audience, cheering, laughing. A few voices back and forth in between. Some panel show, maybe. She wished she had her phone. She decided to count the swirls in the mural over Ria's walls.

***

Cally woke with a start, jerking her head back with a sharp intake of breath as she stopped herself from falling forwards. The clipboard fell off her knee and clattered to the floor.

Fuck.

She picked it up, watching the shape under the duvet stir. *Bollocks.*

Ria lifted the cover and squinted up at her.

'I'm sorry,' Cally whispered. 'Dropped my board.'

Ria rubbed her eyes and sat up.

Cally looked at the blank sheet. *Shit.* Her watch said 1:45am. She quickly initialled down all the missing time-slots, scribbled "asleep" in the observations field and added ditto marks underneath, up to 2:00am. She looked up at Ria, who was running her finger over her lip.

'Does it hurt?'

'Not too bad. Do you know what happened?'

'No, I came in after you were down. You can't remember?'

'I remember hitting my face… on the wall maybe? Or the floor. I can remember you and Mara bringing me back here. But nothing before… was my sister okay?'

'Was she your visitor?'

'Yeah. The one with nice hair. Green coat.'

'She was fine. She wanted to make sure you were okay, but she was fine.'

Cally wanted to ask if they'd fallen out. What was said. How she'd ended up in a restraint.

'How did *that* happen?' Ria asked, holding up her T-shirt edge to show a tear down the side.

'Sorry, I don't know – it was like that when we came in. Could've been a struggle, maybe – before, or when they were getting you on the floor. I don't know.'

Ria stared ahead of her, shaking her head.

'Nothing. I've got nothing. Dee came in. I remember her being pissed off with me for some reason. Then… I'm on the floor, they're picking me up. You take me out and up the stairs. That's it. Fuck. I hope I didn't hit her or something crazy like that—'

'I don't think you did – she looked fine to me.'

Ria sighed and buried her head in her hands.

Cally wanted to reassure her. She felt maternal towards her, somehow. There was only about five years between them, but she saw something so fragile about Ria. Like a little bird with a broken wing. Cally knew what her file said. She knew she'd killed someone. She had psychotic episodes. But they're rare, and any violence was always directed to herself. *Ria is just a mouse in a maze, lost, helpless. This isn't her doing.* That was Cally's instinct. But the same nagging doubt was always there – the murder was so violent. Cally struggled to place Ria in that scene. *She's tiny. Gentle. Kind. It doesn't make sense.* She read the press reports on the case as soon as she had chance to Google it after reading her file. *There was motivation, definitely. Mitigation? Yes. I think so. But… how could anyone—*

'Is that the light from the TV?' Ria asked, interrupting Cally's thoughts.

'Yeah,' Cally said, craning her neck to look out into the hall. 'But I think they've gone to bed now. You want me to turn it off? I'd have to put the hall light on instead, though.'

Ria shook her head.

'Do you want a Kit Kat?' Ria asked, leaning over to put her bedside lamp on. They both blinked and squinted in the light.

'Erm... yeah, I do, actually! I didn't know you had any food?'

'Emergency stash. Come on, I'd be dead if I just ate what you guys see me eat.'

She got up, opened her wardrobe door and rummaged through piles of clothes.

'Here,' she said, handing over the chocolate bar.

'Thanks. I didn't get my break.'

'Do you want some crisps?'

Bless her.

'No, thank you though. This is great.'

Ria sat back on the bed and unwrapped her Kit Kat. Cally glanced down the corridor before opening hers.

'I'm not supposed to,' she whispered. 'Don't tell anyone.'

'Ha. Don't worry. I'm good at keeping secrets.'

Cally finished the Kit Kat in seconds and wished she had ten more. *You should've said yes to the crisps. No. Too much. You shouldn't be accepting anything. Besides, crisps are too noisy.* She screwed up the foil and paper and shoved them in her pocket.

'If you want to sleep, don't feel like you have to stay up – I'm fine sat here,' Cally said, lying. She hoped Ria would stay up and talk to her. She was bored. Ria was always interesting to talk to.

'Oh, no. I won't sleep I don't think. I had a few hours – that's good for me. What time do you finish?'

'Eight.'

'Nights all this week?'

'Yeah.'

'Do you manage to sleep in the day?'

'A bit. It's not great, but you're so knackered it's surprising what you can sleep through when you need it.'

'Yeah. I don't think I'll be able to sleep until I've checked my sister is okay. Can't, though.'

'How come?'

'No phone.'

'You can call her on the payphone downstairs, though?'

'She's a hospital doctor. Works weird shifts. She can never take calls. It's only messages that work for her really. WhatsApp, Facebook Messenger.'

'Oh. Yeah, that's a bit shit.'

'She's the only person I have, on the outside. I get so anxious if I'm not in touch with her. I just wish I could remember what happened yesterday. She's probably fretting.'

'Mara went back to see her, after she cleaned you up. She went back to reassure her.'

'Mara?' Ria asked, raising her eyebrows. 'Oh, Jesus, well in that case I *definitely* need to message Dee.'

'Why?'

'Mara hates me. She makes shit up about me. I swear, half the stuff on my record was probably written by her and it's probably bollocks.'

'Really? Why would she make stuff up?'

Ria shook her head. 'I don't know... it might be because I called her out once, for being a bit rough with one of the ladies. Gwyn, I think it was. She's a bit... enthusiastic, with the restraints, sometimes. I think she's one of those people who is in the job because they like the power, you know?'

Cally nodded. *Definitely. Plenty of those here.*

'Anyway, once we were all in the day room and I heard this scream from up the corridor. There were no support workers around. I went to go see what was going on and there's Mara, sat on Gwyn's back, bending her arm behind her. It was Gwyn who was screaming. So I ran over and tried to get her off. She pulls her alarm, then before I know it I'm on the floor with someone either side of me. I told the head guy – you know, the ward manager – what she did. Since then, she's had it in for me. She wants to make me out to be a liar. And a nutcase, too. Fuck. She'll have told my sister all kinds of crap.'

Ria pushed her hair back from out of her eyes and leaned her head on her palm. 'I just don't want her thinking my recovery isn't on track, you know? I'm doing so well. It's the only thing that keeps our mum going. I haven't seen her for over a year. She can't bear to see me in here. My only way to talk to her is through Dee. And now Dee is going to go back and tell her I'm a lost cause. That you guys should throw away the key. Shit!' Ria drew her knees up to her chest and folded her arms across them, burying her head down into the gap.

'Will they not let you use the computer in the learning suite thing? You could get to Facebook Messenger there—'

'No internet. It's not allowed.'

'I mean, I suppose…' Cally started, knowing she shouldn't carry on. 'You could use my phone? I could bring it in, without anyone seeing—'

'No – thank you, that's really nice. But it wouldn't work – I'd keep having to badger you to check for a reply. Her shifts are all over the place. It could be days before she gets back to me, or it could be minutes. Thank you, though. I appreciate it. No, I think I'll just have to be an insomniac and drive myself up the wall until she next visits. *If* she visits. Depends what Mara said to her.'

Don't say it. Don't.

'How about…' *Fuck, you're doing it.* 'How about if you had my old phone? I've got one on pay as you go – still got a tenner on it, I think.'

Ria looked up at her.

'Really? Does it have data?'

'Yeah – it's old but WhatsApp and Messenger work fine on it. I can bring it in tomorrow?'

'Cally, seriously, do you mean it?' Ria asked, looking like she was going to cry.

Cally nodded. 'Just don't say anything, obviously. And if someone finds it, don't tell them you got it from me.'

'Of course not. They won't find it, I promise. That would be an absolute lifesaver!' Ria clambered off the bed and hugged her. Cally smiled. She could smell Ria's sweat. It was sweet – a stronger, earthier version of her deodorant.

'Don't mention it,' she said, watching her get back on the bed. 'Seriously though, I mean it, don't.'

They laughed.

CHAPTER 29

KIAN

'Fuck off!' he shouted at the back of the door. The banging carried on.

'Fucking queer!' the voices shouted.

Kian paced the narrow strip of floor between his bed and desk.

'Come out.' One voice was right next to his door, breathing through the gap between the frame and the hinges. 'Fucking come out here batty-man, so we can arse-rape you. You'd fucking love that.'

Kian shoved aside everything off his desk onto the floor. Books, pens, his mug and kettle, all crashed down.

'Fuck you!' he shouted back.

'Is that a yes?' the voice shouted. The others laughed. 'Sorry, darling, changed my mind. Don't want to get AIDS. But we've got some broom handles we can help you out with. Or why don't you ask Officer Morgan for her dildo, I'm sure she'd let you use it.'

Laughter rang around the corridor outside. Kian looked at his hands. They were shaking. He clenched his fists and tried to slow his rapid breathing. His head swam. He felt his heart thud against his ribs. Suddenly he lunged forward and grabbed his chair, lifted it and hurled it at the door. The metal legs gouged a chunk of paint off the frame and the wall, the plastic seat bounced off the door and quivered as the whole thing clattered to the floor.

'All right, break it up! Get back to your rooms!' a female voice shouted from down the corridor.

'Don't worry, Officer Morgan, we'll make him clean it before he gives it back.'

The howls of laughter drowned out her reply.

'*Oi! Get in your fucking rooms now!*' a different voice shouted above the crowd. Officer MacLeish.

'All right, don't have a heart attack, you fat bastard.'

Kian heard a scuffle, some struggle.

'You'll do as you're fucking told, and you're going into isolation for that.' Officer MacLeish's voice sounded breathless, harsh.

'You heard him,' said Officer Morgan. 'Go on, all of you.'

He heard footsteps retreating, the laughter petering out with them.

I'm going to kill myself.

The thought came sharp and clear, like flicking the edge of a fine crystal glass. *I have to. I'm going to do it.*

Keys turned in his door. *Fuck off. Please, leave me alone.*

Officer Morgan opened the door, pushing the chair into the pile of papers. She looked at the floor. The shards of white pottery stained brown on one side lay across the floor and over the books. His kettle was on its side, a small damp patch turning the white paper underneath the spout grey. She looked at the desk, then at him.

'Well, at least you didn't break the TV. Come on, time to see Trish.'

'It doesn't help anything,' he said, lying back on the bed, putting his hands over his eyes. 'She's full of shit. Can I please just be left alone? I'm not in the mood.'

'You're never in the mood. Come on. Up.'

He sighed and hauled himself up, shuffling to the door.

'And someone's going to have to pay for a new mug – you or your family – I don't care who. I'm not giving you another. You best hope the kettle isn't bust.'

***

'In the last two weeks, how often have you been feeling down, depressed or hopeless?'

'Not at all.'

Kian repeated the same answer for all the questions, as he did every time they met. He stopped listening. He thought about how he was going to manage to kill himself. *I have got my spare razor blades. You're shit with blood though, Kian. There's the cord from the kettle. Is it long enough, though? The TV cord – that might do.*

'Kian?'

'Hm?'

'I said, in the last two weeks, how often have you had thoughts that you would be better off dead, or of hurting yourself?'

'Not at all.'

'Okay. I heard you had some trouble today. On the wing. Homophobic abuse?'

Kian cringed and shifted in his seat. *Let me go.*

'Do you want to talk about it?'

'No.'

'Did it upset you?'

'No.'

'Officer Morgan said you smashed your room up. Sounds like you were upset to me.'

'Listen, I know you're just doing your job, but please, just leave it, yeah? I don't want to talk about it. I'm fine. No worse than what I used to get in school.'

'About being gay?'

'What? No! Fuck off. I'm not… I don't…' he stammered. 'I mean, the bullying—'

'I still think you should agree to the autism and Asperger's assessment we talked about. It might really help you. So, you're being bullied?'

'For fuck's sake. No. I was bullied at school. A bit. I'm not being bullied here. Just banter. That's all.'

'Right. Does this banter make you feel threatened in any way?'

'No.'

'Angry?'

'No.'

'But you smashed your cell up.'

'I was bored.'

She sighed. 'Kian, these sessions aren't for me, you know. They're for you. If anything is bothering you, this is your chance to do something about it.'

'Like what? Do what about it? Can you get me out of here? What can you actually do to help me?'

'Talk, and explore—'

'No,' he interrupted. 'I don't need to do that. Talking achieves nothing.'

'What would achieve something?'

Killing myself.

'Breaking out of this shithole. But that's not going to happen, is it? So I just have to keep my head down. That's what I'm doing, so just leave me to it. Please.'

She closed her folder and clapped her hand on the back of it.

'Right, fine. I'll take you off the list.'

He blinked. 'What list?'

'My caseload. I have a ton of people who want help. Very little time. So if you don't, you don't have to see me anymore.'

'Oh, well… good. Yeah. That's good.'

She smiled tightly, narrowing her eyes.

'Good. If you want to come back, they just need to fill in a form.'

'I won't. Okay, well… thanks… I'll see you around,' he said, standing and walking to the door.

'Wait – take one of these,' she said, getting up to hand him a leaflet.

LGBT+ in Prison, he read.

He laughed sarcastically, shaking his head, and slammed the door behind him.

Kian screwed the leaflet up. He looked up. Officer MacLeish was walking towards him. He stuffed the ball of paper in his pocket.

'I put a new mug in your room,' Officer MacLeish said as he walked past, with a quick wink. 'Don't tell Miss Morgan.'

'Thanks,' Kian said as he passed him, turning round. MacLeish carried on.

***

Tye. Please tell Dad this is nothing to do with him. Tell him I'm sorry. I don't want this to fuck things up for him. I'm so proud of him, now he's back on the outside. Tell him he has to carry on getting better, that's what I want for him. I wish I was brave, like him. Like you. I'm not. I never was. I know it's going to be harder for him, now you're abroad. Come back when you can.

Try to make up with Mum. Look out for her. I get it, now. How she ended up like that. I feel like that's what would happen to me, if I stuck around. I don't want to stick around for that. She told me never to try Spice, you know? It's funny. She was right. There's a video of me online somewhere. They made me take it. Filmed it on their phones. I don't have a phone, so I can't tell you what to search for. They got other videos of me, too. YouTube took them down.

You always fought my battles for me, Tye. Now I'm on my own, I just can't do it. I was never good at life. You found it so easy. So natural. You made friends. Had girlfriends. Played sports. Looked after me. Looked after Dad. Everyone liked you. So likeable. Even the people who you pissed off still liked you. They couldn't help it. Teachers. The police.

They hate me here. I can tell. Everyone hates me. I can't do this for however many years it takes. If it's this bad here, prison will kill me anyway. I'm just dragging things out. I'll admit it, I'm a coward – I don't want to suffer for longer than I have to. I know there's no life for me on the outside anyway, even if I did last that long. I was never good at it. I know I never would be.

It was a stupid accident that brought me here, but I'm kind of glad it did. It's just helped me see things clearly, faster. Saved me years of being one of those people. The ones neighbours talk about on the news. The guy who kept himself to himself. He couldn't hold down a job. Don't think he had a girlfriend. Or any friends, come to think of it. Only really saw him go to the shop. Put the bin out. That's all there was for me. This has just saved me time. I hate how I got here, don't get me wrong. I hate what happened. What I've done to Bez's family. And that woman's. I hope they get something out of this. They should know that I wanted to help them get closure. Until you've killed someone, you don't know what it's like. You're never the same. I don't sleep. I can see their faces. The face of his mum, too. Her husband.

Like I said before, I wish I was brave, but I'm not. I hope this helps them.

Please thank Nan. She did so much for me. She believed in me. I didn't deserve it. I know this will be hard for you – but please, if you can – thank Christine, too. Nan, Dad and her –

they're responsible for the only time I think I was really happy. Dad and Nan came up with the idea. Dad paid for it, Nan made it happen. Those lessons I had with Christine made me feel like being intelligent wasn't a bad thing. As though it could be an asset. Something that would open doors. She made me realise how far behind I was in so many ways, but it didn't matter – I had time to catch up. I wanted to. I enjoyed it. It was all wide open. It was mine.

Then everything fell apart. It was my fault. All my fault. You warned me. I didn't listen. Don't blame Mum. She wanted me to go back to Nan's. She knew it wasn't right.

I just wanted my mum. I always did. Tell her I love her.

Finally, Tye, thank you for everything. You'll never know how much you did for me. How much you meant to me. There are no words I can write here that do it justice. Enjoy your life. That's what I want for you. This is what I want for me. It's what I want. I'm sorry. I love you all.

Kian

CHAPTER 30
TYE

Fucking heat. The air was so hot, he felt like someone was blasting a hairdryer in his face. Breathing it in felt wrong, like sticking his head in an oven and inhaling. He smiled, shaking his head.

'What?' the voice next to him whispered. Ben. *He's bored. Same as all of us.*

His back, legs and arms ached. *How many hours can you sit against one stone wall, staring at another stone wall, before you go insane?* Tye bent and straightened his legs again.

'Just thinking of my brother,' Tye said quietly, turning his head in Ben's direction. He was on the other side of the doorway, which was missing a door.

'We did this hike for cadets and he was actually worried he might *die*. He was ridiculous. It was probably about twenty-eight degrees and he had a backpack on that would have been lighter than that helmet you've got on. I think it was about 5km, maybe less. Barely a hill in sight.'

Ben laughed, taking off his helmet.

'Yeah. That would've been me once,' Ben said, holding the helmet in front of his face, feeling the weight in his hands, 'I could barely lift my dog Barney upstairs when he came in from a walk and needed a bath. Mum would go ape if he got paw prints on the carpet, so I had to carry him up. He was a pretty big dog, but still. I was useless. But now – I mean, I carried Hopper the other day and he's the size of a fucking tank.'

'He is. And he probably smells worse than your dog, too.'

They laughed. Something sang past them. It flew between their faces, through the open doorway. It burst a small dent in the stone wall directly opposite.

'Fuck!' shouted Tye. 'Down!'

He clung to his gun and spun round on his heels, crouching behind the wall. Another shot. It hit the outside of the wall this time.

'Fucking hell,' said Ben. 'Where's Damer? Fuck's sake.' He had his back to the wall, clinging to his gun.

'He'll be here,' said Tye. 'Put your fucking helmet back on!'

Ben fumbled with the straps. Tye leaned into the blinding heat for a second, gun under his arm, sights to his eye, finger on the trigger. He fired off into the heat, in the direction of a shadow behind a rock, then swung back round behind the wall. *Fuck.*

'We'll be okay,' Tye said, dragging his sleeve across the sweat over his forehead. 'I think there's just one.'

Ben turned round, hesitating, gripping the gun. He tried to see round the wall.

'Stay – I've got eyes on,' said Tye, putting his palm up. Another shot whistled past and hit the wall behind them.

Tye's whole body beat with his heart. He could feel it in his fingers, eyelids, gums, pulsing hard. His breath was short and fast, the dry heat scouring his throat, parching his tongue. He looked at Ben. He could see his fingers shaking as he lifted the sights to his eye.

'Leave it,' Tye said. 'I've got it.'

He swung round again, firing into the white light. Shots came back, hitting the stone outside, another searing past his ear. He fired again. He could see the shape clearly now, a man on his front, in black, watching them, reloading his gun. *Get him. Get him now.* Tye swallowed, aiming for his head. He fired, the gun shuddering under his arm, against his ribs. The man jerked back and fell onto his side. Tye breathed in through his nose and out through his mouth, watching the body for movement. It stayed still.

'Got him,' he turned to Ben. 'Got the—' he stopped. Ben wasn't there. Tye's eyes tracked across the floor to Ben's feet. He was lying on his back, completely still.

Shit. Shit.

'Ben!' he leaned over him and cried out, a noise he'd never heard himself make before, the cry of a cornered animal. Ben's eyes were open, but one was gone. A raw puncture in its place, red and torn, stared up at Tye. He tried to move him, lifting his shoulders and neck, but blood spilled out of the back of Ben's helmet, his eyes still staring, and Tye knew it was useless. He grabbed his radio, hands slippery with the warm red mess.

'Tango 4-3. Man down, request immediate backup. Medical evacuation required.'

He pressed the button again and added, 'Damer... Damer, where the fuck are you?'

'Roger—' came the reply, but Tye didn't hear the rest. Shots flew past him again.

'Fucking hell!' he shouted, crouching back behind the wall. *There's never just one of them. You should've got backup sooner.* He turned to look at Ben, lying with his neck bent to the side now, staring at the roof, blood pooling under him, creeping across the dirt. Tye felt tears rising behind his eyes and tried to stop them. He clung to his gun and closed his eyes, deafening white noise roaring in his ears.

***

'Steadman.'

Tye heard them call his name, but didn't turn round. He stared at the tray in front of him. The shepherd's pie was cold. A grey, congealed film spread over the mound.

'Steadman.'

An elbow nudged him. He looked up. Hopper pointed in the direction of the voice, behind Tye. He turned. Smith stood waiting.

'Sir?'

'Phone call, Steadman.'

He frowned, getting to his feet. *Nan? Shit. What's happened? Dad. He's been sectioned. He's dead. Or... fuck. Ben. What if it's about Ben? Ben's mum. She wants to know. How he died. Who was with him. The look on his face. I can't talk to her.* Tye saw Ben's face, staring up. He rubbed his eyes and carried on walking behind Smith until they reached the admin area.

'Who was it?' Tye asked. Smith handed him a note.

'This is the number. Just add the code.' Smith pointed to the phone mounted on the wall.

Tye took the piece of paper. *Nan. Okay.* He exhaled.

He punched the metal buttons, holding the receiver to his ear. The dial tone was barely audible. He pushed the phone hard to his head.

'Hello?'

Her voice was faint. *Worried. She sounds worried.*

'It's Tye. What's happened?'

'Oh, Tye. It's so good to hear you.'

She's crying.

'Is everything okay? What's happened?'

'It's... it's your brother. It's Kian.'

'What's he done?'

Silence. The crying got louder.

'Nan, what's happened? Is he okay?'

211

'No, he's not. He—'

She broke off, sobbing.

'Nan! Tell me what's happened!'

'He killed himself. Today. Or last night. They don't know which. I can't—'

'What?!'

'They found him… hanging… he left a note for you, Tye, I'm sorry—'

Her voice cracked. He dropped the phone. It swung from the metal cord, back and forth under the box. He watched it swing. He could hear her voice coming in and out, saying his name. He saw Ben's face. Then Kian's. Kian lying there instead of Ben, with the gunshot through his eye, blood seeping out from under him. White noise filled Tye's head, pins and needles spread through his body. *This is a dream. I'm going to wake up now. This is a nightmare. It's not real.*

The black handset carried on swinging, back and forth.

I'm going to wake up. Wake up now. Wake up.

***

He stared out of the window at the landscape drifting past. Grey. Always grey. Afghanistan was blinding white, yellow, orange. England is grey. Grey-green, grey-brown, grey-grey. So dull. He felt his eyes struggling to adjust. His head hurt. Tight, heavy, sharp – the pain wouldn't go away. He didn't mind the cold, the rain. It was fresh – but the darkness, the dullness, was harder to embrace. Darkness was in his head and he couldn't get it out. Every day was grey now. Black when he closed his eyes, grey when he opened them. It was relentless.

The bus lurched to a stop on the road that skirted Talvern Pitts. He stepped off heavily and pushed one foot in front of the other, down the wet, grey road. It felt harder than scaling the mountainsides outside Helmand. Lynne's house came into sight.

He wished he was going to his dad's flat in Stoke. It was a great place. Clean, bright. He thought of his dad's face when they unpacked the shopping. The scotch bonnets, plantains, coriander. Dad's smile. *He was home. So was I. Why am I not going there? Why is Dad not making something amazing in that kitchen?* He could smell it. See his dad's hands, stained with green.

He stood at the gate, waiting. He couldn't seem to open it. His hand was on the thin iron handle, cold, wet. He gripped it, feeling the rain drip down his knuckles. *What am I doing here? I can't. I can't see them.* He looked down the road he'd walked up. The mist gathered in the dip of the valley. It was inviting. A pool of murk, to swallow him up.

He felt a push, a grab, from the side. He looked down. Lynne clung to him. He put his arms around her and stared up the path, through the open door to the hallway. *He's there.* His Dad stood, like a ghost, still and silent. Lynne was talking. Tye patted her back and pulled away, walking up the path. He watched his dad's face change as he approached. It crumpled, cracked, broke. Tye stepped into the hall and reached for him as he saw his knees buckle. He held him, lifted him, sobbed with him.

CHAPTER 31
RIA

You want to kiss her. So do it.

She watched Cally look out of the door, up the hallway. *She's perfect.* Only Cally could make a baggy T-shirt and cargo pants look sexy. The thin black belt with its bunch of keys, ID card, panic alarm – it didn't look the same on her as it did on all the others. She wanted to see her wearing just that, just the belt, around her naked hips.

'No-one's there,' Cally said, turning round, closing the door behind her.

She ripped the Velcro pocket on her trousers open and pulled out a phone and charger, holding them up to Ria.

'Quick – hide them!' she whispered, thrusting them into Ria's hands.

Ria took the bundle and opened her wardrobe, feeling for the box she'd made. She pulled it out and threw it on the bed. The charger and phone fit in the shallow white box, held together with tape. She felt Cally's eyes on her as she bent and reached under the bed, feeling for the gap between the slats where it would sit. It was just the right size to squeeze between them and hold. She emerged, flushed, her head swimming slightly as she stood up.

'How did you get that?' Cally asked.

'Made it in one of the craft sessions. Nobody asked what it was for. I had a story lined up about some ridiculous doll's house I was going to make. That box was supposed to be the start of a four-poster bed.'

Cally laughed.

Ria smiled.

'Thank you, Cally. It means so much to me, to be able to let her know I'm all right. To have some kind of link to the outside world… to remember I'm human, even—'

She stepped towards Cally, holding her gaze, and put her hand on her shoulder. Cally looked at her, she opened her mouth as if to say something, but stopped. Ria kissed her. She closed her eyes and felt Cally's hand round the back of her neck, the other on her waist. Cally kissed her back, hesitant at first, then with an intensity that surprised her. She pulled away.

'I'm sorry,' Cally said, looking at the floor, her hand to her mouth. She lunged for the door and opened it. 'I'm sorry,' she said again, looking her in the eye for a second before she disappeared through the door, leaving it open behind her. Ria heard her footsteps quicken as she got further away.

'Ward round, girls,' Mara's voice rang round the corridor.

***

The blue-white glow lit up her face in the dark. She looked round at the viewing pane in her door. *Nobody will be checking for at least half an hour now.* The background was a photo of a beach. Just like the cover of a Bounty bar. She wondered if it was a beach Cally had been to, or just a stock photo. *We can go there, one day. Wherever it is. When I'm out. We'll go.* She pictured them both in the photo, sunglasses and salty hair, grinning with sun-bleached teeth.

She swiped across to the apps. WhatsApp. No contacts. New contact. Dee. Ria only knew three people's numbers from memory.

Hi there, I'm using WhatsApp, said the caption under Dee's photo. It was an old picture from before she finished medical school, cropped to only show Dee's face with a mock-shocked expression, next to a white plastic model of a skull. Ria knew the bigger photo. It was Dee, stood next to the model skeleton, with her arm around it and its hand cupping her boob. She smiled.

> *Dee, it's Ria. I'm sorry for whatever happened when you came to visit. I can't remember anything – except that I hit my face and ended up on the floor, then they took me away. I'm so, so sorry if I hurt you. If I did, it wasn't me. It was whatever is fucked in my brain. I know you were angry with me for something, but I can't remember what. Whatever it is, I'm sorry. My friend told me Mara spoke to you after. What did she say? Love you, miss you xxx*

She hit the send icon and exhaled.

Google. She searched her name.

Wow.

> *Teenager who murdered her father pleads diminished responsibility*
> > *Girl stabs dad to death, mutilates body*
> > *Psychiatric sentence for girl who killed abusive father*

She closed the browser. *Not now.*

Mum. She created a new contact. *Text her. Saying what? Fuck.*

Ria put down the phone and rubbed her eyes. She looked at the glass in her door. Still no-one. She chewed her thumbnail.

Mum, I'm sorry for everything. Please believe me. I never wanted you to get hurt. I love you. I hope you can forgive me. Ria xx

She typed the message and hovered her finger over send.

Footsteps. *Shit.* She pressed send and quickly turned off the screen, throwing it under her pillow. She lay down on her side and closed her eyes, listening to the footsteps approach. They were heavy. Dave, she guessed. Or Faz.

She squinted, keeping her eyes as closed as possible as she watched the patch of light on her floor. A shadow loomed over it. She watched it disappear, waiting until the footsteps made their way to the other end of the corridor until she retrieved the phone. One more message to send. She closed her eyes and concentrated on the number. The last three digits were just out of reach. Her mind grasped into the air to catch them. *031? 013? Shit. Send it to both.*

Hi, it's Ria here. I'm in a forensic hospital. You probably heard. Doing fine. Got a phone from a friend. I hope you're okay. I never got chance to say thank you for staying with me. It meant a lot. I understand if you don't want to reply, but I'd love to just know if you're okay – Dee said you were posted in Afghanistan.

She typed:

I think I'd rather be there!

Then deleted it. Send. She imagined him on a camp bed in some makeshift barracks in the desert, checking his phone and finding her message. She couldn't decide if he'd smile or frown. Probably roll his eyes and hit delete straight away. She sighed. *Nothing to lose. Forget about it.*

She switched the phone off and sat up, replacing it in its box. Glancing up at the door's window, she crept out of bed and knelt, keeping her eyes on the window as she reached under to secure it back between the slats.

Time to not sleep.

Lying in bed, she stared up at the ceiling. *Mum won't get that until tomorrow. She turns her phone off overnight. Or she used to, anyway. Maybe she doesn't now. She must know that what happened to her was an accident. She has to.*

Dee's words, from her first visit, rang round her head:

She doesn't blame you, she blames herself.

If that's true, why can't she bring herself to see me? She had her stomach pumped. A few days in hospital. But it could've been so much worse. If she'd gone to bed, if the police hadn't got there when they did. Ria could see the wine bottle on the work surface, next to the mortar and pestle on its side, the white powder flung across the marble.

How did she not realise something was wrong? His car was gone. Neither of us were there. What the fuck did she think the powder was? It's your fault, Ria. Don't try to deflect it.

She couldn't help the anger. The bitterness. Ria was trying to ignore the voice that said, *It's her fault, too. She was ignorant. Willingly ignorant, your whole life. She left you alone with him so many times. That was the last time, and she paid for it. If she couldn't see something was wrong, she deserved it.*

No. She didn't. Stop it.

Maybe you wish she'd drunk more of it. Got rid of both of them.

Shut up! She slapped herself across the face. Her cheek stung. She closed her eyes and ran through her preferred version. The sequence of events that she wanted to believe. *Mum gets back from Valerie's. She's already worried, because Dad's car is gone. She calls my name, no answer. She runs upstairs, checks the rooms. Not there. She calls my name again. Runs downstairs, nobody anywhere. Runs out of the back door, calling me. Gets her mobile out, calls me. Calls Dad. Sick with worry, she pours herself a glass of red. She's too distraught to notice Dad's snapped-off ID card on the hall floor, the mortar and pestle, the powder. She drinks the wine as she calls Valerie for help. Then the police. That's what happened. It's not what they said in court, but that's what happened. It is.*

She turned over and put the bedside light on. *You're not sleeping now.* Ria picked up *The Handmaid's Tale* from her bedside table and opened it up at the folded corner. The narrator, Offred, is thinking about her mother. She has been transferred to a penal colony, put to work clearing toxic waste. Offred wants to believe that her mum will get out of it somehow, but she knows that the work will kill her. She's mourned for her already – and she knows she'll mourn for her again, and again.

CHAPTER 32
TYE

'You're on the list though, aren't you?' he asked, replacing his mug on the coffee table. It felt strange sitting on a sofa. Seeing ornaments, rugs, coasters.

'I don't know.' His dad shook his head. 'Takes a long time.'

'But they can't penalise you for this, surely?'

'Leave it, Tye,' Lynne said, opening the biscuit barrel. 'Here,' she said, tipping it in his direction.

'No,' he shook his head, 'no, I won't leave it – it's not right. You had to move here, temporarily, for support. Your son…' He couldn't bring himself to say it. 'What happened would knock anyone. It won't be empty for long. You can move back there soon – what's the alternative? You're homeless? I mean, come on—'

'There are a lot of people who need it more than I do. Don't worry about me, Tye. I won't be homeless. Lynne is looking after me. We just have to be patient, that's all. As long as I take my medication, everything is all right. That flat was great but I just… couldn't be on my own, you know? I just needed someone to check things with. Run things by. That's all.'

'Couldn't you have moved in with him for a bit instead?' Tye asked Lynne.

'Tye,' Ray said firmly. 'It was a one-bedroomed flat on the seventh floor in a building with no lift and your nan has arthritis. That was never an option.'

For fuck's sake. Two steps forward, three miles back. This place is enough to send anyone mad, let alone Dad. Suffocating. Not just the house, the village. The city. The county. Country. This whole fucking country is a shithole. So is everywhere else. Everyone thinks the sun is shining. They think they're happy. It's a lie. All a lie.

He got up and paced the room.

'Go for a run if you've got restless legs,' said Lynne, clicking the lid down on the biscuit barrel.

'Why not? See you in a bit.'

He wanted to get out. He knew all he did was bring them both down. Make them see how shit things were. Remind them of how hopeless it all was.

On the road outside, earphones in, he told himself to stop being selfish. *They need you.* He picked up the pace. It was grey again, but fresh. *You're all they have now. They're proud of you. You're the strong one, the sorted one. The living one.* He slowed down, clenching his fists, breathing in through his nose and out through his mouth. *You're alive. You should be grateful. You do what you have to. Be there for them while you can. Pretend you're loving life over there. Pretend it's the best decision you ever made. Pretend you still give a shit about making them proud.*

He saw Ben's face. Heard the bullets. Felt the blood seeping out over his hands.

Fuck off. He set off again, up the hill, tried to leave it behind. He raised his eyes to the horizon and saw the mill. He sped up. It advanced in his sights, every step bringing the old ruin closer. Boarded up windows. For sale sign. Auction. He slowed as he reached the gate at the bottom of the path.

That night, the car was parked right here. The gate open. The mud was smeared, rough, whipped up across the track.

The mill was black, orange. *Everything is grey and flat again now.* The windows blocked with chipboard, a padlock on the door. For sale at auction, the sign says, with estate agent and auction house logos stamped underneath. Tye held up his phone and took a photo, taking in the mill and the sign together. *You have to reply to her sometime.*

He looked around, scouring the trees. They flickered gently in the breeze. Nothing but leaves, as far as he could see. He whistled, just in case. *They wouldn't come to you, anyway. She. She wouldn't come.* He pictured Bertie, lying on the floorboards. *They mate for life*, Ria's voice said in his head. *Poor Betty.* Nothing came from the trees. He turned and looked down the hill at the village. *Nan's house. Ria's house. Different sides of the same coin.* He put his earphones back in. *Come on. Keep going.*

***

Dad's asleep. Finally. Tye had learned to recognise the change in Ray's breathing. Ray was in the bed Tye used to have, Tye was on the camp bed. He didn't care. *You would've been grateful for this camp bed on that dusty concrete floor in Helmand. Funny how things change.*

He looked over at Ray and wondered how he felt, sleeping in the bed of his ex. Staying at his mother-in-law's, when her daughter wasn't allowed inside. He reached into the open rucksack next to the bedside table and pulled out an envelope. He'd read it once, a week ago. He remembered crying, stuffing it in the rucksack. He couldn't remember what was in it. Not properly. *You don't want to remember, that's why. Tomorrow is the funeral. You need to sort your head out.* He took the envelope under the sheets, opened it up and pulled the letter out, watching his dad for signs of waking. Nothing. He turned on to his front, pulled the sheets over his head and laid the letter out in front of him, shining the torch on his phone over the paper. *Fuck. Come on. Just read it.*

He read it again, watching the tears from his eyes pat gently into the paper, holding the back of his hand to his nose to stop him sniffing. *You do remember it.* The same parts stung his temples, snagged his thoughts, as they had last time.

They made me take it. Filmed it on their phones... They got other videos of me, too. YouTube took them down.

You always fought my battles for me, Tye. Now I'm on my own, I just can't do it.

They hate me here. I can tell. Everyone hates me.

The words made Tye want to vomit. He screwed up his eyes and fought the urge to punch the floor.

He remembered Kian being born. Since that day, he had always felt pain, a physical pain, whenever something bad happened to him. He did whatever he could to stop it. Shielded him, argued for him, fought for him. He remembered when Sian told them Kian was going with her. *I was eleven, maybe twelve. He was eight. I locked us in the bathroom. Said I wasn't letting him go. Nothing she could say would change my mind. I'd stay there forever, if I had to. But Kian wasn't going to do what was best for him. He was never going to listen to me. I knew, really, before he demanded to be let out, that it was coming. I knew he had something with her that I never did. I knew he would follow her, no matter what.*

And you knew you had to let him. He remembered unlocking the door, watching Kian's face go past him, into Sian's arms. He remembered the feeling that something had changed forever. *That it was the beginning of the end. It was the same thing you're feeling now.*

Tye wanted to know who they were – the boys who bullied Kian. The ones that filmed him. He didn't want to see the video. But he wanted to know who he should be hating. Who to blame. He wanted them to suffer. *YouTube took them down. What the hell were they doing to him? Fucking bastards killed him. Every fucker who ever bullied him. They're guilty. And me. I'm guilty. I didn't protect him.*

I can't do it without you.

He sobbed. He couldn't help it. He turned the light off on his phone and lay still, listening. Ray's breathing didn't change. Tye tried to muffle his cries into the pillow, biting down onto it, wishing it would suffocate him.

Until you've killed someone, you don't know what it's like. You're never the same. I don't sleep. I can see their faces.

You're wrong, Kian. You're wrong. I killed someone. I didn't give it a second thought.

He saw the man in black, on his front, reloading his gun. He felt the gun under his arm, going off, the man jerking back and falling to the side. *Just a guy. A guy from the other team in a shooter game. A body. A point scored. He was a blank. That's all he was.* Until Tye read the note again. Now he was a man. Now Tye saw his face, like Ben's, staring up. He had a mum. A dad. A brother, sister. Kids, even. He had a tattoo of his wife's name and asthma. His three-year-old had just learned to kick a ball. His dad had just started chemotherapy. *Stop it. Fucking stop it!* He threw his pillow across the room.

'You all right, son?' his dad's voice drifted over through the darkness.

'No, I'm not.'

***

'I can't do it, Nan.'

'Yes, you can. It's what he would've wanted.'

'No, I mean it, I can't. I really can't.'

'You'll be fine. Just wait until the moment comes, you'll get a surge of adrenaline. You'll be fine.'

He looked out of the hearse window. *You don't get it. I can't. I won't.*

'Why are we doing this in a church anyway?' he asked, folding his arms.

'Don't be disrespectful,' his nan hissed.

'Because I want to,' his dad said, letting a tear roll down his cheek. 'Because it means something to me, okay?'

'Sorry.'

There you go, you've made this day even worse. Grow up. You're a fucking soldier. You're nineteen. Stop acting like you're twelve. Just do it.

He didn't want to see the coffin. He deliberately hadn't looked at the hearse when it drew up to the house, or when they got in the car behind. But now, he had to look at it.

He's in there. That's it. That's him, in there. Done. There's nothing you can do, nothing you can say. He's there. A wooden box. Pale, shining.

Tye stood, side by side with his dad, as they loaded it onto their shoulders. He wished the men behind weren't strangers. The undertakers, making up the numbers. There was no-one else, though. No other people close enough, strong enough. *He weighs nothing, though. Like the backpack on our hike. Fucking hurry up, or I'll smash your glasses and leave you out here.*

They set down the box at the front of the church and took their places. The vicar mouthed some words Tye couldn't hear, then he watched Ray get up and stand at the front, talking about Kian. He'd never seen his dad in a suit before. *He looks amazing.* Tye couldn't listen to what he was saying. He blocked it out. He looked around instead, watching other people's faces. Some kids from school he didn't really know. Friends of Ray's. Friends of Lynne's. Mum.

Try to make up with Mum. Look out for her.
She looks worse than I ever thought she could.

'Tye!' his nan whispered, jabbing him in the ribs.

He turned to see his dad still stood there, waiting for him to come up.

'You can do it,' she whispered. 'Come on. You can face the bloody Taliban, you can do this.'

He stood up, holding his dad's gaze as he walked towards him. They hugged. Tye tried to swallow tears back.

Breathe. He clung to the lectern.

'Kian,' he started, his voice cracking. 'Kian was my little brother—' He broke off, shaking his head, looking over at his dad and nan. They held each other, sobbing. Somewhere on the other side of the church, in his peripheral vision, he could see his mum, doing the same, clinging to the pew. He looked down at his hands, his white knuckles.

'He should be here,' Tye continued, 'reading at *my* funeral. He was the better one. Of the two of us… he was a genius. He was so caring. Forgiving.' He looked up at his mum. 'He had a lot of shit to deal with. Life dealt him a shit hand. He didn't deserve it. And he was worth more. If he had been born somewhere else… in a different family… he'd be going to Oxford now. Changing the world.'

Sian put her head in her hands.

'He was worth more than us,' Tye carried on. 'He was better than what we could give him. He was worth more than what happened to him. He shouldn't be in there.' He pointed at the coffin. 'I should. I was a little shit. He was a great kid. Loved us all. Got bullied for being different. But it was just because he wasn't meant to be where he was. You know how some people say they should've been born in a different time? He should've been born to a different family. He was too good for all the places he ended up. All of them.'

He wiped the back of his sleeve over his eyes and watched

his mum stand up and walk out, one hand over her mouth, tears streaming.

'The truth hurts,' he said, quietly, looking down at his feet. 'It hurts.' He looked up at the open door at the back of the church. The grey began to break into rain.

'He left me a note. It was… pretty much a list of people to thank. Like I'd be giving a speech at an awards ceremony. Ha. Whoever he wanted me to thank and whatever it was for – including me – it wasn't enough, was it?'

He let the silence hang in the air, then looked up at the doorway and released the lectern. He walked down the aisle, out of the church.

The rain felt good. He closed his eyes and raised his face to the sky, letting the drops land on his skin.

'Tye?' a voice behind him asked. It was quiet, hesitant. He opened his eyes and turned round.

'Dee, why are you here?' he asked.

She fumbled in her bag to retrieve an umbrella and put it up, holding it over an older woman standing next to her. The woman stared at him, mascara smudged under her eyes.

'My mum, our mum,' Dee said, pointing to the woman next to her, 'Christine. Wanted to come. She taught Kian—'

'I know, sorry – I didn't recognise you. We've not met,' said Tye, holding his hand out to Christine. She took it and smiled.

'He was a great student,' she said, holding on to his hand still. 'What you said, in there… was true.'

He gripped her hand.

'Thanks,' he said. 'He wanted me to thank you. You made him happy, you know? Your lessons. I don't know. Gave him a taste of what could've been. Kind of cruel, in a way.'

Christine looked at the floor. Dee opened her mouth to speak, but nothing came out.

'Ria messaged me the other day,' he said, looking at Dee. 'She's got a phone, somehow?'

Dee nodded. Christine turned away and walked out from under the shelter of umbrella.

'Anyway,' Dee said, fastening the belt of her mac. 'We have to be getting back. I've not seen you since… you helped with the… the police. And I was supposed to keep you posted. But I didn't. But there wasn't really much to say, to be honest.' She turned to see her mum open the gate of the churchyard. 'Anyway,' she looked back at him, 'you don't need me for that now, so – I better get off. Take care.'

She hurried away after Christine. He watched her go. *You should've asked her if she'd seen Ria. If she's all right.*

He closed his eyes again and lifted his face to the sky, waiting for each drop to land, cold, tiny kisses, melting away into the air.

CHAPTER 33
RAY

Dr Thurlby told me to keep up the diary. Especially now. I don't know, though. I'm not sure it's a good idea for me to go over things. Turn them over in my mind. Again, and again. Pick them apart.

My youngest boy, Kian, died. He died in a youth offenders place. They told us he hanged himself. I didn't want to know. Really, I didn't. He left a note for my eldest, Tye. It mentioned me. He thanked me.

Why didn't he leave ME a note, too? Because I'm not his real dad, maybe. I'm near as, damn it. I raised him, for the most part. I should never have let him go with his mum. He chose her, the second time we split. I respected that. A boy should be with his mother. But I had no idea how bad things would get. The things he'd see. The things that would happen to him. Our house wasn't perfect – but when the kids came along, there were no drugs. That was something.

Sian and I – we had one of those relationships you'd call volatile. But never violent. The odd plate might get thrown, wall might get punched. She hit me, sometimes, but never properly. And obviously, I never hit her back. I have never, will never, hit a woman.

We had a connection, me and Sian – the kind of understanding that you only get with people who have been what you've been through. Come from the same place. We were in the same care home, as kids. Things were different back then. You were in and out of foster families, care homes, whatever. Depending on who could cope with you. Sian had come from the worst life. Lynne was beaten so badly by her dad, she was always at A&E. Once, when she tried to leave him, with Sian, he stabbed her. Sian saw it. Lynne survived, but that's when Sian first went in to care – while Lynne was in hospital. Once you're in the system, it's hard to get out. And Lynne stayed with him, because he said he'd kill Sian, if she left him. Such a mess.

In the end Sian ended up with me and all the other "problem kids" at Alder House. This one guy who worked at the care home used to abuse her, and the other girls. I saw it happen once. He was a bastard. So after that, I said to Sian – we'll get him. We'll take him down. She said she was used to it. Her dad and her uncle did it. At least this guy didn't hit her, too. He didn't hit the girls. He hit boys, though. He used to call me "sand nigger". I didn't even know what that meant. I thought it was some kind of reptile, or an insect. He beat me harder, longer than he beat the white boys. Said I needed it more.

Sian liked my idea of doing something bad to that bloke. She hated him, like she hated all of them. We could've slashed the tires on his car, keyed it, something like that. He'd had that before though, they all had. It wasn't enough. We wanted to humiliate him. Hurt him. We had to get him when his guard was down. We knew people, you see. If we could just get him at the right time, he would be ours. The kids we hung out with down the marsh – they'd been in that home before us. They were seventeen, eighteen by that point. We were thirteen, fourteen. So we watched him, his routine, and made a plan. It all got a bit out of hand, in the end.

230

He always got shitfaced in the pub on a Friday night. So we waited for him to come out and turn the corner down the alley one time, six of us. All in balaclavas. The biggest guy – Tel, I think his name was – knocked him out, straight off. He was ours, then. We all took turns, hitting him – I'm not ashamed to say it. He was still breathing, though. We knew we hadn't killed him. We were only supposed to take his trousers after that. We got a bit carried away. He ended up gagged, tied to a lamppost, stark-bollock naked, with "NONCE" written across his big fat belly in Sian's lipstick. We ran off when he started to wake up.

Partners in crime, me and Sian were. We thought we could be the next Bonnie and Clyde. The reality was so depressing, though. In and out of prison. On and off drugs. In and out of love. Everything changed when she got pregnant. We both vowed that we wouldn't let what happened to us happen to our kid. If we'd carried on the way we were, she'd have lost Tye, one way or another. So we got clean. I got a job at a warehouse. We got a flat. We were finally like normal people. It was hard, of course it was. But we were so proud. When he came along, he was the most beautiful thing I'd ever seen. He still is.

My family, for all their faults, were very religious. My mother in particular. I lost contact with them a long time before Tye was born. Extended family, that is. The last time I saw my mum was when I was twelve, then she died when I was seventeen. I think we'd have reconciled, if we'd had more time. She wasn't well. It wasn't her fault that I was taken away. She was ill. She kept her faith, they told me, right to the end. When Tye came into the world, I found my faith again. It's a comfort. And a compass. My illness took it from me again, for a while. It's helping me to stay better now, I'm sure it is. Sian never understood the whole God thing. I remember her getting pissed off with me for going to church when Tye was a few months old, asking about getting him christened. She wouldn't have it. That girl always had a problem with authority.

She struggled with Tye. These days they'd call it postnatal depression. Maybe there's something they can do about it now. I don't think there was then, really. I didn't realise what was going on with her until it was too late. So wrapped up in myself. I was the breadwinner, the sole earner. I'd been a chancer. A drifter. Then I suddenly had to be the responsible adult and provide for a family. If I came home and she was crying, I thought it was just what happened to new mums. Hormones and that. If she shouted at me, likewise. I thought she was doing well, because the place was spotless. People who are depressed live in filth, don't they? We'd never lived somewhere that clean and tidy in our lives. I thought it was normal – nesting and all that. She didn't have to work, so that's what she did instead. I thought it was a good thing. Now I know it was because she was avoiding him. Afterwards, she said she never bonded with him. Some days she struggled to look at him. She loved him, but she hated him, too.

It was too late by then. She didn't tell me any of that until I found out she was back on the gear. Things fell apart. I couldn't keep track of her. Kept having to call in sick because she wasn't there to look after Tye. They fired me, in the end.

We fought like hell whenever she was home. She came back with these strangers, once. Smackheads. I chucked them out. Then I chucked her out. Told her she couldn't come back until she was clean. Her son needed a mother, not a junkie. I told her, he's NOT going into care. It was as though she'd forgotten everything we agreed. She just cut loose and abandoned ship. Things were desperate. I ended up going to her mum, Lynne, for help. They got back in touch before Tye was born. Things were good between them until Sian fell off the wagon. Lynne was always good to me. Her husband was a horrible man, but he died the year before. Lynne was like me – tried everything she could to help Sian, but nothing worked. In the end she had to turn her away, like I had.

Lynne loved Tye. Her first grandchild. Between us, we made it work. We both got part-time hours at the supermarket and arranged the shifts so someone was always there for Tye. I don't know what I'd have done without her. Me and Tye ended up moving in with her for a bit, after I got behind with the rent, until I had enough for a deposit on a new flat. And here I am again, now, twenty years later. Funny, the way things turn out.

Tye never saw his mum, but it didn't matter. He had us. Then one day, when he was about two, Sian turns up. Seven months pregnant. She has a holdall, dumps it on the floor and says, 'I need help.' Tye didn't even know who she was. He's holding on to my leg, staring up at her. She starts crying when she sees him. I tell her to come in. She's clean, she says. She wants me to forgive her. Wants us to be a family again. I ask her if she knows who the dad is. Says she has no idea. She was on the game. It could be anyone's. But she's clean now. She can't do it on her own. She misses me. Misses Tye. He needs a mother. I just laughed. 'He doesn't know who you are,' I said.

I vented at her a bit. But I knew I was going to have her back. So did she. The mother of your child turns up seven months pregnant and homeless, desperate – what do you do? Send her away? She was still so thin. Other than the belly, she still looked like an addict. She was in bad shape. She was the mother of my son. And she was the daughter of Lynne, who had become like a mother to me. So I took her back. Of course I did.

Kian was born a few months later. He looked just like Sian. Lynne was around to help. They got on better. Things seemed like they could work. Tye preferred Lynne to Sian, but that was okay. Sian only had eyes for Kian anyway. In our messed-up way, we muddled along and by the time the kids were at school, we could've passed for a normal family. Sian was working at the bookies. I was working at Asda. Lynne was back at the school as a dinner lady, coming up for retirement. Sian and I would fight about everything, but we loved each other, we did. I'll always love her. She was my childhood sweetheart. She knew me better than anyone. Still does.

Eight years, from her coming back, we made it work. Then one day, at the bookies, a customer assaulted her. Tried to strangle her. There were witnesses. She had to defend herself, so she smashed a mug over his head. She lost her job. Even though the CCTV showed it all, they fired her anyway. It was hard to get a job after that. There were no jobs for kids with degrees, let alone recovering addicts who smashed mugs over punters' heads. I could see it happening to her, that time – but I still couldn't to stop it. I could see her slipping away from me, slipping back into bad habits. I was at work, the kids were at school. Nobody was there in the day. She stopped turning up for her JSA appointments. Stopped applying for jobs. Started drinking more, smoking weed. Seeing old friends. I tried to pull her back, but it was like she'd seen the self-destruct button and was determined to press it, no matter what anyone said or did. I couldn't have her or her friends around the kids any more, in the end. I wouldn't let her in the house if she was with them. So she stayed away. More and more. We saw her now and then, because she missed Kian. He wanted to live with her. He was inconsolable when she left. Wet his bed, had nightmares. He'd sit on the windowsill in the living room, waiting for her to walk up the road.

One day she came round and said she was taking her stuff. Said she wouldn't come round any more, but she wanted to see the kids regularly. By the kids, she meant Kian. Kian insisted he wanted to go and live with her. I wouldn't have it. I knew some of the places we'd lived before we were clean – I wouldn't keep a dog there, let alone a child. But he kept on at me. I said

234

I wanted to see it before I'd even think about it. It was fine, but she'd only just moved in. I knew how quickly things could deteriorate. I asked Lynne for help. We didn't want Kian to go, but Sian and I weren't married. Kian wasn't mine. What could I do? I didn't trust the social services. In the end, there was nothing we could do except let him go.

Lynne would keep tabs, as best she could. We agreed, as a last resort, we'd get social services involved. In the end, that's what we had to do and he came back. He was never the same, though. A few months, he was there. Just a few months. At that age, though, you're like a sponge. He came back scared of everything. The dark, strangers, loud noises, being alone, being in crowds. He clung to his brother like a limpet. Missed his mum. He was obsessed with checking she was okay – used to call her all the time until she went back to prison.

When Sian went back inside, Lynne and I agreed we should keep some distance between her and the boys. It wasn't fair on them. Especially Kian. That's when I started to get ill. Those boys have had some shit to deal with. I was so proud of how they'd got through it. Now this happens.

Part of me hates Sian. Blames her. Kian wouldn't have been in that place if he hadn't been living with her and met that moron. They say you shouldn't speak ill of the dead, but I don't care. He was a fucking idiot. If you get a stoned kid to drive you between your drug dealings, you deserve what you get. I'm angry with her, for that. For everything. But then, I know what Kian was like, too. He was just as stubborn as her. And I know she hates herself now. At the funeral, Tye was harsh on her. She walked out, in floods of tears. He doesn't know what she went through. Why she is the way she is. He's angry with her. I think he's angry with me, too. I can understand that. Kian was bullied his whole life. We should've done more. I always thought I was someone they could talk to, but being ill changed all that. I wasn't there, even when I was.

They found a leaflet in Kian's pocket, the police. Or ambulance. I don't know which. LGBT+ in Prison was the title. Why couldn't he tell me? Was that what it was about? Was that why they targeted him in there? I don't know. Maybe he wasn't gay. Maybe he was. It just tears me up inside to think that he could've killed himself over it. Is it my fault? I go to church. I'm a pretty traditional kind of guy these days. Was he was scared to tell me because he thought I'd judge him? When I think of the things I've done, the people I've known, the life I lived before the kids. I wish I'd told him more. I wish I'd told both of them more. Then maybe Tye would forgive his mum. And maybe Kian would still be alive.

CHAPTER 34

KIAN

Dying was hard, but not as hard as living.

I remember sitting in my cell, looking at this mug. Officer MacLeish left it on the table for me. He'd put all my papers in a pile, swept up the broken pottery, put my chair back. I'd had a half-hearted go at trashing my cell that morning, you see. While I was out, talking to the counsellor, he put it straight again. Replaced the mug. It was the last straw. This stupid mug, just a plain white mug with a tiny chip in the handle, sitting there. It made me cry.

I'd been thinking about it. Dying. I was always the scaredy-cat. Scared of everything. It all made me anxious. But the thought of dying didn't, somehow. The prospect of the pain scared me – of course it did. But the thought of death – of not being here anymore – didn't. At all. It seemed like a comfort, just out of reach. Like when you have an exam the next day, so you're revising, but it's late and your eyes feel like they're bleeding because you're so tired. Nothing you read is making sense any more, nothing is going in. You just want to go to bed and stay there forever but you have to keep awake and revise, and instead of sleeping you know you'll just toss and turn then have to get up and go to school. Life was like that.

I just wanted to sleep, stay asleep, but people kept making me live this horrible life instead. Life was work, hard work, and I couldn't do it anymore.

This shitty, chipped mug, sat on my desk. MacLeish felt sorry for me. He knew what was going on. Knew what they said, what they did. He knew he wasn't going to stop it. He knew this was my life now, and that's why he felt bad for me. Tidied up my cell, gave me a mug. He probably wanted me to think that someone cares. There are good people out there. Get through it, tomorrow is another day. But that was the problem, tomorrow was another day and I didn't want to get through it.

Good people might be out there, but that didn't change the fact that I wasn't a good person and the people around me in that place were even worse. Good people deserve good lives. Fine. Let them get on with it. That would never be me. Look at Mum. Her life is one massive car crash and she's just bleeding in the wreckage, forever. What kind of life is that? That's what was waiting for me, and I didn't want it. I wanted to sleep.

I smashed a mug. It got swept up and replaced. Nothing I did meant anything. Maybe it would if I kicked up more of a fuss. Maybe if I trashed my cell enough, I'd have ended up in solitary confinement. Maybe if I was honest with the counsellor, they'd have put me on death watch. I didn't want that. I didn't want it taking out of my hands. So the mug was replaced, and life would go on. That's what it said, to me. You're here forever, taking it, the relentless shit that life throws at you, and you'll be grateful that at least you're not dead. You'll lie there and bleed in the wreckage forever, because you're alive.

Some people's lives are all laughter and light, but you know you'll never be one of them. It's impossible. Your life is bleeding, your life is suffering, and it only gets worse from here. You ended two lives that were worth more than yours, you ruined the lives of so many others. You make the lives of everyone you care about worse. You're like a black hole of shit that sucks in everything around it. But you have to carry on, because you're alive and you'll go on living. You carry on. Well, no. My answer was no. I won't.

I wrote a letter for Tye. I knew it would hurt him, what I was about to do – but I knew he could take it. He was always the strong one. He would hold things together. He would look after Dad, Nan. He would even try to make Mum's life less awful, if I asked him to. I knew he would. He would do anything for me. I think it was him, propping me up all that time, really. He's the reason I made it as far as I did. I couldn't lean on him anymore, so I fell. He wasn't there to pick me up, so I stayed down.

Even if things had gone differently – maybe, let's say I hadn't gone to live with Mum. I'd kept up the tutoring. Got into uni. It would have ended the same. When you can't talk to anyone, you can't go out, when there's a big grasping hole tearing at your insides and pulling you backwards every time you try to move forwards – you'll opt out, eventually. It would've ended the same.

I never saw myself in the future. Never saw myself at twenty-one, thirty, fifty. It's like I knew it would happen. I think I knew, right from sitting on the windowsill, when I was eight, watching up the road, waiting for Mum to turn the corner and walk towards me. I knew then that I didn't enjoy living, and that one day I'd decide to stop it.

It was messy, it was painful, but then after a while I was numb. It took a long time for everything to finally dissolve, but now the light is faded to total black, the volume turned down to absolute mute. I can sleep.

CHAPTER 35
CALLY

Shit. How old is she? Eighteen. She's eighteen. Nearly nineteen, but still. She's in a forensic secure unit. She murdered her dad. Nearly killed her mum. She's ill. She's vulnerable. You've basically abused her. Fuck. I should hand my notice in.

'Cal?'

'Hm?'

'I said, stir fry or pizza?'

'Oh. Pizza. I want shit food. And a drink. Is that leftover wine drinkable?'

Tom opened the fridge and lifted the bottle from the inside of the door. He held it out to her. She reached over from the sofa and took it. There was one glass left, maybe two. She unscrewed the cap, watching the TV.

'Tonight, on Newsnight: abuse of mental health patients in secure settings – it's endemic, according to one whistleblower, who has spoken to us exclusively.'

She sniffed it. *That's off.* She took a swig and winced. It tasted like vinegar, but it was cold, and it was alcoholic.

'Rough?' Tom asked.

'Yeah,' she replied, then took another gulp.

'Don't even want a glass? Your day has definitely been worse than mine then.'

She swigged again.

He unwrapped the plastic from around the pizzas and put them in the oven. She knew he wanted her to ask him about his day. She didn't want to. She wished he wasn't there. If he weren't there, she could carry on drinking until she passed out. That's what she felt like doing. But he was there, in the kitchen that shared a space with their living room, and he would be in the bedroom after that.

I'll lock myself in the bathroom for a bit. With those miniatures that Mum brought back from Berlin. He doesn't even know we have them.

'So anyway,' he said, sitting next to her. 'What was so bad? Did you get spat at again?'

'Nothing. I'm just tired. How did your day go?'

She zoned out his answer, turning the TV off to make it look as though she was concentrating on him when really she just didn't want to hear the *Newsnight* investigation. She watched his face and nodded in the right places, making the right noises of agreement or indignation, depending on the tone of his voice.

She sensed the anecdote was ending and zoned back in.

'So I said, look, I'm not going to crucify myself over this because a) it's not my fault and b) it's not my problem, so if you want someone to clean up the mess you'll have find whoever's paid to do that, because I'm not.'

'Jeez. What a fucker. Good for you.'

"Fucker" was a safe description – it could apply to anyone. He nodded. She drained the bottle.

'Anyway,' he carried on. 'We have ten minutes before the pizza's ready if you want to…?'

No, I don't, but I will, because you'll think something is up if I don't and you'll ask me questions I don't want to answer.

Keep him happy. Then you can eat pizza. The you can lock the bathroom door and drink.

***

'Will you tell him, Cal?' Tom's mum asked her, from the other side of the table. Cally smiled, trying to look fresh.

'I'm not his keeper, Neve, if he wants to look like a lumberjack, then I say let him.'

They both laughed. Tom rolled his eyes.

'I'm going to the bar. See where our order is,' he said, standing up.

'Aww, we love you really!' Neve called after him.

'If I could get him to trim it, believe me, I would,' said Cally. 'I don't mind stubble. Or even a bit longer than that – but he's gone full-on beardy now and it just doesn't suit him.'

She had to keep a steady supply of frivolous conversation going so they didn't suspect anything was wrong.

'No. He looks like something from when *we* were young,' Neve said, pointing at her and then Tom's dad, who sat next to her. 'His dad likes it, though. Don't you, Graham?'

'Leave him alone,' Graham said, swirling the head of foam on his pint around the glass. 'I think he looks rather handsome.'

'Who's handsome?' Tom said, pulling his chair out.

'You, of course,' Neve said, patting him on the back.

'Twenty minutes, they said. For the food.'

Maybe if I pretend to be ill, she thought. *I can't take another hour of this. Trying to be breezy. Trying to look and act perfect enough for their son.* She sighed, inwardly, digging her nail into the seat.

'Do you want another drink, Neve?' Cally asked, standing up. *Please say yes.*

'Ooh, go on then. Pinot grigio, please.'

Thank God.

Cally stood at the bar, feeling their eyes behind her, assessing her weight, her clothes, her hair. Were her shoes scuffed? Were her roots dark? Had she ironed her skirt? *If your nail varnish is that chipped, just take it off. Top's a bit tight around the midriff. Is that a fat roll under her bra line? I know what you're thinking, when you look at me. You can fuck off.*

She walked back over with a bottle and two glasses.

'A bottle?' Tom asked. 'Isn't that like twenty quid?'

'No, it's just the house. I mean, if we're both having a large glass, it's pretty much the same—'

'Good thinking, Cal,' Neve interrupted. 'Better value. We're not driving, so why not?'

She took the bottle and opened it, pouring two glasses.

Graham cleared his throat.

'Mum and Dad were just saying, Cal,' Tom said, turning to her. 'They want to lend us some money. For a deposit.'

Shit.

'Oh, wow, I... you don't...' she stammered. 'Are you sure?'

Because I'm not. I'm really not sure, at all.

'A toast!' said Neve, holding up her glass. 'To finally getting on the ladder!'

Tom grinned, clinking glasses with his mum and dad. Cally smiled and did the same, feeling all the blood drain from her limbs and pound round her stomach instead.

Every time she closed her eyes, she saw Ria. Felt her, tasted her. *You have a boyfriend. You're buying a house. She's in a fucking institution. Get a grip. You shouldn't have given her that phone. You definitely shouldn't have kissed her. Calm down. It feels like you're in too deep, but you're okay – if you quit now, never see her again, you'll be all right. It was a moment of madness. You can move past it.* She took a deep breath.

'I'm going to look for another job,' she said, pouring another glass.

'Oh, really? Great,' Tom said, looking at the glass in her hand. 'That place isn't doing you any good.'

'I need to earn more, if we're going to get a mortgage, right?' she said, smiling at all of them.

'What about the masters? Don't you need the experience for it?' Neve asked.

'I've done a few months. I'm still volunteering for that dementia project, so… anyway, I'm not sure if it's what I want to do, still.'

'What do you think you might want to do?' Graham asked.

'I don't know.'

'It doesn't matter,' said Tom, holding her hand. 'You're only twenty-two. It's not like you have to tie yourself to one thing in particular right now.'

'No.' *Except you.*

'Well, here's to new beginnings,' Graham held up his pint. They all clinked again. Cally finished her glass.

CHAPTER 36
RIA

Hey, it's me. Sorry for the late reply. You might have heard from your mum or your sister already about my brother Kian? He died. It was his funeral last week. They were there. I meant to ask them how you were doing, but I wasn't thinking straight. I'm going back out to Afghanistan next week. I don't want to leave my dad, but I have to go. He came out of hospital and was doing really well until this happened. He's back at Nan's now, in Talvern Pitts. I'd forgotten what a shithole it is. Look what I saw the other day:

She tapped the photo. The mill. Windows boarded up, door padlocked, for sale sign up front.

It made me feel bad for Betty. That was her name, right? The raven who was widowed? That sounds ridiculous. I'll stop writing shit now. I hope you're doing okay, considering everything. For what it's worth, if my dad can get out, so can you. I hope you do. Love, Tye xx

Tye. You liked him, you really did.

What happened to Kian? Ria remembered bumping into him once, in the hall. She didn't know who he was, then. It was only later, after Tye confronted her, that she realised. She tried to remember him. Glasses, fringe, awkward. Something about him was familiar, though, even then. The eyes, maybe. The way he looked up at her. *How did he die?*

If my dad can get out, so can you. She shook her head. *It's not the same thing, Tye. He wasn't in forensic. The rules are different here. That's why I have to break them. It's all right though, I'm on it.*

The raven who was widowed. Bless him. Betty will be fine. Ria pictured her that night, on the windowsill, almost invisible against the dark behind her, stabbing the flaccid, flabby length of flesh. She could see it now, rolling away from the beak when Betty nudged it to one side, gathering brick dust in the blood. Then the foot, black wire, seizing it, gripping it still, while the beak tore away. *Yeah. Betty will be fine.*

Kian. What happened?

'Ria – *do you remember me telling you I had a brother?*'

'Yeah.'

'*That he's dead smart but a bit of a loner?*'

'Mm-hmm. *You made him sound like a serial killer.*'

'Ha, yeah. *Well, Nan was worried about him sort of, turning in on himself. Now we're living here, in the middle of nowhere. And we don't know when we'll move back. He'd started skiving. Which is fine, if you're like me. But not him – he actually has a future.*'

Maybe he finally did turn in on himself. Couldn't see the future Tye saw. Mum will know. Dee should, too. She flicked back to the chats list. Dee's reply was still there, unread. Ria didn't want her to know she'd seen it yet. The preview on her screen was enough. *Don't worry*, it said, *you didn't* – that's all she could see. It was enough to put her mind at ease, without having to engage before she knew what to say. She decided to open it and reply.

Don't worry, you didn't do anything wrong. The nurse said it was a psychotic episode. That sounds bad, but you know what she means. You just switched off from reality and saw things, heard things that weren't there, until you came round when you were on the floor. You looked terrified and you were tearing at your clothes, so I think they restrained you because you might've harmed yourself. Can't you remember it at all? I wasn't pissed off with you. I didn't mean to come across like that. I was just frustrated. You were asking about Mum and I couldn't seem to say the right thing. It was my fault. I shouldn't have stressed you out. The nurse said that might've triggered it. I'm sorry. I'm annoyed you've got a phone because you KNOW it's against the rules! Are you taking your medication? You said they hadn't found the right combination yet. Keep going. You'll get there. Much love xxx

You say you're annoyed, but you're pleased really. You're glad I have a phone and you're relieved it didn't come from you. She checked the time. 1:05am. *Do this, then try to sleep. You need to be normal tomorrow.*

Dee, I'm sorry for the late reply! I'm doing well. I'm taking my meds, yes, and I think they're balancing out now. We'll see. I haven't had another incident since that one you saw. I'm so relieved I didn't hurt you. I can't remember it, no – just before and after. That nurse you spoke to isn't a nurse, she's a support worker. She doesn't like me. Could you visit this week? Or next, if you have time? I know you're busy, but I feel like our last visit didn't really count and it does me good, seeing you. I've got my first escorted leave tomorrow. Just walking over to the retail park. Hope I get Cally rather than Mara or Faz. Look round Poundstretcher. Stock up on fags. Get a coffee at the B&Q cafe. The things I can look forward to now! I really don't want to mess it up. I was on the right track to eventually get unescorted leave before the incident when you were there. I was nearly at the top of the tree, then someone kicked me in the face and I fell. Not to the ground, though. Just landed on a branch halfway down. I'm climbing again, now. Come see me if you can, Dee. Love you xxx

***

'How did your leave go?'

'Good. Ended up being with Faz, but she doesn't talk much so I could almost pretend I was on my own. Got my cigs. Got a coffee. Junk food from Poundstretcher. Didn't kill anyone or throw myself under a bus. Mission accomplished.'

Dee laughed. Ria could tell she was trying not to.

'You look good, Dee. You always do. But I like your new hair. Suits you.'

'Thanks,' she said, smoothing the side of her bob with her hand. 'I should've done it ages ago. Takes less time.'

'It makes it look so thick and smooth. Mine somehow manages to be a huge mess and incredibly fragile at the same time. Look.' She stroked a length of hair and watched the broken strands float away from her fingers.

'Don't! You'll have none left. Get them to test your iron – you might be anaemic. Vitamin D, too, and B12. Try to eat something other than shit from Poundstretcher, yeah?'

'I know. I will. It's one of the things on my list.'

'A to-do list?'

'A list of goals they've given me. I have to do them all before they'll consider me for unescorted leave.'

'Wow. Is that like, on the way to getting out?'

'Hopefully. I don't know. If I'm honest, probably not. I know one lady who's been here eight years and she's had unescorted leave for two of those. No nearer going home. I don't know what she did. But people don't spend two or three years in a place like this when they've done what I've done. They're normally here for life.'

'Don't say that. You're not a serial killer.'

Ria looked at the table and started to peel the laminate coating off the edge.

'Ria…' Dee said, leaning towards her. Ria looked up and let go of the plastic.

'…for the record – I do believe you.'

She does. Ria could tell, from her eyes. *She's not just saying that, she does.*

'I'm sorry,' Ria said, sniffing, wiping the tears away from her eyes.

'Don't apologise – shit, I didn't mean to upset you—'

'No, these are happy tears,' she said, looking up at her and smiling.

'The last time I was here,' Dee said, her voice cracking. 'You thought that I… that I didn't, and I just wanted to make sure you know, that I do.'

Dee put her hand on Ria's and squeezed it.

'Oh no, I've started you off now,' Ria said, watching Dee thumb tears away. Dee half-laughed, half-cried.

Go on. Ask her.

'Did he…?'

'No,' Dee shook her head, 'never. I think that's one of the things that made it so hard to process, you know? I really, truly, had no idea.'

'You wouldn't have done, if it never happened to you. It started after you left.'

Dee winced.

'I feel so guilty. I should have been able to tell something was up. I should've been there for you. I keep remembering that time when you turned up to stay with me and I—'

'Dee, don't. It's not your fault. I became good at hiding things. Good at lying. Mum always said, didn't she? I was a compulsive liar, with no moral compass… she still thinks that.'

'No, she doesn't. She's just, got her own demons, you know?'

Ria shook her head.

'Sometimes,' Ria said, peeling the plastic back from the table top again, 'sometimes I wonder. If she knew.'

'She couldn't have—'

'If she didn't, it's because she didn't want to. Years. Four, five years, it went on. Until they split up and he moved out. In all that time, all those nights, what did she think he was doing? I didn't have a lock on the door. Why did she never interrupt? Was she asleep? You're telling me that in all that time, she never once woke up and thought, he's been gone for a while, I'll go see where he is?'

Dee put her head in her hands.

'I'm not telling you anything, Ria, I don't know. That's the honest answer. I don't know.'

They sat, saying nothing. Ria felt anger in her fingers and gripped the edge of the seat.

'Anyway… let's talk about something else,' said Dee, wiping her eyes and straightening her coat. 'This is what got you in a mess last time.'

'All right,' Ria said, taking a deep breath. *She's right. It does you no good.* 'I wanted to ask you something, actually. How did Kian die?'

'How did you…? Ah. The phone. Have you been messaging Tye?'

Ria nodded.

'We went to the funeral,' Dee said. 'Mum tutored him, and it was just at the local church, so...'

Ria waited.

'...he killed himself,' Dee added, fiddling with her bracelet.

I knew it.

'How?'

'Hanged himself. With an electrical cord. In prison. Well, not prison, a young offen—'

'Shit, what was he in there for?'

'Tye hasn't told you?'

'I've only just got in touch with him, after like a year, and the last time we saw each other, well...'

'Right. Yes. He ran over two people. By accident, obviously. One of them died, the other ended up in a wheelchair, and the passenger in his car also died. He was lucky he survived.'

'Fuck. He was so young...had he even passed his test?'

Dee shook her head.

'Didn't even have a provisional. And he'd been smoking too. Weed.'

'Shit. I thought he was a really sensible kid. Just from what Tye said—'

'I think he was, but he'd been living with his mum. She's an addict. Her boyfriend was too. He was the passenger. It was his car. I think Kian went off the rails when his brother left.'

Turned in on himself. Poor Tye.

'He left a note for his brother. So sad.'

They sat in silence, staring at the table. Visiting time was coming to a close. Ria looked around. Most of the visitors and patients had drifted away. There was only one other group left in the room with them. It was Gwyn, with a man and woman. They looked about thirty. Her kids? Daughter and her boyfriend? Son and his girlfriend? Ria wondered what tragedies they would be raking over. *It's all we do in this* room, she thought. *Dissect the past, worry about the future. Anything else is just bullshit.*

'Ria?'

'Yeah?'

'Promise me you won't do that.'

'I won't. Don't worry. I'd have done it by now if I was going to. No. I've got too much to do. Besides, I can't let him win, can I?'

***

Tye, I saw my sister today, she told me what happened to Kian. I'm so sorry. It's just awful. I can't imagine what you're going through or how you're coping. I wish I was on the outside so I could help somehow. I could ask my sister to call in on your dad sometimes, if that would help? She's a GP, but she has done psych rotations in the past. She's back in Talvern quite a lot these days. Are you allowed to use your phone when you're back out there? I miss us being friends. I'm hoping to be out in the next year. When I get out, if there's anything I can do for you, or your dad, or nan – just tell me. I want to be useful in the time I have outside, because I don't think it'll be for very long. My mum isn't speaking to me, so there's nothing I can do for her until she lets me in. Dee needs nothing because she's a superwoman. I'm making a list of people here that I can help. They all have things they want done, even if they don't know it. Which YOI was Kian in? Does your mum feel guilty? You don't have to talk about it if you don't want to. Dee said he left you a note. I hope it gave you some closure. If not, at least you know that you were a comfort to him, if that's the last thing he did. If this message has pissed you off, just ignore me. I'll understand if you don't reply. It's good to have someone to talk to, though. Even if it is just WhatsApp! All the best, Ria xx

She hit send. *He will be annoyed. It's too forward. Gawking at grief. Slowing down to see a car crash. Like when you asked him if his dad had tried to kill himself and he left.* She hoped it wasn't obvious that she was fascinated by it. She hoped it looked like genuine concern. Which it was, in part. She meant what she said about being useful, and about missing their friendship. She felt awful for him. It didn't stop her wanting to know the detail, though. She wanted to know exactly how he'd done it, why he'd done it, what it felt like. She wanted to know if anyone was to blame. If so, how much. She would add them to the list.

A knock on her door made her jump and drop the phone. She scrambled to pick it up and turn it off, throwing it under the pillow.

'Yeah?' she called, calculating what she would do if it was a room search. The door opened. She exhaled.

'Kerry – what's up?'

Kerry stood in the open doorway, grey lines of mascara-tinged tears down her cheeks.

'He's got custody,' she said, tearing a crumpled tissue up in her hands. 'The bastard's got custody because nobody believes me and there's nothing I can do because I'm stuck in this fucking shithole!' She threw the torn pieces to the floor and kicked the wall.

'Shhhh – they'll come and take you down! Close the door.'

Ria motioned for her to shut the door and stood up to hug her. Kerry shut the door and stood shaking as Ria hugged her.

'I'm so angry. So fucking angry. They're *my* children. They can't do this.'

Ria didn't know what to say. She always thought of Kerry as one of her kind, somehow. She was feisty, articulate, cynical.

253

But this was out of Ria's reference library. She watched her pace over to the bed and sit down, drawing her knees up to her chest. *Face it: you're still a teenager, and before you came here, you hadn't even left home. You've done nothing, been nowhere. Kerry's lived all over the place. Had lots of jobs. Had a long-term partner. She's thirty, with two kids. You have nothing to offer here. Say something.*

'Is there anything you can do?'

'No! I *just said* that. I'm fucked. They're fucked.'

'Is he violent?'

'No. He's not violent, he just… it's hard to explain. He's a bully. He's controlling. He ruined my life. Ruined my mind. They're scared of him, I know they are. It's like… psychological torture. But nobody gets it – if you're not black and blue, if the kids don't have broken bones, everything must be fine. But inside, you've disintegrated… it doesn't matter. If you haven't experienced it, you won't understand.'

'I do understand. I promise. You can't let this happen, Kerry—'

Kerry picked up the pillow and threw it across the room.

'YOU THINK I DON'T KNOW THAT?!' she shouted.

'Shhhh! Don't let them—'

She stopped. Kerry was staring at the phone, no longer hidden under the pillow she'd thrown away. Kerry looked at her, then picked up the phone. Ria lunged forwards and grabbed it off her.

'What the fuck?' Kerry whispered.

'My sister smuggled it in for me. Please, I'm begging you, don't tell anyone.'

'How did she—'

'Listen,' Ria said, sitting next to her, lowering her voice. 'I think I can help you. Find him, on here.' She offered the phone.

'What do you mean?' Kerry said, taking it.

'Facebook. Is he on Facebook?'

She nodded.

'Find him for me.'

Kerry looked up at the door.

'Don't worry,' Ria said. 'I'll keep an eye out.'

She got up and walked to the door, peering through the viewing pane. She turned to see Kerry logging in to Facebook.

'You're friends still?'

'No. But he's tagged in old photos.'

She scrolled through her images. Ria watched Kerry's eyes fill with tears as she swiped through photos of her kids. She wiped her sleeve across her face and sniffed. She stopped on a photo, closed her eyes and handed Ria the phone. She took it. The photo showed a boy of about five and a toddler, sat on a sofa on either side of a man. On the man's lap was a birthday cake with a candle in the shape of the number three, lit with a sparkling flame. The man looked about forty years old. *Good looking*, Ria thought. Silver flecks reached from his temples back through his dark hair, making the contrast with his tan more noticeable. His eyes were dark brown, almost black and wide, with thick lashes. *Perfect teeth, perfect jaw. He looks like a dad from a TV advert.* The children had his eyes, but they both had Kerry's smile and her ash-blonde hair. Ria tapped his face. Mick Ashton. She tapped the name. His profile photo was of the two kids sat on a bench, throwing bits of bread to three ducks near their swinging legs. The cover photo showed a sunset over a canopy of trees, broken by a black zip-line with the figure of a man halfway down it, arms outstretched, hands splayed.

'I can see most of his profile,' Ria said, reading his "about" section. 'Doesn't he know how it works?'

'He wants people to pay attention to him and his perfect life. I'm surprised he has any of it hidden at all.'

'Works at Pharmgen. High up?'

Kerry nodded.

'Sales. Drives a Maserati,' she said, shaking her head. 'He thinks it makes him a good dad, because it's an SUV. It makes him a fucking wanker.'

Ria heard a knock.

'Fuck – hide it!' she said, looking at the door. She couldn't see anyone. She heard the door of the next room open and Dave's voice talking about medication.

'He's next door. Quick – go, now, before he comes,' she said, grabbing the phone from Kerry and shoving it in its box. Kerry walked to the door and put her ear to it. Ria thrust the box under the bed between the slats.

'Go!' she hissed.

Kerry opened the door and slipped through, without looking back. Ria exhaled, sitting back on the bed. Dave appeared at the window.

'Was Kerry just in here?' he said, opening the door.

'Hm? Oh, yeah. She had something in her eye. Wanted me to help get it out.'

He frowned. *He doesn't believe me.*

'You're not allowed in each other's rooms. You know that. I don't know what's going on, but stop it, okay? You don't need to get involved, all right?'

'It was just an eyelash—'

'We're doing urine and bloods tomorrow. I'd better not find anything I shouldn't.'

He looked at her, pointing his finger between her and the wall Kerry's room was the other side of. Ria held her hands up, palms facing him.

'You won't,' she said. 'You can search me. I was getting a fucking eyelash out.'

He sighed, stepped back out of the room and closed her door behind him.

***

Hey Ria. I know, it's fucked up. I always thought it would be me that ended up in one of those places. I suppose the army isn't much different though is it? He was in Yarlsden. Fucking shithole. He just didn't belong somewhere like that. He wasn't made for it. They ate him alive. I found a video they uploaded to YouTube of him. They made him take Spice, then filmed it. Look. He said there were other videos that YouTube took down. How bad must they have been? YouTube has so much shit on there. Violent, twisted shit. It's haunting me. I can't stop it. I can't stop thinking about it. I can't stop imagining what he went through. I can't stop hating myself for letting it happen. I can't stop obsessing over those fuckers. It's a good job they're locked up. I'd make them suffer for what they did to him. That's why he did it. Them. But then there's also the fact we all fucked him up before he even got there. So I should make myself suffer too, really. And Mum. Does she feel guilty? I think so. Does that mean I forgive her? No. We all failed him, though. And now I have to go back to Afghan and give a fuck about operation never-ending-shitfest. I would be really grateful if your sister could see Dad from time to time – are you sure she'd be okay with that? I can't lose him too. I just want him to be like he used to be. He was a good dad, you know. He was the best. But he got ill. There was nobody except me to help him and I was fucking useless. Trouble with the police, trouble at school. He didn't need that. I wish I wasn't in the fucking army now. I could look after him, make up for it. We could share a house in Stoke together. I could work, he could cook. Anyway – I'm sorry. I'm rambling. You have enough shit to deal with! How are things with you? Why do you think you'll be back in there soon, if you're getting out? Doesn't that mean you're better? I miss us being friends, too. I don't have anyone to talk to, about what happened. You're the only one. Fuck it. Tell you what, let's both abscond and go live on an island somewhere. If only! I can come visit you, if you like, next time I get leave? Won't be for a while yet but it would give me something to look forward to. I'm so tired. Going to try to get some sleep even though I know I won't. Hope you're well. Love, Tye xx

Ria listened in the dark and watched the light on her floor. She turned the volume down as low as she could without muting it and tapped the link Tye sent. *Mong on spice* was the title of the video.

There he is. The video showed Kian crouching on the floor next to a bed, grabbing at the floor, clawing as though he were trying to dig through it. He was thinner, sharper than she remembered him. Darkness under his eyes that wasn't there when she saw him last. Veins in his neck. His face was twisting, grappling with effort. She could hear him moaning, a hollow sound that made her grip the duvet. Their laughter behind the camera was the only other sound. Suddenly, an arm appeared, then the rest of a boy walked in to shot and pushed Kian over, so he was on his side. *Get back here, Bones,* a voice said. The boy aimed a kick at Kian's side, hitting his arm, then ran back behind the phone. Kian closed his eyes and started ripping his hair out, cycling his legs and saying *no* over and over again. The frame shook with the laughter of the person holding the phone. *Fucking bellend,* the voice said. Kian's eyes opened and he stopped moving, staring at the phone. He put his hand in his mouth and bit down, a noise of pain making its way out from behind it. His eyes started to roll back in his head. The frame quickly panned down to the floor and the video ended.

Ria tapped the profile under the post. She had what she needed.

***

'Li... sorry, Jenny?' Ria said, sitting down on the sofa.

Jenny turned to look at her. She gripped her cards.

'I got something for you.'

Ria handed over the box. It was heavy. Jenny took it, frowning at the cover. Her eyes scanned it, then looked up at Ria.

'It's a different version of solitaire,' Ria explained, pointing at the box. 'Like a board game version. You jump the marbles over each other and try to end up with just one... look...' She took the box back and pulled out the board, the bag of marbles and the leaflet of instructions. She scanned through the different languages.

'Look, here.' She passed the leaflet over, pointing to the text under the Chinese flag. Jenny took it, a trace of a smile touching her lips. She read them and looked at the board, then opened the bag of marbles. She started to place them in the dimples the wood. Ria stood up.

'I'll leave you to it,' she said, fiddling with the hem of her T-shirt. Jenny looked up at her.

'Thank you,' she said. 'You can play, if you like,' she added, smiling.

'That's all right. I have to go get my meds, anyway. But we could figure out how to play with two people later, if you don't have plans?'

'Okay. I'm never busy. Neither are you,' Jenny said, with a half-smile.

'Good point,' Ria said, nodding. 'See you later.'

Turning the corridor, she heard voices from Kerry's room.

'Kerry, calm down. You need to just stop and think—'

'I'm *just asking* for my *fucking fags* and you're treating me like a *child!*'

'You can't go out yet, it's not time. Now—'

The voice stopped. She heard some scuffling, a shout, then Kelly appeared in the doorway, panting. She saw Ria and smiled. The alarms went off. Kerry turned and looked down at the floor in her room then turned back, looking around the corridor, searching for something. She shook her head and set off, walking quickly past Ria, so close she hit her shoulder, as though she couldn't see her anymore. The alarms continued to ring. Dave appeared at the end of the corridor and stopped Kerry.

'What's happened?' he asked her.

Kerry tried to push past him, but he held her shoulders. He looked up the corridor at Ria, then at Kerry's doorway. Ria followed his eye and saw Faz, one hand on the doorframe and the other holding her nose, blood seeping down her chin and dripping onto her top. Ria turned back to see Mara and Dave putting Kerry in a standing restraint, one either side of her. She fought them.

'I didn't do it!' she yelled, kicking her legs so all her weight was on their arms. They struggled to keep hold of her, bending with the weight until all three of them were on the floor, Kerry almost on her back, Dave and Mara kneeling either side, their arms tangled. She kept writhing, jabbing her elbows out, pulling and pushing against them, pushing up on her feet to try to stand.

Faz walked past Ria, still holding her nose.

'Are you okay?' Ria asked, watching the blood spot onto the floor between Faz's feet.

'Fine,' she said. 'Just got to stop the bleeding. Clean myself up.' She looked over at the three bodies on the floor. 'You all right if I—'

'Go,' Mara said, her voice straining. 'Send Jo up though, yeah?'

'No problem.'

'I fucking hate you!' Kerry shouted at them both, reaching to try to bite their arms.

'Right,' Mara said. 'You need to calm down. We're not going anywhere.'

Dave and Mara stayed firm and quiet, occasionally shifting their legs or moving their arms out of the way when they needed to. Kerry shouted, screamed, kicked her legs, tried to stand or shift to one side. She spat at Dave. It landed on his arm. He looked at it then stared ahead, expression blank, still holding her down. Kerry was breathing fast and heavy. Her face was flushed, sweating.

'You can't do this,' she said. 'I'm a human being. This isn't a farm. Fight back!' She raised her head, shouting into the day room where the other patients sat. 'Fight them! You don't have to live like this! You have to help me – we don't have to take this shit!'

Ria didn't move. She felt her ankles creak. A sob rose from between Mara and Dave. Kerry was lying back, her neck arched, head weighing down towards the floor. They leaned down towards the floor, letting her lie flat, loosening their arms to only hold her wrists down. She continued to cry, eyes closed, while they waited.

'I want to go to my room,' Kerry said quietly, opening her eyes.

'Okay,' said Mara. 'We're going to get up. Ready?'

Kerry murmured in agreement.

'One, two, three.'

They kept hold of her, linking her arms, bearing her weight as she stood up.

'Let's go.'

Mara glanced up the corridor to Ria. She shifted out of their way, her back to the wall. Kerry's head was bowed, watching the floor. As they walked past Ria she looked up at her. Her eyes were pink, the skin around them puffy, but her expression was blank. Ria winked at her, impulsively, and got the faintest hint of a smile in return.

'Either get in your room or come in the day room, Ria,' said Jo, at the other end of the corridor. 'Stop lurking. You're always lurking. Nosing in on other people's business.'

'Fuck off,' Ria muttered, opening her door and stepping inside.

'Lovely manners,' she heard Jo reply. She slammed the door behind her.

She exhaled and looked out of her window. *Two hours until tea time. You have to eat what they give you. One of the real meals, on a plate, with cutlery.* The thought made her nauseous. *Don't think about it. I hope Cally's on. She'll mark me down as having eaten, if I ask her to. Anyway. Never mind that. Two hours until they lock you out of your room again. You've got work to do.*

She retrieved her phone and opened the notes tab. There were three entries. *So far.*

Bones
GrimBDaz
Mick Ashton

Ria knew there was at least one more to add, but she knew nothing about them yet. She had to talk to Jenny first.

She typed *Mum,* then closed her eyes and took a breath. She opened them and deleted the word.

Right. Research.

CHAPTER 37

TYE

Nothing had changed. The heat was still dry, the breeze was still dusty. His bed still felt like sheet metal. The canvas over their heads was still the same colour as the floor, the walls, the clothes, the food, the air they lived in. He stared up at the canvas and saw the rocks, the hills, the crags he would trek through tomorrow, clinging to a gun with hands that were somehow wet with sweat and cracked with drought at the same time. He saw Ben's face, the gaping wound staring up at him, the blood pooling. *This is belonging, the advert said.*

He inhaled and closed his eyes. *She still hasn't replied. Probably thinks I'm a fucking dick. Let's abscond and live on an island. God, you're a tool.* He rubbed his eyes and put his hands behind his head. Those nights at the mill. On the jetty, with the fire. He wanted to be there, wanted to see that every time he closed his eyes. But he couldn't, and he wouldn't. *If she can help with Dad, though, that's something. Dee seemed nice. Sensible. Sorted. Steady. Total opposite of Ria. Just what Dad needs. Nan's out of her depth. But Dee could really help.*

He sat up at the sound of a shot. *Fuck.* He looked round. Nobody else moved. He listened, struggling to hear above the blood thumping in his ears. He gripped the edge of his bed. There it was again. He jumped out of bed, shouting at everyone to get up, struggling to get his kit on.

'Shot fired!' he shouted. 'Get the fuck up! Shots!'

A ripple of movement spread across the room. Adam, in the next bunk, swung himself out of bed and up on his feet, doing up his trousers.

'Where did they come from?' he asked, looking round.

Everyone listened, getting dressed, eyes wide in the dark.

'There!' Tye pointed across the room.

Adam switched the light on next to his bed.

'Don't! They'll see!' Tye hissed. 'Listen, there, again!' He put his hands over his head and fell to the floor.

'Tye,' Adam said. 'It's okay, it's not shots.'

Tye heard a murmur of laughter spread around. He looked up.

'Mate,' said Adam, walking round to him, kneeling next to him. 'It's just the clasp on the rope. The metal fastening between them. Hanging off the frame outside. It's clanking in the wind. That's all it is.'

Adam put his hand on Tye's shoulder.

'Fucking hell,' someone across from them said. 'We're all half-kitted up. Jesus. Cheers, Steadman.'

Another person laughed, imitating Tye.

'Don't! They'll see!' they mimicked.

'Fuck off, Brennan, it's not funny,' said Adam.

Tye got to his feet.

'I'm sorry,' he said, looking down at his legs. Adam caught sight of them and stood in front of him.

A dark, wet patch ran from his crotch down to the knee of his khaki trousers.

'Take them off,' Adam said under his breath. 'They won't see.'

Tye quickly undid them and stepped out of them, sitting on his bed.

'Show's over, everyone,' said Adam. 'Let's get some sleep.'

Tye held his head in his hands. He heard them, the mutters, sniggers. He closed his eyes and pressed his fingers into them, trying to push the tears back in.

***

'We have to stop here,' said Brennan.

Tye swallowed and stopped the vehicle, keeping the engine running.

'It's that one, on the right,' Ali said, pointing between them through the windscreen.

'You coming or what?' Brennan said, looking at Tye's hands on the steering wheel.

'Yeah.'

Tye switched off the engine and climbed out, feeling sick. He watched the market as they crossed the road. *Crowded. Noisy. Boxes, bags, everywhere. Could be in them. More likely on that guy there. That woman. That kid. Someone in the middle, trying to take as many out as they can.*

'Fuck!'

He turned and staggered backwards at the beeping horn as it went past him, two young men on a scooter speeding off, gesturing and shouting back at him.

'What the fuck is up with you?' shouted Brennan from the roadside.

'Come on,' said Ali. 'They know we're here.'

Tye wanted to get back in the truck and drive off. For a fraction of a second, he thought he might do it. But he found his body walking towards them, and the door they had to go through. It was the door to an apartment block. The people they were there to see were on the third floor. He felt in his bones that it was a trap. Felt so strongly that he shouldn't go in there. None of them should. Still he carried on, crossed the threshold, walked up the stairs. Brennan in front, Ali behind. It was early enough for the air in the stone walls to be cold, still. The shafts of sunlight piercing through the shadows were merely warm, not yet scorching the steps they fell on.

They're going to kill us. Torture us, kill us, drag us through the market. String our bodies up off the lampposts and stick our heads on the railings. He realised his hands were shaking. He tried to grip his gun hard enough to steady them. The whole thing trembled slightly – he hoped not enough for them to see.

Brennan knocked on the door. Tye closed his eyes. *I love you, Dad.* His eyes opened at the same time as the door.

'As-Salaam-Alaikum.'

'Wa-Alaikum-Salaam.'

The man was older than Tye had thought. His white beard and eyebrows, his open hand gesturing them through, his smile – they weren't what he expected. They followed the man through the hall into a room with bare walls and a window overlooking the market. Cushions lay around the perimeter of the room. Three men sat against the wall opposite the door. They were younger. *One in his twenties, the other two thirties or forties*, Tye guessed. They stood up and shook hands with each of them, then gestured for them to sit. Tye felt ridiculous, with his helmet and gun. Inside someone's home, sat on the floor, being offered tea.

The men talked. Tye and Brennan watched Ali for translation.

'Firstly, they want to thank you for meeting with them,' said Ali. 'And for listening to their concerns.'

'Tell them we're grateful they've invited us and we're keen to find a solution that works for everyone,' Brennan said.

Ali translated. The men nodded. The youngest talked, then the eldest interrupted and carried on.

'It's not the building of the school that they object to,' said Ali. 'They recognise the urgent need for the children to be educated. To return to a normal life. They have been out of school for a long time. It's the fact that girls will be educated there, too.'

'There will be separate classrooms—' Brennan started, but one of the men interrupted. Ali listened and translated.

'We are not against the education of girls, but we are concerned that the presence of girls within the school will make it a target for attack.'

Tye watched the market out of the window while Brennan talked. The square was filled with stalls, carts and people milling between them. Awnings and umbrellas provided shade for most of the traders and their table-tops but some were in full, dazzling sunlight. Tye couldn't make out what much of the produce was, but he could see the vibrant colours. Ruby, lime, gold, coral. Life in the base was so beige. He longed for colour. He watched one trader carefully unpacking azure blue pottery onto his shelving unit. The colour was so rich, it took his mind to a perfectly clear ocean from above, watching the flecks of white foam rise and fall gently, tiny silver glimmers of fish darting beneath them. Then he was down in the water, swimming with Kian, both of them diving down, floating over the reef, somersaulting under the water, grinning at the shoal gliding past them.

'We'll be there,' said Brennan. 'Please thank them.'

Ali translated.

They said their thanks and goodbyes.

On the way down the stairs, Tye felt the heat of the sunlight shafts. *Time's moved on. We must've been there a while.*

'The fuck is wrong with you?' said Brennan as they crossed the street.

'What?'

'I'm going to talk to Sarg. You're a liability.'

'I'm a... why? What did I do?'

'Exactly. What did you do? Nothing. Do you even know what we agreed?'

They climbed into the vehicle. Tye started the engine and set off, racking his brain. It was useless.

'No, okay, I don't. I was watching the market, I thought I saw something dodgy—'

'Ali, back me up. He's worse than useless, right?'

Tye could hear Ali shifting uncomfortably behind him.

'Maybe,' Ali said, hesitating. 'Maybe you came back too soon. Have some time off. Your brother—'

'Don't bring my brother into this. I'm fine. Don't you think I would've stayed with my dad longer if I could? There are rules, you can't just—'

'What Ali means is—'

Everything was white, blinding white, then black. That second was so loud, Tye felt his skull burst under the pressure, his ears rupture. He was in the air, his whole body weightless in the neon white, then buried, every inch of him was being pushed down, down into the earth. He was sure his ribcage had shattered, lungs collapsed, his guts were somewhere in the clay next to him and his limbs shorn clean off, he was only conscious because his brain was in its last oxygen, last blood, before it died.

Kian, I'm on my way.

CHAPTER 38
CALLY

'I've got another job,' she said to Ria. 'I'm leaving in a couple of weeks.'

'What? Why?'

She watched Ria grip the handles of the shopping basket until her knuckles were white.

'I just, I'm not sure this it the right thing for me. I'm doing my masters in the autumn, I need experience of a few different settings... the course qualifies me as a psychologist, you see, it's really competitive, and...'

Ria looked down at the floor, then at the automatic doors. Cally watched her take a deep breath, then look her in the eye.

'Is it because—'

'No. Look, I'm really sorry about that. I shouldn't have done it. I never brought it up, because—'

'You regret it?' Ria lowered the basket and looked at her feet, a solitary tear running down her face.

'Shit, don't... no, it's not that... I just, someone in my position shouldn't... it's wrong to—'

Ria dropped the basket and hugged her.

'Please don't go. You're the only thing that's keeping me alive in that place, you know? The only thing!'

Fuck. Fuck. She felt her warmth against her, smelled her hair. She wanted to kiss her again, but she pulled away, putting her hand on Ria's shoulder.

'It's okay, we'll still be friends,' she tried. 'I'll come and visit—'

Ria kissed her. She let her do it, for a second, because it was heaven. *You have to stop her.*

'Please, don't,' she said, pulling away. 'There are people around. Look, I'm really sorry. I never intended for this to happen. I thought I'd just be here a few months, move onto something else. I didn't mean to get involved... so I'm sticking to the plan. Moving on. I have to, for both our sakes.'

Ria wiped her palms over her eyes and picked up the basket. She breathed in through her nose and out through her mouth.

'You're right,' she said, sniffing, smoothing her hair. 'I'm sorry. You're right. I don't know what came over me. I'm... happy for you. And don't worry, I won't say anything. You have to help me, though.'

Ria watched her closely.

'What do you mean?' Cally asked, the intensity of Ria's stare making her step back.

'I brought your phone out with me, because I was going to call my sister. She doesn't work Sundays. I have my card, because we're shopping.' She lifted up the basket. 'So really, I have everything I need. You'll make sure Dee gets my other stuff, yeah?'

'What are you—'

'The only thing I don't have is solitude. I'm supposed to be on my own to do this. You're going to have to give me that. More than that, you're going to have to cover for me.'

Shit. She's absconding.

'Cover for what, Ria? I'm not leaving you—'

'Yes, you are. You have to.' She put down her shopping basket. 'We're going to the cafe in B&Q. You go up and order, I'll leave while your back is turned. Give me a head start.'

'Ria, I can't—'

'You owe me that much, Cally, don't you?'

'Where are you going?'

'A few places. You don't need to know. Better not to. Listen, when you realise I'm gone, take your time looking for me, yeah? As far as the CCTV is concerned, you've done nothing wrong. Go to the toilets. Look around the shop. Ask them to put a call out. Look round the rest of the retail park. *Then* you can raise the alarm.'

Fuck. She really means it.

'Ria, it's my career—'

'It's my *life*! Look, you don't come out of this badly at all. Your back was turned, I bolted. What were you supposed to do? On the other hand… being sexually involved with a patient?' She raised her eyebrows and shrugged her shoulders. 'What's worse?'

Cally's stomach felt as though it had fallen out and bounced down the aisle. Her legs nearly gave way. She took a step to right herself and tried to steady her breathing.

'I tell you what,' Cally said, loudly. 'We don't need any of this stuff, but I definitely need a brew. Let's go to the cafe in B&Q.'

She looked around at the man stacking shelves at the end of the aisle and the woman with a pram walking past them. The woman smiled politely. The man went on stacking.

'Good idea,' said Ria, grinning. 'Let's go.'

***

Cally waited in the queue. Her back was turned completely, so that all she could see were the cakes sat in the counter display cabinet. As the queue moved, she didn't even dare turn sideways to walk forwards. Instead she sidestepped, still staring at the cake, too scared to put her eyes anywhere else.

'Look good, don't they?'

She glanced to her left. An old lady was smiling at her, then at the cakes.

'Yes. I can't decide which to have,' she said, conscious that her voice was trembling and her lip shaking a little.

'Don't worry, love, they have the same choice every day. Get one now, then come back next week for another. That's what I do. Made my way through them now!'

'Ha, good idea.'

She felt sick.

'Next!'

Cally ordered, taking as long as possible. She waited at the counter after paying, still facing the wall.

'We'll bring it over, shug,' the woman behind the counter said.

'Oh, really? Great, thank you.'

Her arms and legs were buzzing. The feeling was halfway between pins and needles and the feeling you get just before you start to run – the stretch of an elastic band before it fires across the room. Finally, she turned round. *No Ria*. Just the empty seat where she had been.

She walked over to the table and sat down, looking around, craning her neck to see up the aisles nearby. She stood up and looked over at the counter. The woman was placing her order on a tray. Cally sat back down and waited for her.

'Thanks,' she said as the tray was placed in front of her. 'Thank you.'

The woman left. She looked up the aisles again and stood up. She left the coffee and walked out of the seating area and round the corner to the toilets. Cally felt as though she could feel her heart beating in her neck. In the toilets, she glanced at the CCTV camera in the corner above the sinks and walked to each cubicle, checking the doors. One was closed.

'Ria?' she asked. No answer. She knocked on the door. 'Ria, is that you?'

'Sorry love,' an older voice replied. 'That's not me.'

'Oh, sorry. I'm just looking for my friend.'

'No problem.'

The toilet flushed. *Fuck. What now.*

A woman in her fifties emerged and made her way to the sinks.

'Have you tried the cafe?' she said, turning on the tap. 'Or the homeware aisle. I could get lost in there. Some lovely things on sale. Look, I got this—' The woman lifted a garden lantern out of her bag.

'I will,' Cally said. 'Thanks.'

'Only four—' she heard the woman continue as she pushed through the door to the shop floor.

Go up and down each aisle. Shout her name. Go to customer services. Ask them to do a shout-out. She checked her watch. Five minutes had already gone. *That'll give her another fifteen, surely. Five waiting around at the desk, giving them my info. Twenty looking round the other shops. Ten to walk back up. Nearly an hour's head start. That's enough.*

***

'Good day?' Tom asked.

Cally shook her head.

'Handed in my notice.'

She poured the wine into her glass then offered him the bottle. He took it, but didn't pour any for himself. He put it back in the fridge.

'Not go down well?' he asked.

'Wasn't that. Someone absconded. While I was with them.'

'Fuck! What happened?'

She drank half her glass in one go. She felt him watching her. She didn't care.

'Just in B&Q. We were in the cafe, I was ordering. When I turned round, she'd gone. They still don't know where she is.'

'Jeeeez. Are you okay?'

'Yeah, I'm fine. I mean, I'm glad I handed in my notice before that happened, obviously. And that the other place have already said yes.'

'It wasn't your fault, though – she bolted while your back was turned, what were you supposed to do?'

Cally took another mouthful of wine, letting it burn her tongue before she swallowed.

'They said she'd probably come back. Most of them do, after a few days. Doped up, few war wounds. They come back of their own accord, because they don't have anywhere to go. Or they want the meds. Can't cope outside.'

'What if she doesn't?'

'Sometimes the police bring them back. All the services know she's absconded. It's unlikely though. They've got too much on. Not enough staff. They won't be doing much to find her, beyond the standard enquiries. She'd come on a lot. She's not a danger to the public or anything. It's more for her own safety than anyone else's. It was Ria.'

'Who?'

'A girl. Quite young. Nineteen. Never figured out exactly what was up with her. Hallucinations sometimes. Self-harm. Possible BPD. Possible schizoaffective.'

'What did she do?'

'Killed her dad.'

'Fuck.'

'He'd abused her from a young age, though…'

'Still. You never mentioned her.'

'No. Didn't really know her.'

CHAPTER 39
RIA

Sorry it's taken me ages to reply. It's Ria, by the way. I'm on a different number, but it's definitely me! Had to ditch the other phone. I asked my sister about your dad, she's happy to check up on him now and then when she's back in Talvern. I hope that helps. She wanted you to know she's not a mental health professional, blah blah blah, but she's happy to do it as a friend of the family. Weird phrase. I guess Mum knew Kian. I knew you. Mum and Dee met you once. Anyway, whatever she needs to make herself feel like she's not intruding. She's back every few weeks. I'll keep you posted.

I'd love to see you, when you're next back. You might not be able to come and visit me. It depends. I'm not there at the moment. I'll probably be back there soon enough, but they might not let me have visitors for a while. We'll see.

You're right – if only we could both abscond and live on an island, hey? Well, I took your advice. Sort of. Temporary absconsion, anyway.

I had this mural on my wall, in my room at the unit. Did it with a black marker pen, before they confiscated it. It's huge. Takes up all the walls. Big swirls and sweeping patterns, like a tattoo. There's a huge pair of wings in there, just like Betty's would be, if she were the size of a dragon. Big, black, beautiful wings. There's detail in the feathers, the spines. They were so pissed off with me. Decided to let it stay though. No point painting over it until I left. Maybe they've done it by now. It doesn't matter though, because she's still there. And here. There was a girl in the middle of it, you see. A girl, with those wings. Me.

When I killed my dad, it wasn't a spur of the moment thing. I'd wanted to do it for so long. Since the age of eight, I'd thought about it. The different ways I could do it. Just fantasy, of course. I was a kid, he was a fully-grown man. Then he left. I still thought about it. Less, though. It faded.

I grew up. A problem teenager. Like you. I was getting there, though. Getting over it. Could've done well in my exams, gone to uni, got a job, whatever. I'm pretty sure I could've been normal, more or less.

Then he came back. I couldn't ignore it any more. He would ruin my life, all over again. The hate was too strong. It just took over. I knew I had to do it. It went from this dream I had, a futile hope I turned to when I was weak, to a completely real prospect. It wasn't a fantasy any more, it was a real thing that had to happen, otherwise he'd destroy me. It had come down to me or him, and I was never going to let him win. I was going to destroy him.

You want me to say I did it in self-defence, or because I was out of my mind. I can't. I didn't, and I wasn't. Not that it went how I planned, though. It was so much better.

I tried to poison him. How else could I do it, really? He was bigger than me, stronger than me. I couldn't get hold of a gun. It was the only way I stood a chance. But he found me, putting the powder in his wine. He tied me up, took me to the mill. I was so sure he was going to kill me. He showed me Bertie's body. Said no, he wasn't going to kill me. He wanted me to live, so he could go on torturing me forever. No use to him dead, was I?

What I did wasn't self-defence, I knew he wasn't going to kill me then. I believed him. Besides, if things had gone according to plan, he'd have been dead already. Killing him was premeditated. It just went off script, that's all.

There I was, tied up, beaten up, on the top floor of the mill. He wanted to keep me alive so that he could keep me suffering. He knew he could keep me quiet. He wanted to make me into his creature again, just like I had been. He was going to fuck me. First of many, I bet he thought. Undid his trousers.

I had my knife, I used it. Fuck, did I use it. I can't lie, it was the best feeling I've ever had. I'll never be that high again.

I know there are people out there who are like I was. Scared. Suffering in silence. Fantasising about the day they can use a knife, a gun, their bare hands, whatever – to finally get even.

I used to think about the worst ways to die and play out the scenarios in my head. We went to a zoo in Budapest once, when I was twelve. You went into a room where there were railings that you looked over and down below you, a long way, were these enormous crocodiles. Just sat, one on a fake bankside, one lying in the water. I remember being absolutely terrified. There was no way they could get up to us, but there was nothing between us and them. No glass, no net, no bars. Just distance. Someone leaning over, further than I dared – their sunglasses fell off their head, splashed into the water. The crocs didn't react. Everyone laughed nervously and joked that he should go in after them. Dee said the crocodiles were fake. They hadn't moved, they must be. Then the one on the bank sidled into the water. We all stepped back. I remember thinking, push him. Push him. Just maybe, if I could catch him off guard, make him lose his balance. Just maybe he would go over. That was one of my favourite ways for him to die. I *thought about it a lot. I got as close as I could, in the end.*

These people who are out there, who are paralysed with the hate of someone who has tortured them, ruined them – I can help them. They're scared, stuck in this box they daren't break out of. Scared of the consequences, scared they'll fuck it up, scared of becoming a monster, whatever. So they'll never do it. But I can do it for them. I smashed my way out of the box, you see. Burned it to dust. I'm scared of nothing. I feel bad for them, that they'll never have that feeling I had. It was fucking amazing. No matter. I'll have it for them.

That girl on the wall is me. Bigger than everything. Beautiful black swirls and feathers. Sweeping, majestic. I can fly. I have flown, and it's glorious. I am an avenging angel.